Fighting for Her Wolves
Hungry for Her Wolves, Book Five
A Reverse-Harem Paranormal Romance
Tara West

Copyright © 2019 by Tara West
Published by Shifting Sands Publishing
First edition, published July, 2019
All rights reserved.
This book is protected under the copyright laws of the United States of America. Any reproduction or other unauthorized use of the material or artwork herein is prohibited.
This is a work of fiction. The characters, incidents and dialogue are products of the author's imagination and are not to be construed as real.
Edited by Theo Fenraven.
Artwork by Becky Frank.

WHEN LONE WOLF ANNIE Thunderfoot's human brother is threatened by a crazed shifter chieftain, she flies to Texas to diffuse the situation. She's thrust smack in the middle of a shifter civil war, and the insane chieftain is her mates' father. Annie's dreams of finding her fated mates are crushed when she realizes they are being manipulated by a madman.

Before she can fight for the men who want to claim her, she must first uncover her alpha's dark past and convince him he's worthy of love. Her plans are put on hold when a tricky demon threatens her, forcing her to choose between fighting for love and saving her soul.

Dedications

TO THEO, GOD OF GRAMMAR, blessed by the Ancients, and tasked to save my ass with your red pen of shame. Thank you, thank you, thank you.

To Ginelle, thanks for always coming through with great suggestions.

To Sheri, thanks for always being there when I need a beta.

Laura, your medical advice has been invaluable. Thank you!

Cary, thanks so much for helping make my Spanish scenes more authentic.

Chapter One

ANNIE FROWNED AT THE bead of sweat that had slipped down her cleavage. Holy shit, it was hot in Texas. She looked at her adoptive Uncle Van, sitting beside her in the back of the truck. As always, his eyes were sharp as he stared out the windows, not even bothering to wipe the moisture that beaded on his brow.

Fanning her face, she leaned forward, grasping the back of her brother's seat. "Hey, Roy. I'm dying back here."

"Sorry." He nodded at the weathered truck dashboard. "A/C's on full blast."

"Ugh," she groaned. "I'm not going to last a week in this hell pit." She eyed the dash, noting how both air vents were pointing toward her other adoptive uncle, Alaskan Amaroki chieftain, Tor Thunderfoot. The big shifter's shoulders were wide enough that he needed his own zip code, and his long, peppered black hair did appear damp from sweat, but he could've given her a little air.

She looked out the window at the sea of grass and bushes. She'd been expecting dirt and tumbleweeds. Texas wasn't as beautiful as Alaska, but it would do. Still, she wouldn't have flown here if the Texas chieftain hadn't threatened to kill her brother. After she put the asshole in his place, she planned to stay inside the comfort of an air-conditioned house until it was time to return home to her mountains.

"About accommodations." Roy said nervously, his gaze flitting to Tor before catching Annie's eye in the rearview mirror. "My apartment is only a one-bedroom, but you can have my bed, Annie, and I'll take the sofa."

"Aw, thanks." She smiled at her brother, patting his shoulder and hating how stiff he felt. He sure was wound up. Then again, he was a brand new federal agent, working as a liaison between the American government and the Amaroki species, and they had put him smack in the middle of a shifter civil war.

Uncle Tor, who hadn't said more than two words since they'd disembarked from the plane, cleared his throat. "She's staying with us."

When Roy's gaze darted to the grumpy shifter, Annie swore she heard him shart his pants.

Though the cutting edge to Tor's voice had sliced through the air like a razor, she refused to be deterred. She hadn't seen her human half-brother in months. She wasn't about to pass up the opportunity to spend quality time with him.

"Why can't I stay with Roy?" Instantly regretting the whine in her voice, she bit her lip when Tor turned and gave her a sharp look.

"You know why, Annie."

Damn. She turned up her chin, forcing herself to sound calm. "But I thought I was coming here to see him."

Tor answered with a grunt, indicating the discussion was over. She got that the friction among the shifters in the Laredo tribe had created a hostile environment, but this was their war, not hers. Tor had no reason to worry about her safety. Until the Alaskan tribe had discovered her and brought her to their reservation, she'd been living on her own. She loved being surrounded by her own kind, but she knew how to fend for herself, too.

Folding her arms, she glared at the back of Tor's head, ignoring Van, the pack's tracker, when he chuckled. She shot him a glare. Though he was smaller than Tor, there was something more feral about him. It probably had something to do with his sharper canines and the way he could look at her as if he was looking through her. He unnerved her, though she wasn't about to show it. She held his gaze until Roy hit a pothole, forcing her to look away. At least she pretended she'd been forced.

Resigned to her fate of death by boredom, she cracked the window, hoping the breeze would cool her. She sniffed the air, surprised when she caught the scent of something familiar, a musky smell more tantalizing than fresh-baked chocolate brownies. She sniffed again, the smell tickling her senses before disappearing. Strange. What was that, and how could she get more of it?

She vigorously rolled down the window, stuck her head out, and swore when she could no longer smell that delicious scent. Whimpering her sorrow, she hung out of the truck, panting while her heart raced and her libido cried *more, more, more!*

She gasped when she was jerked back by a strong hand, barking and snapping at Van to let her go.

The fine lines framing his eyes deepened. "What the hell?"

Her chest heaved like she'd been running a marathon, and for a moment, she forgot where she was or what she'd been doing, her head was so fogged with memories of that heavenly scent. She released a slow breath as the truck came to a stop. Everyone was looking at her as if she'd grown a second head.

"Well?" Tor demanded, his voice dropping to that deep protector baritone that rattled her insides.

How could she answer when she couldn't define what had happened to her? One second she'd been mind-numbingly bored and the next her heart was racing so fast, she wanted to jump out of her skin. She crossed one knee over the other, an uncomfortable ache settling between her legs. And that's when it hit her. That scent belonged to male wolves.

Please, Ancients, no!

Her fated mates couldn't be living in Texas's sweaty armpit, smack in the middle of a civil war.

ANNIE FELT AS IF SHE was walking in a dream when her brother helped her out of the truck. She frowned at the fresh, jagged scar on his temple, knowing she should be furious with the wolf who'd put it there, but she was too dazed to think about much else other than that heavenly smell. She'd heard her mates' scent would draw her to them, but she'd had no idea they would smell so damn good and make her so freaking horny.

When Roy slammed the door, she noticed for the first time the huge dent on the driver's side, like a rhino had head-butted it. Had he been in an accident? Why hadn't he told her?

"Come on," Roy said, tugging her toward the long, red brick ranch house.

She walked like she had a stick wedged up her ass, trying hard to quell the desire that pounded like a drum between her legs. She had no idea who the hell these wolves were, but she sure hoped they presented themselves fast, and that they hastened the mating ceremony. As much as she didn't want to live in Texas, her sexual desires eclipsed all her misgivings.

"Annie, you okay?" Tor whispered as he flanked her other side, walking with her up the gravel path toward the young family of shifters.

She plastered on a smile when the woman waved at her. "I-I don't think so."

"You scented your mates?" he asked.

She grimaced. "Unfortunately."

"They probably scented you, too," he continued. "Let's hope they're not foes to the Coyotechasers."

"Yeah." Annie swallowed a lump of apprehension. She'd been so distracted by her libido, she hadn't even thought of that. The Coyotechasers were the pack that had basically usurped the old chieftain. She and her uncles would also be staying with the Coyotechasers during their visit.

"Why didn't you tell me you found your mates?" Roy hissed.

"I did," she snapped. "Why else do shifters try to crawl out of moving trucks with their tongues hanging out?"

Before he could answer her, a broad-shouldered man with a mop of dark hair and skin the hue of rich Texas soil, whom Annie assumed to be the Coyotechaser chieftain, called to them from the porch.

"Welcome, Chieftain Thunderfoot and family." He descended the porch steps, looking pained, as if he'd returned home from war.

Behind him were his three brothers, all similar in complexion, with tight lines framing their eyes. Even the gamma had a haggard look. She wondered if Amara had been mistaken when she'd told Annie her aunt and uncles were in their thirties and forties. They looked to be in their fifties. Their four sons, all with the same coloring as their fathers, stood behind them, chins held high and far too controlled for children. The oldest couldn't have been more than thirteen.

Tor surged ahead of Annie and met the large alpha halfway up the porch steps. "Chieftain Coyotechaser."

Annie noted how the Coyotechaser alpha stood one step below Tor, a sign of deference to the older chieftain. They shook hands, clapping each other's backs.

"Call me Cesar," the Coyotechaser alpha said and nodded to the family gathered behind him. "My brothers Alejandro, Ben, and Andre, and this is our mate, Ioana."

Ioana, who had a little girl balanced on her hip, offered Annie a warm smile. Ioana looked very much like an older version of Amara—a pretty blonde with dazzling silver-blue eyes.

Tor grunted, gesturing behind him. "My brother Van and our niece, Annie."

Annie was nervous when all eyes turned to her. She forced a smile, feeling heat creep into her cheeks when Tor shot her a dark look.

Stay out of their heads, his warning reverberated in her mind.

Annie wasn't sure how, but Tor always knew when she was reading minds, and he'd made it clear on more than one occasion that he didn't appreciate her magical gift of telepathy.

Doing her best to block their thoughts, she waved, her feet rooted to the spot as she clung to her brother. "So nice to meet you all."

Ioana came down the steps, carrying her little girl with large hazel eyes and her fathers' dark hair and complexion. "Annie," she said in a thick Romanian accent, "my niece Amara has told me so much about you."

"Oh." Annie bit her lip, then backed up a step as Ioana approached, fearing the shifter would smell her heat.

"Is something wrong?" Ioana stopped, frowning. "You don't look well."

She didn't know what to say. Her brain had been porridge ever since the incident in the truck.

Tor scowled. "She scented her mates on the way here."

"Oh?" Ioana narrowed her eyes, plastering on a smile. "Where did you smell them?"

"We'd just crossed onto Amaroki land," Tor said. "Far east side."

Annie's heart hit her stomach when the Coyotechasers' faces fell like dominoes.

Chieftain Cesar dragged a hand down his face. "Vidar's side of the reservation."

Annie struggled to speak past the ball of nervous tension clogging her throat. "Is that bad?"

Cesar shared dark looks with his brothers. "Vidar was our chieftain before the split. Actually, his brother Hodr was, but he was killed twelve years ago."

"Killed?" She clung tighter to Roy, her knees turning to jelly. "How?"

"Shot by drug smugglers crossing the border," Cesar answered.

Her hands flew to her mouth. "Oh, no."

When Roy wrapped an arm around her shoulders, she pressed into him. She'd always considered herself a strong, independent wolf, but she clung to her human half-brother like a lifeline. Why had the Ancients thought to pair her with Texas wolves in the middle of a civil war?

Cesar scratched the back of his head, looking uncomfortable. "Are you sure it was on the east side?"

Tor's face was a mask of stone. "Positive."

Cesar crossed his arms, giving Annie an assessing look that made her want to crawl out of her skin. "Then let us pray to the Ancients Annie didn't scent Vidar's sons."

Ioana turned to him. "It has to be them. None of Vidar's other followers are of age."

"What's wrong with Vidar?" Annie blurted, then felt stupid for asking. Roy had already told her the old chieftain had attacked him and told him on many occasions he wanted to kill all humans.

"He's gone mad." Cesar shook his head. "He's the reason we had to split."

"But what happened?"

"Long story." Cesar grimaced. "If I were you, Tor, I'd take her back to Alaska before they catch her scent."

"But I just got here," she cried.

"Good idea." Tor jutted a finger at Roy's truck. "Get back in, Annie."

She crossed her arms, leveling Tor with a glare. "Seriously?" She wasn't leaving until she knew Roy was safe. Also, she couldn't help herself. She wanted to meet her mates, even if their dad was nuts.

"Fuck me!"

Annie flinched when Cesar swore, his eyes narrowing on something behind her.

Collective swearing and grumbling ensued as the Coyotechasers grabbed shotguns from inside the house. Holy shit! She spun around, dread settling like a lead brick in her gut, and saw an old blue truck barreling down the winding dirt road leading to the ranch house.

"W-what's wrong?" she stammered, but she knew. Her mates were coming.

Roy threw up his hands and rolled his eyes. "Here we go again." He brushed open his suit jacket and settled a hand on the gun at his hip.

Her heart hammered. "What are you doing?"

Shadows fell across Roy's features. "These wolves are dangerous."

"Ioana!" Cesar boomed, raising his shotgun. "Take Annie and the kids inside."

Annie held her ground, shrugging off Ioana when she grabbed her shoulder. "I'm not going anywhere." She glowered at Cesar. "Why do you need guns?"

"Because they'll have guns," he said. "They always have guns."

Tor pointed at the house, his voice dropping to an ominous rumble. "Go inside, Annie."

She raised her chin, refusing to be intimidated when his eyes flashed a blinding gold. "And let them think the Coyotechasers are holding me against my will?"

Tor swore and shared a look with Cesar.

Cesar nodded to his mate and children, who disappeared inside. His two younger brothers guarded the door, shotguns raised, while the other alpha joined Cesar on the gravel driveway.

She faced the truck when it screeched to a halt and four men jumped out. She thought her knees would buckle when they gave her feral looks. One word popped into her head: *mine.*

The one she assumed was head alpha, broad-shouldered and tall, with sun-kissed skin and dark, shoulder-length hair, aimed a shotgun at Cesar's chest. "Give us our mate."

He didn't flinch. "We're not holding her hostage, Magnus. She's a guest at our house."

Magnus? She whispered his name softly to herself. Yes, he looked like a Magnus.

The brother Annie presumed to be the second alpha raised his shotgun and leaned across the hood of the truck. "Give her to us!"

He looked much like Magnus, with the exception of his eyes, which were even more feral. A long scar cut across his cheek. Tension radiated off him in pulsating waves, and she knew he was a shifter used to fighting. The thought both unnerved and excited her.

Tor stood beside Annie, growling. Van pushed Roy out of the way, flanking her other side.

"Lower your weapon, Raine," Cesar boomed at the second alpha.

"We will when you release her," the wolf named Raine answered.

Raine and Magnus. She had two names, but as she looked into their glowing, golden eyes, she was no longer hot and bothered for her mates. She was annoyed. Give her to us? Did they think she was their lost pet?

She surged ahead of Tor and Van, ignoring their warning growls. "Do I look like a goddamn prized cow to you?" she spat, then thumbed at Cesar. "You heard him. I'm a guest of the Coyotechasers. Now lower your fucking guns!"

She did her best to quell the shaking in her limbs as she took several more agitated steps toward her mates before stopping beside Cesar.

"Don't go any farther, Annie," he warned.

She forced a smile. "I won't."

Both alphas blinked at her. The gamma and beta shared wide-eyed looks before lowering their weapons.

"I'm sorry," Magnus relented, standing down, though he still held a finger on the trigger. "I don't know what came over us. We were only concerned about your safety." His pouted, reminding her of a contrite child. She would've thought he was sexy with his square jaw, high cheekbones, and wide hazel eyes, but trespassing on someone else's property and waving guns around was anything but.

She turned to Tor, frowning. "The Ancients are mistaken," she said loud enough for her voice to carry. "I'm not mating with idiots."

She ignored her mates' collective gasps and grumbles.

Cesar cleared his throat. "More trouble." A truck was kicking up a cloud of dust as it barreled down the dirt road toward the house. "The Wolfstalker elders."

"Chieftain Wolfstalkers to you," her mates simultaneously boomed, raising their guns once more.

Holy fuck! They weren't just idiots, they were willful idiots. The worst kind of stupid. No way was she breeding with those backwards-ass tree-humpers.

Cesar spit in the dirt, laughing. "They ain't our chieftains."

Annie shook her head, feeling like she was at ground zero after a testosterone bomb explosion.

Tor left Annie to join Cesar.

Annie swore under her breath.

"I was hoping your first meeting with the Wolfstalkers would have been under better circumstances," Cesar said to Tor.

After the truck screeched to a halt, three men stumbled out. They barely resembled their sons, having long, scraggly hair and distended beer guts. One of them had an eye patch and dragged his leg as he walked.

"What in devil's name is going on?" the biggest man, who also had the biggest belly slurred like a drunk, waving a pistol in the air.

Magnus turned to him, unalarmed by his father's appearance or erratic behavior. "We scented our mate, Father."

The old man narrowed his eyes on Tor. "What are the Thunderfoots doing here?"

Cesar cleared his throat. "I asked them to come, Vidar, in hopes they could help us negotiate a truce."

Vidar spat a wad of tobacco in the dirt. "This feud ain't none of their damn business."

"It's our business now," Tor said evenly, though Annie sensed the rage simmering beneath his cool façade. "I won't let our niece mate into a tribe in turmoil."

Vidar pointed at Cesar. "Tell the Coyotechasers to forfeit their false claim to the chiefdom, and there won't be no turmoil."

"You know we can't do that." Cesar aimed his gun at Vidar's chest. "Now get the hell off our property."

"Fine." Vidar threw up his hands, ignoring the guns Cesar and his brothers were pointing at him. "Give the girl to my sons, and we'll leave."

Annie shrank back. "I'm not going with them." No way in hell was she getting tangled up in some crazy pack's drama.

Vidar's eyes shifted and his nose lengthened as he gave her a look that would make a lesser wolf cringe. "Do you know who I am, girl?"

She refused to break eye contact. She'd battled werewolves, for fuck's sake. She wasn't about to let a crazy drunk intimidate her. "I don't give a damn who you are."

Vidar snarled at her, then turned to Tor. "Is she always this disrespectful?"

Tor let out a low chuckle. "You're provoking her."

"Who is she?" Vidar asked Tor, acting as if she wasn't standing right in front of him.

"My name is Annie," she blurted, balling her hands into fists in an attempt to control her rage.

Vidar refused to look at her. "She's the half-human?" he asked, his leathery features scrunching up as if he'd sucked on a sour lemon.

She was tired of his games. "I am." She gave him another challenging look.

He looked her over with a smirk before turning to Tor once more. "Does her human blood make her weak?"

She gaped at him and then at his useless sons, who'd somehow managed to fade into the background, giving the madman center stage.

"Hello." She waved wildly. "I'm right here."

Tor shook his head, snickering. "She's a strong shifter and will make a fine mate for a chieftain's sons."

Vidar rubbed his chin with the barrel of his pistol, a demented look in his bulging eyes. "That is yet to be determined."

"I beg your pardon," she snapped, a wave of anger flushing her face. "I'm a daughter of the Ancients."

Vidar shot Tor a pointed look. "Is this true?"

Wow. Could the guy be any more of a chauvinist asshole?

Tor nodded. "She is their daughter. Our ancient gamma mated with her mother."

"Interesting." Vidar flashed a grin. "Come, boys," he said to his four slack-jawed sons. "Before this bitch's scent turns you into fucking retards."

Holy fuck. Annie clenched her fists until nails broke skin. She'd never wanted to punch anyone so badly in her life.

Vidar jerked Magnus back, making him drop his gun. Everyone ducked when the weapon hit the ground. She gasped, shocked when Magnus's hand fell with the gun. What the hell?

His cheeks turned as red as an overripe apple as he picked up the gun and attached prosthetic with his other hand, balancing them on an arm which ended in a stump. Magnus was missing a hand? He turned away, eyes downcast, and threw the weapon and fake hand in the back of his truck. He climbed inside, followed by his brothers. They looked like naughty children who'd been caught pilfering the cookie jar. Balancing his stump on the steering wheel, Magnus backed out of the driveway, his cheeks still pink, and he tore off behind Vidar's truck without a backward glance.

Gaping at the retreating trucks, her anger with her mates turned to pity. What had happened to his hand? Her pity quickly turned back into rage. The missing hand didn't give Magnus and his brothers the right to act like Neanderthals, and why hadn't they spoken up when their father disrespected her?

She turned to Tor. "Did that crazy drunk call me a bitch?"

"He did."

"I'm sorry, Annie," Cesar said. "That is his nature. Now you can see why peace between our tribes is impossible."

His brothers stood beside him, mumbling agreement.

Annie had to work hard to unclench her teeth. "Are his sons like him?"

Cesar shared looks with his brothers. "As far as we can tell, no." She sure as hell hoped he was telling the truth and not trying to placate her.

Squaring her shoulders, she watched the trucks turn onto the main road. "They'd better not be, or I'm ripping off their balls and shoving them down their throats."

ANNIE STARED AT HER food and then glanced down the long table, made out of what appeared to be an old barn door. It accommodated the Coyotechasers, their children, and their guests. The spread was amazing. Platters of steaming barbeque, pickled vegetables, tamales, and cornbread, as well as jugs of homemade tequila Cesar promised would burn their eyebrows off were scattered across the table. After Roy, Tor, and Van spluttered and coughed on the fire brew, she refused a drink.

She was too upset to eat much. She felt bad, because the Coyotechasers had worked so hard on the meal. She pulled a thin layer of cornmeal off the tamale husk and chewed. Texan food was delicious. She could definitely get used to tamales and brisket. Then again, she was going to have to if she mated with the Wolfstalkers.

She set down the empty husk and pushed away her plate.

Ioana balanced her daughter on one knee and placed a hand on hers. "Are you okay?"

She frowned at the cornmeal crumbs by her plate. "My fathers chose fools for my mates." Legend was that the Ancients were the ones who paired up wolf packs with their mates.

"I'm sure they have their reasons," Ioana soothed.

She spoke around the lump of sorrow and fear wedged in her throat. "What if they grow up to be like him?" When Ioana looked away, she wasn't reassured.

"Their head alpha, Hodr, was a fair and wise leader," Cesar said and stabbed a piece of meat.

Well, that was promising. Maybe her mates would turn out to be more like him. "And you said he was killed by drug smugglers?"

Cesar nodded, his expression grim as he and his brothers set down their silverware. "We had a tradition among the Texan Amaroki. When young wolves first shift, they run the canyon with their parents."

She shared curious looks with her brother. "You *had* the tradition? So you don't do it anymore?"

"No. It's too dangerous. When Magnus first shifted, his alpha and gamma fathers and mother took him to the canyon. They stumbled upon drug smugglers. They were shot. Magnus and his gamma father Sami were injured. Hodr and their mates were killed."

Well, shit. The food soured in her stomach.

"Is that how Magnus lost his hand and why Sami has a limp and eye patch?" she asked.

"Yes." The lines framing his eyes deepened. "Sami's injuries go deeper. He hasn't been able to shift since that day."

Alejandro, the Coyotechasers' second alpha, shot his brother a scowl. "He turned into an incompetent drunk."

Cesar let out a groan. "All the remaining Wolfstalker elders did."

"What's worse is Vidar blames Magnus for their deaths," Ioana added.

The look of pity in Ioana's eyes filled Annie with a mixture of shame and sorrow. Alphas weren't supposed to be pitied, especially not those destined to become chieftains.

"What did Magnus do?" she asked and held her breath, afraid to know the answer.

Cesar shrugged. "Not enough apparently, and Vidar has never forgiven him."

"But wasn't he just a kid?"

"He'd only just learned to shift." Cesar's expression hardened. "But Vidar still blames him for not doing enough to protect his mother."

"He lost his goddamn hand!" She pounded the table, apologizing when Ioana and her young daughter flinched.

"I know," Alejandro said. "What's worse is that Vidar also blames all humans for his mate's death."

"All humans?" Moisture evaporated from her throat.

Roy laughed nervously and tossed back another shot of homemade tequila. "He's not too fond of us."

"He tried to cut ties to the American government," Cesar added.

"How?" Annie asked.

Cesar poured a splash of tequila into his shot glass and gazed at the amber liquid. "He ordered the betas serving in the Army to abandon their posts."

"Seriously?" She looked at Roy for confirmation and was dismayed when he nodded. "That's desertion."

"I know," Cesar said. "Most of them refused to heed his orders."

She eyed Cesar intently. "Then what happened?"

He made a spluttering noise. "He tried to banish the betas who refused to follow his orders."

"There was no way we were standing by while our brother was banished." Alejandro nodded to his beta brother, who remained stoically silent. "We ordered an emergency meeting. About two-thirds of our tribe sided with us and elected us as the new chieftains."

Tor grimaced. "I take it Vidar didn't handle that well."

"Every day there is some new drama," Cesar grumbled. "Packs are no longer allowed to split up. The Wolfstalkers have cornered smaller packs and beat them to bloody pulps. They've driven away the last two government liaisons. We went without a liaison for six months while we waited for Agent Miller."

Roy laughed, his gaze nervously flitting about the table. "Now we know why they sped up my training."

"You've handled your assignment better than men twice your age," Cesar said. "We appreciate you sticking with us this long, even after Vidar tried to kill you."

Annie laid a hand on Roy's arm. "What did he do?"

"That dent in my truck." He hung his head. "That was him."

Her hand flew to her throat. "He ran into your truck?"

"Yeah, with his fist." Roy wiped a bead of sweat off his brow with a trembling hand. "He was in protector form."

"Obviously," Annie muttered. Alpha wolf shifters could transform into more than just wolves. They could also shift into giant Sasquatch beasts standing ten feet tall, with wide, barrel chests and the power to rip out full-grown trees by their roots. "Then what happened?"

All color drained from Roy's face. "He jerked me out the window. I swear he was about to rip me in two, but Raine convinced him to let me go."

She touched the scar on his forehead. "Was that how you got that?"

"Yeah." He shrugged. "He'd shattered the window before he pulled me through it."

Holy freaking Ancients! Annie did not want to bond with that family. It didn't matter if his sons weren't like him. She didn't want to have to deal with a crazy father-in-law on a daily basis. "I can't mate with them."

Tor cleared his throat. "I'll take you back to Alaska tomorrow."

"We can't do that." A growing migraine pounded the back of Annie's skull. "Vidar tried to kill Roy."

Roy stiffened. "I can handle myself, Annie."

"He can crush you. He can pop off your head like you used to do to my dolls."

All color drained from his face. "What do you propose we do?"

Her gaze swept the table. "If the Ancients chose me for a reason, maybe it was to bring peace to the tribe."

Cesar shared knowing looks with his family. "There's no negotiating with Vidar."

She already knew that. She didn't want to negotiate with that chauvinistic donkey-dong-sized douche-nozzle. "No." She clenched her hands to quell the tremors that made her heart race like a speeding train. "But maybe I can negotiate with his sons."

Again the Coyotechasers shared knowing looks.

"What?" she asked Cesar.

"They're afraid of him," Cesar answered grimly.

"B-but," she cried frantically, "Raine stood up to him when he tried to kill Roy."

The table broke into a cacophony of noise.

"That one time," Cesar finally said. "But there have been countless other times he's gone off the rails, and his sons have done nothing."

Well fuck. Her future mates were dumbasses *and* pussies?

She pushed back from the table, the food in her gut giving her instant indigestion. "Well, they'd better grow a set, because I'm not mating with them until they do."

Chapter Two

ANNIE TOSSED AND TURNED in bed, trying to fall asleep, but she had too much on her mind. Were the Ancients angry with her? They had to be, to punish her with such awful mates. She swiped away hot tears, wiping them on her pillow and cursing herself for crying. She'd survived the foster care system, rape attempts, and even ravenous werewolves. She could survive being mated to four idiots. Couldn't she?

She didn't remember how or when she fell asleep, but surely she was dreaming. She found herself at the bottom of the most beautiful canyon, carved into a *V* with a waterfall splashing into a shimmery pond at the narrowest point. She sat on a rock ledge overlooking the water opposite the waterfall, smiling at her distorted reflection in the ripples. She gasped when a man's face showed up beside hers but didn't jump to her feet and defend herself. She recognized his alluring scent and his handless shadow. Slowly she turned to Magnus, saddened though not surprised by his frown.

He held up the arm with the missing hand, and his thought projected into her head. *I'm a useless protector.*

She stood and gently settled a hand on what used to be his wrist, now just a lump of angry, scarred skin covering misshapen bone. She searched his eyes, where flecks of gold, brown, and green swirled together like rare jewels. "You are enough of a man for me." She squeezed, her heart clenching when he pulled away, tucking his arm behind him.

I'll never be able to protect you like I should. He caressed her cheek with his knuckles. *Love you like I should.*

"You don't need two hands to love me." She grabbed his solitary hand and kissed the palm, her eyes fluttering as she looked up at him. "You just need one heart."

She thought it odd how familiar she was being with him when they'd never touched before. How she knew him so well in this dream but didn't know him in real life. Perhaps her soul knew his. Maybe that's why she'd recognized his scent.

"I want to love you, Annie." He spoke aloud, searching her face with a look akin to desperation, his irises swirling a blinding gold and back again. "You don't know how badly."

She pressed her hand to his chest, feeling the pounding of his heart beneath her palm. "Then love me," she said with an urgent whisper. "Don't overthink it, Magnus. Just love me."

With a low growl, he dragged his fingers through her hair, skimming the back of her neck before tracing down her spine and cupping her ass.

She shivered at his touch, instinctively wrapping her arms around his neck, sighing when his arms circled her waist. Her mouth sought his, pressing into his full lips with a groan, pleased when he opened his lips to her. She teased him with the tip of her tongue, clutching his collar like a lifeline while tasting his succulent essence. Great Ancients, he tasted even better than he smelled.

He deepened the kiss, then gently laid her across the rock. She cried out when his hand explored her chest, squeezing one breast before pinching the nipple into a hardened peak, then repeating the action on the other breast.

She felt his frustration as he growled into her mouth. He wanted two hands to explore both breasts at once. Instead he ripped open the buttons on her shirt, exposing her breasts to the elements.

She arched her back while he rubbed one bare breast, then the other. The feel of his skin branding hers was so exquisite, so perfect, how could he think he wouldn't be able to please her?

When he trailed kisses across her chin and down her neck, his lips finding the hard peak of one nipple, she sighed, cupping his head while he sucked her.

"That's it, Magnus," she begged. "Please, please don't stop."

He answered with a grunt, then kissed her from her breasts to her navel.

Her legs fell open when he kissed her mound, nuzzling her tight button and then kissing and nibbling the tender spot until it swelled with need.

She opened her eyes in surprise when she felt two hands spread her thighs. Magnus's second alpha brother, Raine, flashed a wicked grin before scraping her thigh with sharp fangs. She tensed, then relaxed, when his teeth grazed her just enough to make that ache between her thighs unbearable.

Her legs spread like melted butter, her eyes rolling into the back of her head when Magnus began to suckle her sweet spot like a calf trying to draw milk, swirling his tongue around the sensitive flesh and making her cry to the heavens.

When two familiar men knelt beside her, she held out her arms to them, giggling when they nuzzled her neck and toyed with her breasts.

Magnus pulled away and sat back on his heels, frowning while his brothers lavished her with kisses.

"Magnus," she called, waving him toward her.

He didn't move, resting a hand on his knee and hiding the arm with the missing hand behind his back.

"Magnus," she cajoled. "It's okay. Please come to me."

But he sat as still as stone, lines etched deep into his face.

She was about to call to him again, then sucked in a sharp hiss when Raine slid a thick finger into her pussy. She cried out when he tunneled into her while stroking her inner thigh with the other hand. His brothers continued to nibble on her breasts and neck. She wanted to call to Magnus to join them, but the pleasure was suddenly so intense, she could barely breathe, much less speak.

Raine's finger hit a magic spot that awakened every nerve ending in her body, lighting her on fire from the inside out. With a low growl, his eyes shifted from chestnut to a blinding gold as he fucked her harder, faster. Her climax came without warning, the impact so cataclysmic, she was paralyzed beneath his touch, crying out Raine's name and then shuddering when she fell over the edge, her pussy throbbing against his fingers like a heartbeat.

Raine let out a low, deep chuckle before falling on top of her, the tip of his thick erection pressing into her swollen juncture.

She blinked at him and placed a hand on his chest. "We can't have sex."

He arched a thick brow. "Why not? Are you the only one who gets pleasure?"

"No, but I know the rules. Head alpha goes first." She nodded to Magnus, who simply sat there, a lone tear sliding down his cheek. "Magnus," she said. "Do something!"

But he simply blinked at her, saying nothing.

She squirmed under Raine, trying to scoot away, swearing when his brothers pinned her down.

"Hey!" she cried. Then she yelled when his face shifted to that of his drunken father, Vidar.

She shifted, snarling at him when he refused to back down, her senses overwhelmed by the putrid stench of stale whiskey. When he lunged for her, she lashed out, grabbing Vidar's neck and giving him a good, hard shake. Coughing and sputtering, she spit out a mouthful of feathers. When her eyes shot open, it took her a moment to realize she had a pillow in her mouth, or what was left of it. She spun on the bed when Tor burst through her door as a ten-foot beast.

"Annie, what's wrong?"

Whimpering, she tucked her tail between her legs, looking around at the mess of feathers everywhere.

"I think she had a nightmare." Ioana ducked under Tor's massive arm and sat beside Annie, stroking her neck.

She cringed as the entire Coyotechaser family, kids included, gathered in her doorway and the hall. How embarrassing.

"Go, everyone!" Ioana shooed them away like they were stray dogs. "Give a girl some privacy."

When they left her alone with Ioana, she sighed in relief and shifted back into human form, digging under the covers for her nightgown, which was in tatters.

Ioana handed her an oversized T-shirt from her suitcase. "Is everything okay?"

She slipped the shirt on over her head. "I had a bad dream."

"What happened in it?" Ioana threw her a pair of underwear.

A shudder coursed through her as she remembered how much her mates' touch had aroused her. "My mates were touching me." Averting her eyes, she slipped into her undies, hoping the thin cotton would be enough to soak up the moisture between her legs.

Ioana arched a brow, a subtle smirk tugging at her lips. "And?" *You go girl,* Ioana's thought projected into Annie's head.

How fucking humiliating. Ioana knew she'd had a wet dream.

She looked around the room, anywhere but into Ioana's assessing gaze. "Magnus pulled away when Raine tried to have sex with me." She shivered again and rubbed warmth into her arms. "Then Raine turned into their father. He tried to rape me, and Magnus did nothing to help me."

Resting a hand on Annie's arm, Ioana searched her eyes. "I think he would help if it ever came to that."

"It felt so real." She bit her lip, repulsed by the memory of Vidar's hands on her. Even though it had only been a dream, she still felt unclean, soiled by his touch.

"It's natural to dream about your mates," Ioana said. "I had several about mine before we bonded."

"But what about the part with their father?"

Ioana grimaced. "Well, that part was unusual, though the man is frightening, so I can see why you'd have that sort of dream. Nothing to be ashamed of." Ioana flashed a smile that didn't quite reach her eyes.

"Do you think they have dreams about me?" Annie clutched her chest, imagining what she'd be doing in their dreams.

Ioana's grin turned positively wicked. "I know they do."

She wondered if their erotic dreams had also ended badly. "I hope they defended me in their dreams."

Ioana looked away. Her silence wasn't reassuring.

TIRED OF STARING UP at the ceiling and thinking depressing thoughts, Annie finally dragged herself out of bed. The morning sun was barely peeking over the horizon when she stumbled into the kitchen.

The open room with the new white cabinets and a breakfast bar that faced the living room was devoid of people, save for Tor and Van, who were sitting at the counter, elbows resting on the gray granite, clutching steaming cups of coffee while they eyed her expectantly. Figured they'd be awake at the butt-crack of dawn. She was beginning to wonder if they ever slept, or if they simply haunted her door, making sure the boogie man didn't run off with her. She eyed the sofas where they'd spent the night. Their blankets were neatly folded on the edge of an armrest, their backpacks tucked away in a corner of the room. They'd hardly left a trace of their existence, while Annie had shredded her host's pillow and woken everyone up in the middle of the night.

"How did you sleep?" Tor asked.

She shrugged, knowing full well they knew she'd had an erotic dream. There was nothing those two didn't know. "Meh."

Tor cleared his throat. "We've received word from the Wolfstalkers."

Her breath caught in her throat, and she gaped at him like a deer caught in highbeams. "And?"

"We've been invited to dinner," Tor said without inflection.

Her erratic heartbeat came to a grinding halt. "When?"

Tor gave her a stony-eyed look. "Tonight."

Annie stiffened. "I'm not going over there."

Van arched a brow. "You want to negotiate peace, don't you?"

She crossed her arms, pent-up anger making her temples ache. "I want better mates."

"You don't even know them yet." Tor flashed an annoyingly patronizing smile. "You may like them once you get to know them."

She fought the urge to roll her eyes. "I doubt it."

Tor's eyes narrowed to slits, and his voice dropped to a commanding rumble. "Dinner is at eight."

Eight? That was late—not for her, but for a pack of drunks. If they were anything like her mother's boyfriends, the closer to nightfall it got, the worse their demons became. She wasn't looking forward to seeing Vidar at all, but the steely look Tor gave her made it hard for her to disobey.

"Fine." She threw up her hands. "What do I do until then?"

"Roy will be here soon," Van said and took a long drink from his coffee.

She glared at both of them, impatiently tapping her foot. "But I'm not allowed to leave with him, right?"

Tor shook his head. "It's not safe."

Not safe? Had he forgotten she'd killed a freaking werewolf? That she'd lived on her own for almost a year? Turning on her heel, she marched to her bedroom.

"Where are you going?" Tor called.

"Back to bed," she called over her shoulder. "Wake me up after the apocalypse." Though she'd wanted to slam the door, she feared the others in the house wouldn't appreciate being woken up by her tantrum.

She needed alone time to regain her composure while she adjusted to the idea of dinner with her cowardly mates and their drunk, abusive father. What could possibly go wrong, other than Annie losing her cool and ripping Vidar's throat out?

She flopped on the bed, mentally calculating the time difference between Texas and Alaska. Amara would be asleep and probably wouldn't appreciate a phone call, though she really needed someone to talk to. At the very least, she wanted to hear her dog Mako's sweet bark. How she missed him and wished she could've taken him with her to Texas. If she did end up mating with the Wolfstalkers, she'd send for him. She couldn't live in Texas without him. But she was getting ahead of herself. No way in hell was she mating with the Wolfstalkers until they learned to stand up to their father. Until they proved themselves worthy of her. She looked at the ceiling through a misty haze. What if they didn't stand up to him? Or worse, what if they turned out to be just like him? She couldn't possibly mate with them if that was the case, which meant she would be destined to live as a lone wolf. How positively depressing.

ANNIE SAT ON THE PORCH swing, sipping a cold soda and watching the cows roam across the expansive field, munching grass. Beside her, Roy palmed a can of beer, looking like he had a lot on his mind. She thought about prying but knew it was wrong. She had never found the right time to tell Roy about her mind-reading capabilities, so popping into his head would be worse than spying. Roy had to get the words out on his own.

Finally he cleared his throat. "I looked her up."

She froze. "Who?"

He grimaced. "You know who."

Her shoulders sagged. Of course she did. She gave him an expectant look. "And?"

His voice was flat. "She married a rich old man twice her age."

"What?" A bitter laugh escaped her. "Mom's a gold-digger? Say it isn't so. Did you talk to her?"

"No." He frowned into his beer. "It's too risky. If she asked what you or I was doing, I wouldn't be able to explain."

"She won't ask." Annie rolled her eyes. "She doesn't care." A knife of rejection twisted in her heart at the mere thought of the woman who'd abandoned them, forcing them into foster care.

"She had to leave." Roy's voice rose and his cheeks reddened. "She and Dad had a loveless marriage even before Dad's accident."

Swearing under her breath, Annie refused to call that man her dad. Not after he'd sat in his wheelchair and said nothing as CPS took them away. She'd been relieved when she learned her true fathers were the Ancients, the first wolves, immortals who watched over their packs from heaven and sometimes graced Earth with their presence. She squared her shoulders. "First off, he's *your* dad, not mine. Second, she could've taken us with her."

Roy's face fell. "That's cold, Annie. He thought you were his child. He loved you like you were his."

That was a lie. He'd loved nobody. His only purpose in life was to pop pills and feel sorry for himself, even though it was his bad karma that put him in the wheelchair. After her grandparents died, he'd taken her cousin Amara's inheritance on the grounds that he was to raise her. Instead he left her with her abusive, druggie mom and then turned his back on her when she was forced into foster care. The Ancients had punished him for his selfishness. Amara told her that the car crash that had left him paralyzed had been no accident. The Ancient alpha Amarok had caused the crash by appearing on the road before him in his apelike protector form, scaring him so badly, he'd hit a tree. After the accident, the man Annie had thought was her father withdrew from the world, preferring to stay in a perpetual state of drunkenness or drug addiction. Their mother, refusing to watch her husband deteriorate, had spent most of her time away from home with various boyfriends. Sometimes she'd even been bold enough to bring her boyfriends home, flaunting them in front of her crippled husband.

"He didn't even fight when they took us away," Annie whispered through a constricted throat. Every time Roy insisted on talking about their parents, she felt like an elephant was sitting on her chest.

"He's a quadriplegic," he snapped. "What was he supposed to do?"

Annie looked at him through narrowed eyes. "That didn't mean he couldn't fight for us."

He crushed the empty beer can in his grip. "He asks about you."

Her breath hitched. "What do you tell him?"

"That you're living with friends in Alaska." He flashed a boyish smile. "He wants you to call him."

Every muscle in her body tensed. "I have nothing to say to him."

He tossed the empty can on the floor and kicked it down the stairs. "Annie, you're not being fair."

"*I'm* not being fair?" Annie's pitch rose along with her ire. "Look at how they treated Amara."

He slouched, looking at that empty beer can as if it was his heart he'd kicked down the stairs. "That was wrong."

"Ya think?" She couldn't conceal her venom. Roy knew what his father had done to Amara and how hard her life had been because of it. He seriously couldn't expect her to feel sorry for the man.

"Taking her inheritance was Mom's idea," he mumbled, "not Dad's."

As if that made it all right. "He could've stood up to her, but he didn't, and Amara suffered because of it."

"So you won't call him?" His voice cracked, reminding her of his awkward puberty stage.

She groaned, her inner-wolf scratching at the surface, howling to break free and run far, far away. "Stop." She abruptly stood, making the swing shake and squeak. She had to get the hell away from Roy. She knew from experience there was no shutting him up when he got in these dark, depressing moods.

"Okay, fine." He heaved an overly dramatic sigh and pouted. "Where are you going?"

"Inside." It was almost time to go see the Wolfstalkers. "I have to get ready for my dinner date from hell."

Chapter Three

ANNIE PICKED AT HER undercooked hamburger, feeling more like she was the main course. She stole cautious glances at her mates. Tor and Van flanked her, growling at them when they stared at her for too long. She had never been more grateful for their presence than at that moment and not just because they served as good shields from her mates. They were also protecting her from the constant glares she was getting from Vidar.

The old wolf and his two brothers were stupid drunk. Maybe that's why the gamma didn't realize the food was undercooked. She couldn't believe the condition of their house. Her mates mentioned they'd been cleaning all day in anticipation of her arrival, which made her wonder exactly how dirty it had been before, because there was still food stuck to the walls and spider webs in every corner. Not to mention the entire place smelled like rotten cabbage. She understood her mates' gamma father probably had a hard time keeping up with housework, with only one eye and such a pronounced limp, but the rest of the family could've helped out more. Who thought cheese stuck to the walls was the definition of a clean house?

No fucking way was she living here.

Annie took a bite of bland broccoli, hoping she wouldn't get salmonella from it. She didn't smell anything odd, which she took as a good sign. Magnus stared at his food with only one arm on the table. The other was stuffed in his pocket as if he was ashamed to reveal his missing hand.

Second alpha Raine acted like first alpha. He gave her bold looks, like he was undressing her with his eyes. It was unnerving and maybe a little exciting. He'd been the one to greet her at the door and hold out her chair before she sat down.

His brother, Jax, the beta, handed her a burger that was still half raw. Jax had a feral look about him, like all betas, but he also had a subtle, sweet smile.

His dark hair was buzzed short, but from what she'd heard, he'd followed Vidar's orders and never enlisted in the military. She couldn't help but wonder if he'd cut his hair that short to defy his father.

Frey, the youngest of the brothers, had a difficult time controlling his trembling hands. He ended up sloshing half a glass of lemonade down his arm before he set it in front of her plate. Frey had a deer-in-the-headlights look whenever she caught him staring at her. He also had the typical gamma baby face, with squeezable cheeks and an infectious smile. She'd smiled at him a few times and been rewarded with a goofy grin and flame-red cheeks.

She'd wanted to pop into her mates' heads, but she'd been too terrified to try. What if she heard something she didn't like? Besides, she knew it was an invasion of their privacy. She'd hear their thoughts soon enough after their mating. If that ever happened.

"So, Annie," Vidar slurred, spilling his mixed drink all over the table. "Rumor is you killed a human. Is that true?"

Wow. So he was finally addressing her? He hadn't said two words to her since she'd sat at the table, and now he wanted to talk about the time she was forced to defend herself against a rapist? The way he smiled at her, a wild gleam in his eyes, made her flesh crawl. She refused to be intimidated by him. "Yes."

His eyes lit like fireworks. "How did you do it?"

What a sick fuck. Did he really think she'd want to talk about something so traumatic? She set her fork down and folded her hands in front of her. "I really don't like talking about it."

"Nothing to be ashamed of." Waving his drink in the air, he splashed amber liquid down his arm. "If I could kill every damn human on this planet, I would."

She eyed him coolly. "My brother is human."

"I know." He flashed a fanged grin. "So how'd you do it?"

Her spine stiffened, her veins turning to icy sludge. "I've already said I don't want to talk about it." She shuddered at the memory of the taste of Gus's coppery blood filling her mouth when she'd shifted into a wolf and bit down on his neck. She hadn't meant to kill him, but the big, drunk bartender had nearly knocked her unconscious when he'd thrown her against the table and torn off her clothes. Instinct had taken over, and she'd reacted as a trapped, savage wolf.

His smile faded as he leaned toward her, his eyes shifting from brown to gold. "You realize I'm the fucking chieftain, don't you?"

Tor and Van growled until Vidar leaned back, his eyes returning to brown.

Even though her heart was racing, she forced a note of indifference into her voice. "I know what you are."

Stupid fucking cunt! Vidar's virulent thought smacked her like a frying pan to the head. Vidar grabbed his steak knife, a look of pure murder in his eyes.

What a dick! No fucking way was she breeding with this asshat's sons.

Tor threw a protective arm in front of her and spoke in a low, ominous rumble. "Put down the knife, Vidar."

"Father, did you see beef prices have gone up?" Raine asked in a voice so upbeat, it had to be forced. He stared down his father.

Though she was grateful for his intervention, she wondered why his alpha brother didn't intervene as well.

"Shut up," Vidar slurred and pointed the knife at her once more. "You're a mouthy bitch." *And you need to be taught respect,* he projected into her head.

When Vidar glared at her, it was as if a thousand tiny spiders were crawling across her skin. Teach her respect? How about she teach the asshole some manners?

Tor's growl was eclipsed by Raine's roar. His eyes shifted and his nose lengthened as he jumped up and drove his steak knife into the table beside his belligerent father.

Vidar wrapped his fingers around the wooden handle of Raine's knife and jerked it out of the wood. "Stand down, son," he whispered.

She shivered. In that whisper, she felt the force of Vidar's ominous threat in the marrow of her bones. For some reason she was more terrified of Vidar's threats to her mates than to her. The hair stood up on the back of her neck, and her protective instinct roared to life.

Refusing to stand down, Raine picked up another knife, chest heaving, the scar across his cheek turning from pale white to pulsing red while he glared at his father.

When Vidar pushed back his chair, Annie knew she had to act.

"I ripped his goddamn throat out." She jumped up, pointing her fork at Vidar's chest. "Call me a bitch again, and I'll show you how I did it."

Vidar's red-rimmed eyes turned murderous. He picked up a fork and snapped it in two.

Tor and Van stood, too, flanking her with steely expressions.

Holy shit. Annie hadn't thought this through. She'd been trying to diffuse the tension between Raine and his father, but she might have made the situation worse.

Vidar gazed at her for a long, tense moment, his drunken brothers stumbling to their feet, clutching their knives as well. Raine's brothers got up, though Magnus was the last to stand, hanging back and warily eyeing his family.

Annie clutched her fork like a lifeline, tension a knot in her gut. The testosterone in the room reached an all-time high. Every wolf shifter was growling, and she had no idea how to get Vidar to back down. Despite her nervousness, she narrowed her eyes at Vidar and read his thoughts.

Goddamn bitch. She'll turn them against me if I'm not careful.

So he was scared of losing his sons' loyalty. Good. She refused to break eye contact and let him intimidate her.

He did something unexpected. He tossed back his head and let out a hearty laugh. Whatever was so funny, she had no idea. Vidar's thoughts hit her like a gust of wind, nearly knocking her back. He had many thoughts at once, and they were too jumbled to make sense. That's when she realized he was beyond batshit crazy.

He let out a chuckle so deep, it reverberated through her bones. Losing control of the knife, he bent over, clutching the table. His brothers soon joined in while everyone else stared at him as if he'd lost his fucking mind.

After wiping moisture from his eyes, he pointed at Annie. "She's got bigger balls than my sons. They're going to have a hell of a time taming her."

Anger flushed her cheeks. "Nobody's taming me," she said through clenched teeth.

"You think so?" The words rang with humor and condescension, making the wolf inside her want to snap him in half.

Still holding the fork, she crossed her arms. "I know so." She knew his bout of manic laughter was a way to diffuse the tension, and she should have followed his lead if she wanted peace between her mates and their fathers, but she couldn't help herself. It suddenly dawned on her that she hated the man more than any of the sleazy boyfriends her mother had paraded in front of the family while her "father" said nothing from his wheelchair.

Raine lowered his weapon, clearing his throat. "Annie, would you like us to show you around the ranch?"

She shrugged, relieved that he'd given her a way out. "Sure."

"She hasn't finished her meal." Vidar said.

She scowled at what was supposed to pass for edible food. "I've lost my appetite." Truthfully, she was ravenous. What she wouldn't give to be home in Alaska, eating one of Rone Thunderfoot's mooseburgers with a side of his beer-battered onion rings and a homemade strawberry milkshake. She missed his food. She also missed being around sane shifters.

"Go ahead," Tor said as he sat down. "Vidar and I need to talk."

THE RANCH WAS IN THE same condition as the house. Fences needed mending, and the barn was full of holes, making it look like a big red block of Swiss cheese. Annie didn't have much, but she took pride in what little she did have. She understood the fathers were drunks, but couldn't their sons have repaired things?

Noting how Magnus trailed behind them like he was the pack leper, she kept her distance from the other three brothers as they showed her a field with several dozen grazing cows. At least their livestock appeared to be healthy. She cast several wary glances over her shoulder, noting how Magnus always looked away, keeping his stump stuffed in his front pocket. What was wrong with him? Was he that self-conscious over his missing hand, or was it something more? And why the hell had he let Raine do all the heavy lifting with their father? Wasn't he supposed to be head alpha? His inaction meant he didn't care or he was a chickenshit. Either way, it didn't bode well for her.

"Did you want to see the stables?"

She blinked up at Raine, who motioned to an old dilapidated building that looked like it should have been condemned.

"Or maybe the barn," the beta named Jax said, a smile tugging at his mouth. "We've been rebuilding a '65 Chevy."

"Twice now he's called me a bitch." She glared at them, including Magnus.

Jax thumbed at his second alpha. "Raine stood up for you."

Crossing her arms, she focused on Magnus, who leaned against the fence, staring out at the field as if she didn't exist. "Not enough."

Frey cleared his throat, voice shaking like wobbly glass. "We'll talk to him later."

"Not enough."

Raine threw up his hands and shared a hopeless look with his younger brothers. "What is enough?"

"You're men," she spat, poking Magnus's side while brushing past him. "You figure it out."

Anger fueling her movements, she strode to their rental truck. Magnus hadn't even grunted when she'd jabbed him. What the fuck was wrong with him?

She'd just reached the truck when a strong hand spun her around. She blinked up at Raine.

"There's something you need to know about our dad," he said.

"He's a major fucking asshole," she snapped.

The frown lines around his eyes made him look far older than mid-twenties. She briefly remembered him telling her at the table that he was twenty-five, and Magnus was twenty-six. Jax had just celebrated his twenty-third birthday, and Frey was twenty-two, two years older than her. They were hardly boys, so what was the problem?

Releasing a slow breath, Jax said, "Yeah, he's an asshole, but he wasn't always this way. He's been like this since our mother and father were killed."

"That's no excuse."

Raine held out both hands in an apologetic gesture. "We're sorry for his behavior. He's not usually this bad, but he's been drinking."

Seriously? As if that was an excuse for poor behavior? Disappointment in her mates widened a hole in her heart. "You need to quit making excuses for him."

Jax frowned. "We're not making excuses."

"You are." She lunged toward him, poking his chest. "You can call a monster by another name, but he's still a monster."

Eyes widening, Jax stared down at the spot where she'd jabbed him, a hurt look in his eyes as if she'd just shot him through the heart with an arrow.

"What are you doing?" Raine asked as she climbed into the backseat.

"Waiting for my uncles to come out."

"Don't you want to see the ranch?"

"Not really." She scowled at Magnus, who'd stayed by the fence. He was still gazing at those cows as if in a trance. He didn't give a damn about her. "I won't be mating with you, so it doesn't matter." She angrily wiped away a tear while the sun set behind a copse of oak trees.

"What do you mean you won't be mating with us?" Raine cried urgently.

"Do you honestly think I want to marry into this family? Bring up kids in the middle of a civil war?"

"It won't turn into a civil war," Raine said. "Our father will cool down."

"Yeah, he does this from time to time." Jax's smile appeared forced. "The tribe will make up."

She pulled back her shoulders, more resolved than ever to put distance between her and these pathetic shifters. "They should've never split."

Raine dragged a hand through his hair. "You're right, but the Coyote-chasers—"

"Make better leaders than your dad. Isn't it obvious that your father is out of his fucking mind?"

Raine grimaced slightly. "He will cool down."

"Until the next time and the next." She rolled her eyes. "I'm not putting up with a father-in-law who calls me a bitch or mates too weak-spined to tell him to shut the fuck up."

Jax threw up his hands, then thumbed to his older brother. "But Raine—"

"Yeah, thanks, Raine," she snapped. "What about the rest of you?"

"We stood with him," Frey said, his boyish face marred by a heavy frown.

When her attention shot to him, he looked at his dirty, scuffed boots, his cheeks reddening.

She glanced at their oldest brother, who still hadn't moved from the fence. "He didn't." Technically, Magnus had stood with them, but he'd been the last to get up, and he hadn't said a word to his father. As head alpha, he should've been first to defend her.

Raine gaped at her, unable to defend his brother. Slamming the door shut, she pulled out her phone and scanned her messages while ignoring the three brooding brutes outside.

So much for her foolish dream of finding mates to complete her and spending the rest of eternity with them. These men were unsuitable. They weren't strong and brave, like the Thunderfoots. Maybe Vidar had been right when he'd said she had bigger balls than his sons, and that was the problem. She couldn't imagine what their children would be like, but one thing was certain—she wasn't raising a pack of pussies.

She sent Amara a text, asking how her husky Mako was doing. When Amara fired back an image of Mako cuddled up with Amara's two big dogs, her heart sang. He was so happy in Alaska with his best friends. One more reason she couldn't mate with the Wolfstalkers. Mako would be heartbroken if she left him behind, and he'd be equally crushed if she moved him to Texas. Why couldn't the Ancients have chosen Alaskan mates for her?

RAINE LEANED AGAINST the fence, staying in view of the truck where his mate had barricaded herself. Not that he blamed her for not wanting to spend time with them after the way their father had treated her. He should've done more when he'd called her a bitch, like break a glass dish over his head, but such an act of violence would've probably called for more violence and put Annie at risk of getting caught in the middle.

Raine's two younger brothers stared at Annie like two mutts drooling over frying bacon. They had every reason to want her. She was a beauty, with long, smooth hair the color of midnight, alabaster skin, and bright blue eyes. Her generous curves made his dick as hard as iron, especially that sweet, round ass. He'd love to dig his fingers into those soft globes while ramming her from behind.

"Why is she so mad at us?" Frey's lower lip hung down as he stared longingly at Annie's truck like a starving child drooling over a cupcake. "It's not our fault our father's a dick."

Jax leaned against the fence and cast Magnus a furtive glance. "This wasn't how I envisioned our first date."

"Me neither," Frey said.

Magnus didn't respond. He just kept staring at the field of grazing cows, his face a mask of indifference. Raine's blood boiled. His brother should've been leading the fight to win over their mate.

Jax jerked upright as if he'd been jolted by a cattle prod. "We can't let her go back to Alaska."

"What are we supposed to do?" Frey asked.

"Exactly what she told us to do." Raine shrugged, casting Magnus a sideways glare. "She's right. We didn't do enough when Father insulted her."

Swearing, Magnus pushed off the fence and faced the rolling, grassy hills. "She expects too much of us," he grumbled.

Ah, so the brooding alpha brother had something to say after all.

"No, you expect too little of yourself," Raine grumbled. "You're the oldest. We should be following your lead, and you should have been first to defend our mate."

Magnus's eyes flashed gold. "With this?" He thrust his stump in Raine's face before shoving it back in his pocket.

"Stop using your disability as an excuse." Raine was so pissed, he was seeing red. "I could kick that old man's ass with one hand tied behind my back. So can you, so stop being a pussy." To emphasize his point, Raine shoved one hand in his pocket and pushed Magnus with the other.

Magnus backed up a step, hurt flashing in his eyes before he turned and marched to the barn, refusing to spare any of them a backward glance.

"Damn you, Magnus!" Raine shook a fist at his retreating back. "Why don't you get mad for once?" What the hell was the matter with him? Raine had been hoping that Annie's presence would bring Magnus out of his shell, but he hid behind his disability even more with her around. If Raine didn't know any better, he would've thought Magnus didn't want to be loved. "Don't fuck this up for us!" he hollered, and a moment later Magnus slammed the rusty doors shut.

Raine started to go after him, but Jax latched onto him. "Leave him alone."

"I can't." Raine shook him off. "Don't you see we need Magnus on our side?"

"He won't help us until he's ready."

"We can't do it without him." He scowled at Annie's truck. "Stay here and keep an eye on her." Then he marched to the barn with purposeful strides.

Throwing open the door, he waited a moment while his eyes adjusted to the dim light. Magnus was at the workbench, slamming tools around while tearing apart an old carburetor.

Feeling Magnus's tension radiating across the dirt floor, Raine approached his brother cautiously. "We can't stand up to Father without you."

Crashing a wrench on the counter, Magnus looked up at him with blazing eyes. "What good do you think it will do?"

"He called our mate a bitch. We can't let that slide."

Magnus let out a bitter laugh, tapping his head with the end of a screwdriver. "You don't think his words are burning a hole through my skull right now?"

Something about the hopeless look in Magnus's eyes made Raine's anger deflate like a popped balloon. "She thinks we're cowards."

The creases in Magnus's brow deepened. "Maybe she's right."

"Damn you." How could his brother be so apathetic? "Get mad at that asshole for once!"

"You think I'm not mad as hell?" Magnus roared, punching the wooden bench and creating a fist-sized hole. "Every time I stand up to him, he just reminds me of what I am—half a wolf."

He gazed at the damage Magnus had done. Their fathers had destroyed everything else they owned, but Raine and Jax had spent days building and sanding that bench. Was it too much to expect one thing in this shithole to stay intact? He looked at his brother, his heart stopping at the pain he saw in his glassy eyes. He knew Magnus had been transported back to the night of his fourteenth birthday, the night everyone's lives went to hell.

"Her death was not your fault," he whispered as Magnus hung his head.

Not a day had gone by since his mother was murdered that Raine didn't miss her, but not once in his mourning did he ever blame Magnus for her death.

Balling his hands into fists by his sides, Magnus shook his head. "I didn't move fast enough."

"You were a kid. It was your first shift."

"Even if it wasn't my fault, I'm still only half a man." Magnus held up his stump.

Walking around the bench, Raine placed a hand on Magnus's shoulder. "Only if you believe it, brother."

Magnus's face was screwed up so tight, Raine didn't know if his brother was on the verge of crying or about to punch him in the face. "You didn't see the look in her eyes when my hand fell off!"

Raine blinked hard as he recalled the incident yesterday when Magnus's prosthetic had fallen. "She was shocked," he said, trying to keep a straight face.

He hadn't seen Annie's expression, and even though he hardly knew her, he got the feeling she wouldn't be turned off by Magnus's injury.

Magnus frowned at his boots. "She was repulsed."

Frustration surged through him. Yeah, it sucked that his brother had lost a hand, but it happened twelve years ago. For fuck's sake, he needed to get over it. "Magnus, stop torturing yourself before you end up just like him." Without waiting for his brother's reply, he turned and marched back out, his heart dropping to his stomach when he saw Tor Thunderfoot pulling out of the drive, Annie sitting in the backseat with her head down.

He hadn't even gotten a chance to say goodbye. Damn their Father for ruining their evening, and damn Magnus for letting him!

Chapter Four

ROY PUT HIS TRUCK IN park and shut off the engine. After blowing on his steaming coffee, he chanced a sip, swearing when he burned the roof of his mouth. Damn. He'd have to go into the sheriff's office without caffeine. He wasn't ready for this shit before the butt-crack of dawn. He set the coffee in the holder and climbed out, grimacing when he slammed the door and heard the window rattle. That backwoods repair shop had done a shoddy job. He'd need to take his truck to a real body shop the next time he had downtime and extra money.

The sun still hadn't risen, and the gravel drive was barely lit by the rusty lamp overhead. He dragged his feet up the creaky steps of the historical old house turned police station, surprised to find so many deputies inside the small office, all of them on edge, hands on holsters when he walked through the door. They should recognize him by now. One of the deputies took him to the back room with Sheriff Gonzalez.

The old sheriff had leathery brown skin and a bushy gray handlebar moustache. He glanced up from the desk. "Sorry to wake you up so early, amigo."

"No problem," Roy answered. "Thanks for calling me."

"Three dead this time. Migrant workers. All were disemboweled."

Roy's stomach churned. "Same as before then?"

"No. We got a witness this time." The sheriff stood. "A farm worker. She doesn't speak much English, though."

Roy froze. If this witness could identify the Wolfchasers, he would finally have justification to bring in Vidar and his brothers, and possibly even their sons. He hoped not the sons, for Annie's sake. "Can you interpret for me? My Spanish is still rusty."

"Sure." The sheriff waved him to the back room.

A young, pregnant woman with long, black hair pulled back in a braid sat on the sofa with a female deputy, holding a cup of coffee with trembling hands.

"Esmeralda," the sheriff said to her. "Roy Miller *es un agente federal. Puede hacerte algunas preguntas, por favor*?"

Esmeralda looked at Roy with wide, frightened eyes, then rattled off a bunch of rapid Spanish.

Roy looked to Sheriff Gonzalez, who shrugged. "She thinks you're INS."

Roy flashed her a smile, discouraged when she shrank back. "Tell her I'm not going to deport her. I'm only here to ask her questions."

The sheriff translated so fast, Roy could hardly keep up. He reminded himself to to take some online Spanish courses when he found the time.

"I need to know what she saw," Roy said.

Before the sheriff could translate, the girl answered. "*Chupacabra.*"

Roy arched a brow. "Chupacabra?"

"She's an artist." The sheriff handed Roy a piece of lined paper. "Even drew us a picture."

Roy studied it carefully. He didn't know much about art, but he knew the drawing was detailed. Too detailed, showing the profile of a mangy animal that looked like it was part cat by the arch of its back. It hovered over a screaming man, a long rope of intestines hanging from its sharp fangs. Roy had heard the legend of the chupacabra from the locals but assumed they'd seen an Amaroki mid-shift. This thing looked more like the description Annie had given him of a werewolf, with its long, pointy snout, scraggly fur, gangly legs, and long claws that looked like eagle talons. But it couldn't be. Werewolves were only found around haunted forests, and Texas didn't have one. Did it? One thing was certain, it didn't look like an Amaroki, which both relieved and confused him. What the hell was that thing?

"That doesn't look like a wolf. Ask her if she's sure it wasn't a wolf." Maybe the girl had exaggerated the monster's appearance.

"No, no." She vehemently shook her head, not waiting for the sheriff to interpret. "Es un chupacabra."

Roy let out a frustrated groan. He'd spoken about the chupacabra legends with the Coyotechasers. They'd assured Roy they were only fables.

"Do you mind if I keep this?" he asked the sheriff.

"Go ahead. We've already scanned it."

Roy pocketed the picture and looked at the woman once more. "Gracias."

She nodded, turning away and wiping moisture from her eyes.

The sheriff escorted Roy back to his office. "One of the victims was her husband," he said. "She's still in shock."

Roy felt pity for the woman and her unborn child. Whatever this beast was, he was determined to root it out before anymore innocents were killed.

The sheriff reached into his desk, pulled out several photographs, and handed them to Roy. He studied what appeared to be images of animal tracks.

"These were at the scene of attack," the sheriff said. "You can keep them."

"Thanks." Roy studied them. The tracks definitely didn't look wolf. They were narrower and deeper, which would match the sharp claws from the drawing.

"The boys are coming back with coffee and breakfast tacos if you care to stay," the sheriff said as he sat at his desk and motioned for Roy to take a seat across from him.

"No," he answered, a heaviness settling in his chest as he stared through a crack in the door at the young woman curled up on the sofa, looking like a frightened child. "I need to get back."

He was in no mood to eat after looking at that detailed drawing. He'd been craving breakfast tacos when he'd woken up, too. Spicy chorizo and egg tacos made living in this hellhole somewhat worthwhile, but he wasn't sure when he'd be able to eat after looking at the horrified look in that poor man's eyes as the beast ate his entrails.

"When you gonna tell me what the FBI is doing investigating wolf attacks?"

"Wish I could." He patted the drawing in his pocket. "Thanks for your help."

He trudged to his truck like his feet were made of concrete, thinking of the trail of destruction the beast had left behind in the past few months. An eerie howl resounded in the distance, making him pick up his pace while resting a hand on his holster. He jumped in the truck and started the engine, then gripped the steering wheel with trembling hands. Dammit, he knew he'd signed up for freaky shit when he agreed to work for the FBI as an Amaroki liaison. He'd been foolish to think they'd all be like his half-sister, Annie. This job didn't offer enough hazard pay for the shit he had to put up with, and he feared it was about to get a whole lot more dangerous.

ANNIE KNEW SHE WAS dreaming, but, again, it felt so real. She was sitting on a ledge beside the waterfall, where it emptied into the pond. Looking across the misty vapors rising from the pond, she saw four shadows standing on the opposite ledge and knew they were her mates, for the largest shadow had an arm that ended in a stump. Though she could barely make out their faces, their golden eyes pierced the fog. What did they want? One of them stepped forward, his face slowly coming into view. She recognized his square jaw and piercing eyes. Raine. He stretched an arm out to her, but she shrank back. How could she go to him? The chasm between the ledges was too great. There was no way, and she wasn't about to jump into the water. She had no idea of its depths. What if she injured herself or worse, drowned under the waterfall? No, she couldn't cross. They'd have to find a way to come to her. But would they? She stood there for what felt like ages, the sounds of her shallow breathing overshadowed by the roar of the waterfall. She waited and waited, but her mates never moved. They expected her to cross that chasm alone, to blindly throw herself into the abyss without any help from them. Though she'd been abandoned as a teen and shuffled about in foster care before striking out as a lone wolf, never in her life had she felt more alone than at that moment.

She woke in a sweat, heart racing and limbs trembling as she recalled her dream. She sat up, rubbing the sleep from her eyes, and looked out her window. She'd no idea what time it was, but the sun wasn't up yet.

She jumped at the sound of whimpers outside. When she pulled back the curtains, her heart skipped a beat. Four familiar black wolves with silver eyes were looking up at her.

"Fathers?" she whispered.

Come with us.

Not needing to be told twice, she opened the window, slipped out of her nightgown, and shifted into wolf form. She leapt from the window to the grass, surprised to see all four of her fathers were no longer shadows, but in solid form. They motioned for her to follow, and so she did, chasing them through fields, over rolling hills, and then onto rocky ground. Her tongue was lolling out of her mouth and her tail was dragging by the time they reached a wide canyon illuminated by the moon. The canyon was deeper than it was wide and stretched for miles.

Amarok turned his nose to the sky and let out a powerful, deep howl. Her other fathers followed suit, and she joined them. When they finished howling, she followed them along a narrow trail that led to the bottom of the canyon.

We shouldn't be here, she projected, tail tucked between her legs as she slid down rocks. *This is where my mates lost their alpha father and mother.*

Amarok flicked her nose with a bushy tail. *You will be safe with us.*

She followed them all the way to the floor of the canyon, where they ran and ran, only stopping to drink from the river before they were off again. Strangely enough, they ended up at a waterfall, one that looked similar to the one in her dreams.

After they traversed a rocky slope to a flat rock overlooking a misty pool of water, she was awestruck. It was the same as in her dream, with an almost identical slab across from the pool. She remembered staring at her mates standing on that slab, waiting for them to find a way to her. She sat, wrapping her tail around her legs. How could she have dreamed this place when she'd never been there?

She noted how her second alpha and gamma father stayed behind, perched on top of the cliff like sentinels. They were watching for danger.

Her birth father, Fenrir, nuzzled her with a low whine. *We've longed to see you.*

Her ears flattened against her skull. They'd longed to see her, yet they'd left her alone all this time? *Then you should've come sooner.*

We are always with you in spirit, Amarok answered, then lifted his muzzle to the moon. *We can't form from the shadows unless the moon is full.*

Where were you when I was fighting werewolves? she asked accusingly, because she certainly could've used their help when demonic wolves had been trying to kill her.

Guarding inside the portal, Amarok answered.

Inside the portal? she asked. She didn't remember seeing or hearing them when she'd neared that place.

Why do you think you didn't see other demons while Katarina kept it open? Amarok asked.

She gave pause, stunned. *I just thought they hadn't found their way out yet.*

Amarok let out a low growl, the black hair on the back of his neck standing on end. *They knew the way. We fought them back day and night until the witch closed the portal.*

All moisture from her mouth suddenly evaporated. *Oh. Did any escape?*

Amarok and Fenrir puffed up their chests, and their laughter reverberated in her ears.

One, Amarok answered, *but we tracked her down and dragged her back to hell.*

Her ears twitched as she recalled the vengeful ghost who could transform into a snake. *Was it Katarina?*

No, and Katarina wasn't a demon. Not yet. His gaze swept the sky. *She was still in spirit form, or we would've been able to send her back to hell ourselves.*

Fenrir licked his paw. *The demon was a tricky bitch who led us on a hunt across North America.*

Annie's heart thudded loudly in her ears. *Did you catch her?*

Amarok flashed a fanged smile. *Of course.*

She heaved a breath of relief. *Oh, thank the Ancients.*

You're welcome, her fathers answered in unison, their tails simultaneously thumping.

Annie's tail instinctively thumped. She'd used that expression so many times, she'd forgotten the Ancients were sitting in front of her. Her tail thumped harder, warmth flooding her when Fenrir nuzzled her again. *Now that the portal is closed, there won't be any more risk of demons?*

Fenrir sat back on his haunches, his lips pulling back in a snarl. *There's always risk of demons.*

We've been guarding portals these past thousand years, and in that time a few have slipped through, Amarok said, the words dark and deadly.

Annie froze. *Where are they?*

If we knew where they were, Amarok answered, *we'd have captured them by now, but do not fear. They are afraid of Amaroki.*

Her chest deflated with a groan of relief. *That's good.*

They can't control us like they can humans, Amarok added.

Annie swallowed. *They control humans?*

Amarok solemnly nodded. *Some of them can possess humans, but they cannot possess Amaroki. They can't break our magical barriers, not unless an Amaroki ventures beyond the veil of a haunted forest.*

How can we tell which humans are possessed? Annie asked apprehensively.

You have the unique ability to read minds, Fenrir answered. *That is how you tell. A demon's thoughts are dark and self-centered. You may also notice an occasional flash of red behind their irises. But again, do not worry. They fear the Amaroki.*

I do not worry for myself, Annie said. *I worry for my brother.*

We understand, Fenrir answered. *But like I said, demons fear the Amaroki. Your brother is safest when he's close to us.*

She let out a low whimper. *Are there demons nearby? Is that why you're telling me this?*

We picked up the scent of one on our run. Fenrir growled. *We can't tell how old it is.*

And can't you consult those ancient scrolls of yours to see what will happen with the demons?

Who do you think wrote the scrolls? Amarok chuckled. *We cannot see what the future holds when demons are involved. Their dark magic muddies the water.*

Annie's heart thudded so loud, it sounded like a freight train driving through her ears.

I think we've had enough demon talk for one day. Amarok's tail went limp. *Our purpose wasn't to upset you.*

I've fought werewolves before. Annie willed her racing heartbeat to slow. *I can handle demon talk.*

His tail thumped again, brushing dirt and debris into the water below. *We saw you fighting the werewolves.*

Her ears perked. *You did?*

You were very brave, he answered, his deep voice softening. *We're so proud of you.*

Really? She tilted her head, whimpering. *So you're not mad at me?*

Amarok jumped to all fours and rubbed her neck with his thick muzzle. *Why would we be mad?*

You paired me with idiots, she blurted, an ache stabbing her chest at the thought. Why couldn't they've paired her with brave mates who didn't have a douchey father?

Amarok sat, his brow drawing low. *It's true we do have a hand in bondings but not like you think.*

Oftentimes, we cannot deny an obvious bond, Fenrir explained, *just as you cannot deny your instincts when you find yourself attracted to the Wolfstalkers.*

She looked down at the waterfall splashing into the pool. *They are cowards.* She knew she was being harsh. Raine had stood up to his father for her, but he hadn't done enough. None of them had.

Their fear of their father is a deep-rooted seed. It is not so easy for them to dig it out.

If she'd been in human form, she would've laughed out loud. *Is that a nice way of calling them pussies?*

Amarok pressed against her while Fenrir flanked her other side.

Your youngest mates are ready to stand up to their father, Amarok said, *but they cannot do so without Magnus.*

She bristled. *He's the biggest pussy of them all.*

He carries a heavy burden of guilt, Fenrir answered. *It is wrapped around his heart like a noose.*

He's being ridiculous, she said, refusing to allow Magnus to get a pass so easily.

To you, maybe, Amarok said. *An alpha's primary job is to keep his women safe. He failed with his mother. He thinks he's not worthy because of it.*

She turned to him with a whimper. *He was just a child.*

Amarok shook his head. *He was a man.*

Barely. The irony that she was making excuses for Magnus wasn't lost on her, but it had been his first shift. How could they hold him responsible?

When Amarok gave her a fanged smile, she knew she'd been set up. He'd wanted her to defend Magnus, damn him.

Until he can forgive himself, believe in himself, Amarok said, *he will not have the courage to face his father.*

How does he forgive himself? she asked. His mother had died over a decade ago. If he hadn't forgiven himself by now, would he ever?

Amarok gave her a pointed look. *He needs the support of a strong woman.*

Fenrir nuzzled her once more. *And you are the strongest woman in all the Amaroki.*

Anger and resentment welled in her chest. She couldn't help feeling like she was being punished for her bravery. *So that's why you paired me with them? You want me to teach an alpha how to be a leader?*

No. Fenrir's voice softened. *Teach him he's worthy of love.*

How do I do that?

Let your heart tell you what to do, Amarok said.

Her heart? What kind of bullshit was that? How was she supposed to let her heart guide her when she felt only resentment toward the wolves who were destined to be her mates?

A warning howl from above interrupted her thoughts.

Amarok's nose wrinkled as he sniffed the air. *We must be on our way.*

She scented the air, too, thinking she smelled the blood of humans mixed with something else, something she couldn't place. Her fathers flanked her while they ran back to the Coyotechasers' home, never letting her get too far ahead or behind.

By the time they reached the lawn, she was mentally and physically exhausted. She turned to them as the morning sun peeked over the horizon. *Will you visit me again?* She hated the note of desperation she projected, but she so longed to spend more time with her fathers.

Of course, Amarok answered wistfully.

Her heart sank when their solid forms became shadows, then faded into nothing. She crawled back through the window, slipped into her pajamas, and sank into bed. Too tired to grieve their absence too long, she fell into a deep slumber, wondering if she'd dream about her fathers or her mates and praying she'd find the strength to help Magnus.

ANNIE WOKE TO THE SOUND of Roy's low murmurs, followed by Cesar's heated whispers. The sun had risen. She got out of bed and cracked open the door.

"None of our shifters look like this," Cesar said.

"What about the Wolfstalkers?" Roy asked.

"This isn't even a wolf," Van Thunderfoot said.

"Then what the hell is it?" Roy demanded.

She tiptoed to the kitchen. They were standing at the island counter, passing around a piece of paper. She glided between Roy and Tor, and caught a glimpse of a scraggly beast that looked part werewolf, eating what appeared to be a bowl of spaghetti.

Tor placed the picture on the counter, clucking his tongue. "Did it ever occur to you that the witness was lying?"

"Annie," Roy said. "You've fought a werewolf. What do you make of it?"

She picked up the picture, her jaw dropping when she realized the bowl of spaghetti was a human's innards. The look of pain etched into the victim's features made her stomach roil. She didn't think she'd ever purge that image from her brain. She shifted focus to the beast. It definitely had werewolf features, like the long, pointy snout and sharp fangs, but it was smaller than those she'd fought and walked on all fours, whereas werewolves walked upright.

"We found bloody paw prints around those attacked." Roy handed a picture to Cesar. "What do you make of them?"

Cesar rubbed his beard and passed it on. "They could belong to a wolf."

Roy's features hardened. "This is the third attack in two months."

Cesar's shoulders fell. "I will call a tribal meeting."

Roy arched a brow. "Will the Wolfstalkers come?"

"I doubt it. Do you think this is them?"

"The elders maybe." His gaze flitted from Annie to Cesar. "Nobody hates humans as much as they do."

Annie's gut twisted. It was bad enough her mates' fathers were drunk assholes. Could they be murderers, too? "But they risk bringing the American government down on their heads."

Cesar shook his head. "That's the problem. I don't think they care."

Chapter Five

ROY HADN'T EVEN FINISHED writing up his report when he received an urgent call from his father's nurse. Some days he regretted moving him to Texas, but the assisted living homes were much more affordable here than in Oregon, taking only half of Roy's paychecks after Dad's social security paid part of it. It was either that or Roy stuck his father back in a state-run home. His father had nearly died in the last one he'd been in when they'd left him in bed too long and his bed sores had become infected. Never again would he let that happen, which meant Roy would have to to eat ramen noodles and live in a run-down apartment for the rest of his dad's life, but at least he'd be safe.

Heaving a resigned sigh, he punched in the code to get through the side gate, which he preferred to the hospital setting at the front entrance. The courtyard was pretty—a collection of wooden benches surrounding a massive live oak, the branches of which shaded the courtyard and half the building. Two residents sat in wheelchairs under the tree, heads hanging, their downcast eyes dull.

What a sad place. He hated that his quadriplegic father was forced to live with dementia patients, but what choice did he have? Taking care of him was a full-time job, and Roy had to work.

After walking through the gate, Roy had to punch in another code to get through the front door, and yet another one to get through the next. The residents were trapped, and none of them knew it except for Dad, who'd been trapped by his body, not his mind.

Gloria, the head nurse, a pretty Hispanic woman with large mocha eyes and endless thick lashes, was helping an elderly woman into a rocking chair.

"Thanks for coming, Roy," she said and waved him toward the dining room, where elderly patients mindlessly gazed at plates of mushy food. "I'm hoping you can talk some sense into him."

His father was sulking in a corner, wearing his usual scowl. Roy checked the time. It was half past five. Dinner had been served half an hour ago, but his father's plate hadn't been touched. Dad didn't realize how good he had it here. The cook always made him a special plate of real food, not the mush the other residents ate. The nurses showed his favorite movies in the common room, and his generation's music played in the halls. He was the only resident who had a say in how the facility was run, yet it still wasn't enough. He was miserable, and Roy was at a loss about what to do.

"Hey, Dad." Roy forced a note of enthusiasm into his voice as he cautiously approached him. "Your nurses tell me you refuse to eat."

"What's the point?"

Roy sighed. How many times would they have this argument? "Dad, they're going to get food into you one way or another."

"Again, what's the point?"

He knelt beside Dad and grasped his frail hand. How odd it was to be in the position of having to treat his father like a child. He remembered when Dad had been strong enough to hoist Roy over his shoulders and carry him around the yard as if he weighed nothing at all.

"The point is that I don't want you to die."

Roy knew he was being selfish. Dad wanted to end his misery, but Roy couldn't let go.

Dad's face fell. "I'm a burden to you, Roy. I'm a burden to everyone."

Roy squeezed his father's hand, wondering if he felt his son's touch. "You're not a burden to me."

His throat constricted with emotion. Why had he thought moving Dad to Texas would make him happier? He was still miserable and still intent on making everyone else around him unhappy, too. Resentment toward his depressing father rose and then that resentment was quickly replaced by guilt. These feelings of resentment and guilt had been a vicious cycle for Roy ever since Dad's car accident. How he wished he could be free of this emotional burden. That familiar feeling of anger toward Annie made an appearance. Even though she had recently discovered her true father was an ancient Amaroki god, as far as Roy was concerned, his father was Annie's father. He'd raised both of them, after all—at least until the accident. He'd doted on Annie and treated her like a princess, and she didn't have the decency to ask Roy how their old man was doing.

Roy sat in a chair beside him, ignoring his scrutinizing gaze.

"It's Friday night," he said accusingly. "You should be out with a young lady on your arm, not at a nursing home with your invalid father."

"Oh, you thought I came to visit you?" Roy teased. "How do you know I'm not here for the pretty nurses?" He quickly glanced at Gloria, who was spoon-feeding a resident. He'd thought about asking her out many times but had always chickened out. How would he take a girl out on a date when he couldn't afford to fix the A/C in his truck?

His father's chuckle was short but sweet. Roy hadn't heard his laughter in too long.

"Have you heard from your sister?" Father asked.

Roy tensed. He asked about Annie every time he visited, and every time Roy had to make up some excuse why she never came with him. "She's doing well."

"Still staying with Cousin Amara?"

"Yeah." Roy averted his eyes. He still hadn't told Annie their dad was in Texas. He feared she'd refuse to visit him.

"Your mother and I didn't treat Amara well."

Roy was at a loss for words. He rarely talked about Roy's shifter cousin.

Father's eyes misted over. "Is that why Annie won't talk to me?"

Roy struggled for the right words to say but in the end decided to settle on the truth. "Yeah," he breathed. He couldn't shield him forever, and he needed to know the reason for Annie's absence. She had a lot of reasons for avoiding him, but his treatment of Amara had been her main excuse.

Father's eyes radiated even more despair, and he swallowed a visible knot in his throat. "How is Amara doing?"

"Really well," Roy said. "Married with kids." He decided to leave out the part about Amara's four husbands, and her shifting and healing abilities. Father wouldn't believe him, and Roy had been sworn to secrecy.

Father arched a brow. "What's her husband like?"

"Treats her like a queen," Roy answered, summarizing the traits of all of Amara's mates into one fictional husband. "Good job. Great with the kids."

"That's good." He gave a pained smile that didn't mask the sadness in his eyes. "She deserves happiness."

"She does," Roy agreed. He thought of Amara often, especially her magical ability to heal. Too many times he'd tried to summon the nerve to ask her to heal Dad, but he had no idea what to say to her. Annie had said their father's car crash was no accident, that he'd been run off the road by one of their Ancients as punishment for his treatment of Amara. Roy agreed Father had needed to be taught a lesson, but a lifetime in a wheelchair seemed a bit harsh.

"I wasn't a good uncle," his father continued. "I shouldn't have let your mother...." He looked down at his legs. "Looks like karma got me back."

Nurse Gloria showed up with a clean fork and napkin. "You ready to eat now, Mr. Miller?" She jabbed the fork in a pile of noodles swirled high on his plate. "The cook made spaghetti, your favorite."

Dad made a face. "I told you I'm not hungry."

"Please," Roy begged. "For me."

After releasing a litany of swear words that would have made a sailor blush, his father finally relented and opened his mouth. The nurse fed him a bite.

Roy stood, stretching his legs. "I'll let you eat in peace. I'll be back tomorrow."

His father swallowed and made a grunting noise. "How's your job going?" The pitiful look in his eyes tugged at Roy's heartstrings. He hated leaving, but he did have a life. This evening he was supposed to take Annie out for drinks, and he had to pick her up before happy hour ended. No way could he afford full price.

He thrust his hands in his pockets. "It's going."

"Did you know my son's in the FBI?" Dad asked Nurse Gloria.

"Yes," she said and laughed. "You tell me every day."

Embarrassed, Roy wondered what else his father had told Gloria about him.

A wide smile split his father's face. "I'm proud of him."

Warmth flooded his chest at the look in his father's eyes.

Gloria patted Dad's wrist. "You should be."

Roy's breath hitched. Now would be a good time to ask Gloria out, but he couldn't summon the nerve. She could do better than a broke secret agent. He backed up a step, nearly tripping over his own two feet and inwardly cursed himself for acting like a hormonal teenager.

"Thanks, Nurse Gloria." He gave her an awkward nod and was way too self-conscious to say anymore. "See ya, Dad."

He quickly walked away, his mind blank as he tried to recall the secret codes to open the front door. After an orderly helped him unlock it, he rushed out of the building without a backward glance. Once again, resentment, followed by guilt washed over him. If he didn't have to donate half his paychecks to his dad's care, he could afford to take Gloria someplace nice. But it was no use lamenting what would never come to pass. Roy was trapped in his mundane life, with no way out and no hope for a real future.

ANNIE PACED THE PORCH and watched the road. Though she appreciated her solitude, the house had been too silent today. The Coyotechasers turned out to be the best kind of hosts; they left her alone. They worked sunup to sundown on their cattle ranch, leaving her to brood about her crappy future. After getting no word from her mates or their fathers all day, she didn't know if she should feel relief or apprehension. Roy had texted ten minutes ago that he was on his way to take her to happy hour, and she still hadn't told Tor and Van about it. She appreciated that they cared about her safety, but their overprotectiveness was too stifling. She'd been on her own for years before they came along. She could handle herself for a few hours.

She tensed when she saw Roy's truck coming down the dirt road. Casting a surreptitious glance over her shoulder, she wasn't surprised to see Van Thunderfoot sitting on a rusty chair with his legs propped up on a railing, watching her like a hawk.

He arched a thick brow. "What are you and your brother planning, Annie?"

Feigning indifference, she picked grime from under her fingernails. "Just a few hours away together."

His dark eyes flashed yellow. "When were you going to tell us?" Lowering his legs, he slowly rose to his feet. "I need to get Tor."

"Alone together," she whispered just loud enough for him to hear as he turned to the front door.

Shoulders stiff, he said, "Nope."

Her heart plummeted. How did she know this would be his reaction? "Come on." She fought to keep from whining. "What exactly do you think will happen to me while I'm with a federal agent?"

"That's the thing. We don't know what's going to happen."

Geez, these wolves were way too neurotic. "I haven't had any alone time with Roy."

"We'll sit at a different table." His features hardened. He wasn't giving up.

She rolled her eyes. "You'll be watching us, listening to us."

"We'll be watching the crowd, listening to the crowd," he said. "Amaroki men protect their women."

She threw up her hands. "Roy will have a gun."

Van didn't say a word as he stared at her, his stony eyes unwavering.

She returned the look, impatiently tapping her foot. "You're not backing down, are you?" Though she appreciated that he cared about her safety, she couldn't help feeling annoyed. "We're taking separate trucks."

"You can't ditch us." A muscle twitched in his jaw. "I will find your scent."

Of course he would. He was the second best tracker in all the Amaroki, right behind his son Luc. She flashed a wicked grin, innocently batting her lashes. "I wouldn't dream of ditching you, Uncle Van."

He growled as she brushed past him and grabbed her purse off the kitchen counter.

RAINE HAD GIVEN MAGNUS enough time to sort out his mood. He'd waited all day for Magnus to say something, anything, about Annie and their father, but his brother never said much beyond a few grunts. Raine's patience had finally worn out. He refused to let Magnus's cowardice interfere with his chance to have a mate and children.

He tracked Magnus to the stable, where he was saddling up his horse, Bulwark, a big, black steed with a stubborn streak and a fiery temper. Bulwark only listened to Magnus, and only with gentle coaxing. Too bad he wasn't as patient with his brothers as he was with his horse. Raine couldn't deny that he was jealous of the time and attention Magnus gave to the animal, isolating himself from his family for hours while riding Bulwark alone in the desert.

He frowned at Magnus when he mounted Bulwark one-handed. "Where are you going?"

"Bluebell got through the fence again. I'm going after her. Want to come?"

Raine was surprised by his brother's request. "Sure."

He quickly saddled up his horse and met Magnus outside. Bulwark was impatiently trotting along the fence. Raine nodded to his two younger brothers, who were busy repairing the broken fence. The entire perimeter needed new fencing. Hell, it had needed to be replaced for ages, but their father refused to spend the money.

When a piece of wire snapped and lashed Frey's cheek, he cried out, then clamped his lips shut, quickly looking around.

He's inside watching TV, Raine projected.

Frey's shoulders slumped, and he rubbed the bloody welt. *Thank the Ancients.*

Raine shook his head, frowning. Frey shouldn't have been afraid of his natural reaction, but Father would've called him a pussy and whacked him upside the head. Sadly, Vidar was Raine's birth father, a second alpha just like him. Back before his alpha father and mother had been killed, Raine remembered Vidar had been strict, but he hadn't been an asshole. Now he was a bitter old drunk, a cancer destroying his family's happiness.

They found Bluebell on the outskirts of their thousand-acre ranch, grazing beside a large live oak.

Bulwark let out an angry neigh to let the Longhorn know he was unhappy with her desertion. She swished her tail once and turned her back on him, not caring what he thought of her.

Magnus swung off his horse and grabbed a bucket of feed, rattling the pellets inside and calling to the cow. She looked over her shoulder and then returned to her grass.

Magnus threw down the food, kicking the can. "Goddamn stubborn female."

Raine bristled at Magnus's tone. "You talking about the cow or Annie?" Because if it was Annie, he and Magnus would have a problem.

Magnus shrugged and grabbed his rope. "Both."

Raine dismounted, eyeing his brother coolly. "You want a mate who hangs her head while our father abuses her?"

"No."

"You want our father to treat our mate the way he treats you?" Raine prodded.

Magnus's cheeks turned as red as a Texas sunset. "I didn't say that."

Raine threw up his hands. "Then how the fuck do you expect her to act?"

"Did you come here to help with the cow or bitch at me?"

Raine refused to relent. "She'll go back to Alaska if we don't do something."

Magnus expertly threw a rope around the cow's head, deftly landing the loop around her horns and cinching it around her neck. "What do you expect me to do?" Tying the rope to his saddle horn, Magnus climbed back on Bulwark.

Raine mounted his horse. "It's time to put that madman in his place."

Magnus let out a sinister chuckle. "And do what with him?"

Raine's vision tunneled, and something inside him snapped. "Did you lose your fucking hand or your fucking spine, Magnus?"

Magnus's face went from red to purple, and his eyes looked ready to bulge from their sockets. "I lost my fucking mother!"

"She was my mother, too, and we've never blamed you." Raine's heart clenched at the hopeless look in Magnus's eyes.

But pity quickly turned into resentment. He was sick and tired of catering to his father's anger and his brother's depression. This was no way to live, and their mate deserved better. He turned away, unable to stand the pathetic look in Magnus's eyes another moment.

Steeling himself, he resolved to try to reach him once more. "Stop punishing yourself, stop punishing us. Only the madman blames you."

"He's our father," Magnus whispered.

"He's an ignorant drunk."

When Magnus hung his head, Raine was unable to contain the litany of swear words that escaped his lips. "Fine," he grumbled. "Our brothers and I will take care of him, but when the time comes, you'd better damn well back us."

He trotted back to the house. Let Magnus stew in his misery another night. Raine wanted no part in it.

Chapter Six

ANNIE SAT AT A TABLE in the bar, pleased when nobody asked for her ID. Not that she was intending on drinking, anyway. Her twenty-first birthday wasn't for a few more months. She hid a smile when Roy ordered a beer, and the pretty waitress carded him. Though he was barely twenty-two, he had the same baby face from his middle school days.

Roy slouched in his seat, casually looking around the place, which was covered with vintage memorabilia like cookie tins, old magazine covers, and license plates.

He puffed up his chest. "Do you need me to buy you a beer?"

"Aw, how cute." She teased. "No, thanks. One of us needs to be the designated driver."

Truthfully, that wasn't the reason she'd rejected his offer. Roy had been obsessing about paying for their night out all evening. Not out loud, but he'd been thinking it. She couldn't help but invade his thoughts. He'd been so on edge when he'd picked her up. He was broke, thanks to having to pay for his dad's room and board. Annie wondered if Roy's father appreciated his son's sacrifice. Annie couldn't count the number of times she'd spoon-fed Roy Senior or changed his shitty colostomy bags. He hadn't thanked her once. The only time he'd spoken was to tell her when she was doing it wrong. She had no idea where Roy had moved him to, but he should've left him at that state-run hospital.

"Well, this is nice," Roy said as he dunked a tortilla chip in salsa.

"I guess so." She dipped a chip, her attention shooting to Tor and Van, who were looking at her from behind their menus.

"They're only looking out for you, Annie." He clasped her hand, his blue eyes foggy. "You're lucky to have so many people who care about you."

"You've been melancholy lately." She bit her chip, and the salsa exploded on her tongue in a symphony of cilantro, onion, garlic, and tomato. She leaned forward, narrowing her eyes. "What's up?"

She wondered if she'd ever get the nerve to tell him about her mind-reading powers. If he knew about her ability, their relationship would change. They'd finally reconnected after years apart. She couldn't imagine losing him again. He was literally the best thing she had in the world, even better than her mates, who as far as she could tell, were too browbeaten and manipulated by Vidar for her to ever form any real connection with them.

His shoulders fell. "It's Father."

She arched a brow. "*Your* father?" It was more a statement than a question. She'd tried many times to get it across to Roy that Roy Senior wasn't her father. Maybe if she said it enough times, he'd take the hint and stop talking about him.

"*Our* father." He flashed a tight smile. "He raised you, too."

She blinked hard. He couldn't be serious. "He popped pills and felt sorry for himself while CPS took us away."

"He's disabled," Roy said, the hurt look on his face as if she'd just kicked his puppy. "He's paid for his sins ten times over."

Annie fought the urge to roll her eyes. "Do we have to talk about him tonight?"

"He misses you," Roy rasped, giving her another hurt look.

"I need to go to the bathroom." She abruptly stood, pushing back her chair. If she'd known Roy had only taken her out to give her a guilt trip, she would've stayed home.

"It's over there." Roy pointed.

"Thanks." She wanted to add that she could smell the way to the restroom, but she stomped away instead. When she returned, he'd damn well better change the subject or she would demand he take her home.

She paced too long, needing time to cool down. Luckily, she was the only one inside the three-stall bathroom with the paint peeling off every door and romantic Latin music filtering in overhead. Leaning against the sink, she steeled herself to return before Tor and Van barged in. She stared at the silver lining her irises, willing the color to fade to blue and ignoring a woman who walked into one of the stalls. Her inner-wolf was still too angry about her talk with Roy.

Annie didn't have time to examine her feelings, not that she wanted to. Roy had awakened the deep, dark pain from her childhood she'd rather forget. Whenever he brought up Roy Senior, all she could remember was that look of apathy he'd given her when CPS took her away. He seriously didn't give a shit that their family had fallen apart. He was probably more worried about what would happen to him than to his children, that self-loathing, selfish son of a bitch.

She stepped aside when the woman exited a stall. She was a tall, curvy redhead in her mid-thirties, wearing way too much lavender perfume. Bleh. The shit smelled awful.

Annie fanned her face, trying not to gag.

"Hello there," Redhead said, flashing a smile that made Annie's flesh crawl. She washed her hands. "You're awfully young to be in a bar."

Annie bristled when Redhead looked her over with a gleam in her luminous hazel eyes, as if she was mentally undressing her.

"It's not a bar," she snapped. "It's a restaurant."

Redhead's smile widened, revealing unnaturally white teeth. "How old are you?" She reached around Annie for a hand towel, coming far too close to her personal space, her nostrils flaring as if she was breathing in the scent of Annie's hair. Fucking creepy.

She instinctively stepped away, coughing into her fist when Redhead's perfume singed her nostrils. "Why is it any of your business?"

Redhead wiped her hands and face, balled up the paper towel, and pitched it in the basket. "I was just going to ask if you need me to buy you a drink."

"No, thanks."

Redhead toyed with the frayed end of a woven belt cinched around her waist. "If you change your mind, my name is Sharon. I'll be at the bar."

When Sharon held out a hand, Annie backed away, scowling at long white fingers curved like talons.

What a delicious little slave you would make.

Sharon's thought made Annie's blood run cold.

"I won't change my mind," she snarled. Whatever kinky shit this woman was into, Annie wanted no part of it.

Sharon sauntered out the door with a condescending smirk. Annie thought she saw red flash in her eyes. Warning sirens went off in her head when she remembered her fathers telling her that demons had red eyes. Sharon couldn't be a demon though. Her fathers had said they were afraid of the Amaroki. She stared at the paper towel Sharon had thrown in the trash. After a moment, she wrapped it in a clean paper towel and shoved it in her pocket. Sharon's scent might come in handy later.

When Annie returned to her table, Tor and Van eyed her with interest. Then she looked over at Sharon, who was sitting across from a tall, broad-shouldered black man with a shiny bald head, her bare foot blatantly stroking his crotch. They stared at each other so intently, she wondered if they were speaking telepathically. She had no idea if demons had such powers, but it seemed odd how their gazes were locked on each other, their mouths quirking and twitching but otherwise unmoving.

When Sharon caught her eye and smiled, she quickly looked away, feeling as if a thousand tiny spiders were burrowing into her skin. Just one look from that woman, and she felt unclean. Sharon had to be a demon. When Roy launched into another sob story about Roy Senior, she pretended to be interested, but she was trying to probe Sharon's mind. Soon words began to filter into her head.

What is it? a deep, dark voice asked.

That girl, Sharon answered.

They *were* speaking telepathically.

She's a beauty, the man's words slithered across her senses like a serpent.

Sharon toyed with the rim of her margarita glass, covertly giving Annie more coy glances. *She smells like a wolf, but she has too much human blood.*

Maybe she is part human.

No. Shifters don't mate with humans.

That was one thing she'd gotten wrong about the Amaroki. Good. The less she knew about Annie's kind, the better.

You sure?

Don't be an idiot. She abruptly sat back, removing her foot from his crotch. *I've been in this dimension for four hundred years. I've never seen a wolf/human pairing.*

Four hundred years! Holy shit. Sharon didn't look older than thirty-five.

Sharon's companion leaned toward her. *What is she to them?*

I don't know, but she is being watched by those two wolves. Sharon inclined her head at Van and Tor, who were talking over drinks and four baskets of polished chicken wing bones, seemingly unaware of the two demons at the bar.

We have enough human slaves. The man latched onto Sharon's wrist. *Do not think about it, Balban.*

Balban? Was that Sharon's demon name?

Sharon pouted. *But she is so pretty, Aosoth.*

The veins in his neck popped out. *Those wolves are too protective of her.*

Of course they are. Sharon—Balban—smiled venomously. *She's a delicious little virgin.*

Aosoth rubbed sweat off his bald head. *You smell her virginal blood?*

I do. Balban's eyes practically rolled into the back of her head. *It's heavenly.*

He mopped his face and head with a napkin. *She'd fetch a high price, but she's not worth the risk.*

Oh, they never are. Balban's demonic laughter rang in Annie's ears. *But this one is such a challenge. How can I resist?*

Great Ancients! Fear solidified Annie's veins to ice. This demon was willing to risk fighting shifters for her virginity? She had to get the fuck out of here. Her attention snapped to Roy, who was waving a hand in front of her face.

"So you'll go?"

"Yes," she absently answered, unaware of what Roy was asking her. She abruptly stood, smoothing invisible wrinkles down her pants. She felt the demon bitch's eyes boring holes through her skin. "I'm ready to leave."

"We haven't even ordered yet," Roy said.

She dug into her purse and threw ten dollars on the table, enough for Roy's one beer. "I want to go, Roy. Now."

He frowned at the money but didn't object to her paying. "What's wrong?"

"Nothing," she lied. "I-I don't feel well."

She waved at Tor and Van, who also stood. Tor arched an inquisitive brow, but she looked away, clutching her purse tightly.

She marched to the exit, pleased when Tor and Van followed. She just prayed the demons wouldn't follow, too.

ROY GRIPPED THE STEERING wheel with whitened knuckles, staring at the winding pothole-filled road. "Annie, are you going to tell me what's wrong?"

"Nothing's wrong." She looked over her shoulder, relieved when she saw Tor and Van were close behind them. "I just don't feel well."

"Did you catch their scent?"

She gaped at him. "Whose?"

"Your mates."

"Oh." She heaved a sigh of relief. "Yes. That's why I wanted to leave." She wasn't ready to tell him a demon wanted her. He'd probably get himself killed going after her or worse, be forced into slavery.

Her head snapped back when Tor honked his horn behind them. She watched in horror as an old pickup truck with monster tires nearly ran Tor and Van off the road, spinning dust in its wake as it barreled toward Roy's truck.

"Watch out!" she screamed, clutching his arm.

Roy slammed on the brakes as the truck swerved into his lane, nearly clipping his front end. A familiar redhead was behind the wheel.

Roy sped up, tailgating the driver and shaking his fist. "Goddam crazy drivers!"

Annie looked back at Tor, whose glowing golden eyes shined bright in the dark cab as he closely followed Roy's truck. The guy looked seriously pissed off.

"Are you okay?" Roy asked with concern.

"Yeah." She absently nodded. The demon's truck left them behind in a cloud of smoke.

"I've seen her around town. I'm calling the local sheriff." He jabbed a finger at the windshield. "He'll handle that crazy bitch."

"Just let it go, Roy," she mumbled, a chill wracking her. She suspected the sheriff was no match for two ancient demons.

He emitted a few curse words, and she knew he wouldn't listen. She had to let Tor know before the demon caused harm to innocent civilians. Not that Balban probably hadn't already caused harm, considering she and her demon friend had been talking about human slaves.

By the time Roy pulled into the drive, Annie's limbs were mush from the nervous tension that had zapped all her energy. She'd fought werewolves, for Ancients' sake. A couple of demons shouldn't have frightened her so much.

Then again, werewolves were mindless eating machines, easily taken down with a well-aimed silver blade. How in the fuck was she supposed to kill a demon?

"I'm going to bed." She cracked open the door. "Be safe, okay?"

He gave her a stony look. "What's gotten into you?"

She shrugged, unable to answer.

"I'll be by tomorrow morning to pick you up."

"Okay." After she got out and slammed the door, she turned back. Wait. What the hell had she agreed to?

Roy was already pulling out of the drive, his cellphone to his ear. Dammit. He was calling the sheriff. Even more reason to tell Tor. He'd know what to do.

When Tor and Van parked and got out, grumbling and red-faced, she knew they were still pissed off about the demons who'd tried to run them off the road.

Her legs felt encrusted in ice as she bridged the distance between them, her heart thudding in her ears.

"That damn, crazy human," Tor grumbled.

"And she was on Amaroki land," Van added.

Tor rubbed his face. "I'll alert Cesar. She passed several *No Trespassing* signs to end up on that road. She could have gotten us killed."

"I think that was her intention," Annie said, twisting her fingers. "And she isn't human. She's a demon."

Tor lifted a brow. "How do you know this?"

"I listened to her thoughts. Her name is Balban, and her partner is Aosoth."

Tor's eyes widened. "Those are demon names."

"I saw them sitting at the bar," Van said. "I didn't like the way the woman was looking at you."

Though the relentless evening sun beat down them like they were shriveling pieces of meat under a heat lamp, a chill went through her. "She was acting strangely in the bathroom. She wanted to buy me alcohol." Remembering the paper towel, she pulled it out of her pocket and handed it to Van. "Here's her scent. I took it after she wiped her face."

Van sniffed it with a snarl and then handed it to Tor.

"Good job, Annie," Van said. "Her scent is strong. We'll easily find her."

She didn't know if she should feel relieved or more worried that he could find Balban. She didn't want anyone she cared about getting hurt.

"She doesn't know what I am. She's confused by my human blood." She decided to leave out the part about the demon wanting her virginity. Tor and Van would only encourage her to mate early, bond with four cowardly sons and be forced to live with their abusive father. "She knows you're wolves, and she doesn't care about the risks," she warned. "She wants me."

Tor let out a low whistle. "Great Ancients."

Sniffing the paper towel again, Van closed his eyes.

"I also heard them talking about sex slavery," she said.

Van's eyes shot open. "What do you think the trackers here do? They work the border, apprehending pimps and rescuing slaves."

"But there's a new ring, and they haven't been able to apprehend their leaders." Tor said. "Now we know why."

"She said she's been on Earth for four hundred years." Annie wrapped her arms around herself and scanned the horizon. She could hear the Coyote-chasers inside the house, eating dinner, and she wanted to join them. She felt too exposed outside, as if the demon was nearby, watching her. "I don't understand why she'd want me. My fathers told me demons were afraid of Amaroki."

Tor thoughtfully rubbed his chin. "The Ancients visited you?"

"The other night." She turned toward the direction of the canyon, longing to be with her fathers once more. "They took me on a run."

He frowned. "There will be no more running, Annie."

She hung her head. "I understand." But she was far from happy. Her life was going in the wrong direction, and she had no control over it. She felt like she was stuck in a speeding car with faulty brakes, and she'd crash any moment.

"Let's get inside." Tor held out a hand to her. "I need to consult with Raz. She knows more about demons than I do."

She took his hand, comforted by his strength. He wasn't her father, but he made a good surrogate. Van flanked her other side, sweeping the horizon as they walked up the porch steps.

She blinked up at Tor when they reached the porch. "Maybe it's best if I go back to Alaska."

His features seemed to melt. "Either that or bond with your mates."

She jerked away and stepped back. "I'm not bonding with them." Was he crazy? Had he forgotten the way Vidar had treated her? And Magnus's cowardly inaction?

Tor shrugged, his cheeks coloring. "They would keep you safe."

She jerked open the screen door. "I seriously doubt that." She walked into the front room with a heavy heart. Tor was trying to shove her off on her mates. Clearly she was a burden. Marching straight to her bedroom, she wiped away hot tears and flopped on her bed, angry with herself for crying. Hell, she didn't even know why she was crying. She'd been rejected by her parents. Tor's rejection shouldn't have been any different. So why did it feel like he'd wedged a knife in her chest?

AFTER MAKING SURE HIS father had eaten his dinner, Roy hung up with Nurse Gloria. He swore under his breath when he saw Redhead's truck on the side of the road. It was a beautiful truck, a classic Ford, probably a '72, the kind Roy could only dream of when half his salary went to his dad's care. It was cherry red, with orange flames going down the sides and monster tires. The redhead who'd almost run him off the road leaned against the truck while her friend struggled with a flat tire. That truck had to have cost a bit of money to restore, yet the driver didn't know how to change a flat? When the redhead flagged him down, he knew he should've kept driving, but he wanted to know if she'd been drinking. If so, he was calling the sheriff.

As he got out of the truck, he smelled an odd, cloying perfume, like a mixture of strange spices and lavender. His dick hardened as he inhaled again. How the hell did perfume do that? His nostrils flared when he got a good look at the woman leaning against the tailgate of her truck. She wore a tight, knit dress and knee-high boots that exposed her mile-long legs and tempting curves.

She was probably a good ten years older than him, but Roy preferred older women. Not that he intended to try anything. The big bald black dude changing the tire was probably her boyfriend, and she drove like a crazy woman. He had enough problems in his life. He didn't need one more. But something about her drew him to her like a moth to flame. Was it her large, hazel eyes? Those full tits? Roy couldn't help but stare, she was so damn pretty.

"Thank you for stopping." She batted her lashes and stuck out her chest, displaying her cleavage like a peacock showing off his feathers.

Alarm bells went off in Roy's head. Instinct told him to run and run fast, but curiosity and something he couldn't define propelled his feet forward. It was as if she held him in a trance.

He jutted a shaky finger at her chest. "You're the woman who almost ran us off the road."

"I know, and I'm sorry." Her plump, cherry red bottom lip made him think of kissing her. "I don't normally drive so crazy. Our tire blew out, and I lost control. We ended up in a ditch."

Roy was hit with another burst of that tempting perfume and stepped back when she stepped forward. "You think I'm a goddamn idiot?"

"What?" Her eyes bulged. "No."

Her companion rose, clutching the tire iron. The tire was fixed, so why had she flagged him down?

He rested a hand on his holster. "You drove down the road on all four tires."

She shared a confused look with her companion. "You're mistaken."

"No." He braced his feet apart and squared his shoulders. "You are, if you think I'd fall for this crap."

"I'm telling the truth." She placed a hand over her heart, a pained look in her eyes as if Roy had attacked her with a verbal spear. "I swear."

Roy wasn't buying her charade, but even though he knew she was trying to deceive him, he had this overwhelming desire to kiss her. What the hell was wrong with him? The perfume smell grew stronger, ensnaring his senses like he was being wrapped in invisible tentacles.

"I'm calling the sheriff." He flashed his gun. "No funny business. I'm a federal agent." He reached for his phone.

"Roy, please." She edged closer to him, preceded by that alluring perfume. "We can work this out."

He clutched the phone like a lifeline, momentarily disoriented, unable to remember if he'd dialed the sheriff or not. "How do you know my name?"

She licked her lower lip and brushed a hand across the swell of her breast. "I overheard you and the pretty girl named Annie talking at the bar."

He was momentarily mesmerized by the sight of her nipples poking through the thin material of her dress and the fragrance that continued to slither around his senses like a sensual serpent. The alarm bells faded, replaced by an overpowering surge of lust. He blinked, shaking the fog from his head. At some point, his phone slipped from his fingers.

"You followed us from the bar?"

"We were on our way home, too." She let out a sultry laugh, one that made his balls tighten in anticipation. "It's a small town, Roy. People are bound to meet up in a few different places."

She nodded at the bald black man, whose grip on the tire iron was unnerving. Instinct told Roy he was in grave danger.

"I never said you could use my first name. It's Agent Miller to you."

"Very well, Agent Miller." She advanced toward him while unbuttoning the top of her dress, allowing him a glimpse of ample cleavage. "Let's say we forget about this whole thing."

When she reached for him, he stumbled back, nearly tripping over his own feet. He wanted her like he'd never wanted a woman before, but she was dangerous. Wasn't she? "Don't touch me!" Roy saw a flash of red in her eyes as she lunged for him. He was barely aware of pulling the trigger of his gun, the ricochet sounding off. He looked into her wide, frightened eyes and then saw the crimson bulls-eye blooming on her abdomen.

Dear god, what had he done?

"You stupid human!" she screeched, her eyes shifting to glowing crimson. "This was my favorite body!"

What the fuck was she?

With a roar, she launched at him even as he fired another shot.

When she encircled his neck with bloody fingers, he tried to fight her off, but something odd happened. His vision dimmed, and he was sinking into his body as if his soul was shrinking. He fell into a pit so dark, he couldn't see his hands in front of his face. Surrounded by gloom and depression so overpowering he wanted to die, he curled into himself and let out a strangled sob.

Dear God, save me.

Chapter Seven

BALBAN FLEXED HER FINGERS and opened her eyes. Changing bodies was such a nuisance. So many different parts to learn, not to mention new identities and all the bothersome relations and health problems that came with new skins. Though Balban was a succubus, stealing bodies wasn't her favorite pleasure. She preferred sex and drugs to swapping skins.

This one came with awkward dangly parts, and Balban identified as a woman, preferring large, smooth tits to a hairy chest. She had been using the pretty redhead for well over three years, and had had many satisfactory sexual partners with such a fine figure. Balban was sad the man-boy had made her lose such a valuable human skin. She blinked up at the red eyes of her companion.

"Balban?" Aosoth asked. "Is it you?"

"Of course it's me," she snapped. "You idiot."

Aosoth crossed meaty arms over a broad chest, giving her a derisive look. "Damn."

After Aosoth helped her sit, she scowled at her flat chest. "I don't like male bodies."

"I liked your other body better, too," Aosoth said.

Of course he had. Aosoth had made her generous cleavage his personal playground, probing it with his tongue and dick. Now he would have to settle for male on male sex unless he rejected her as a lover. She couldn't risk that happening. He had been her best lover since she lost Sitri. He was nothing compared to Sitri, but he had been gone a century, cursed to hell by cruel shifters who'd cut his life on Earth too short.

Somewhere deep in the pit of her new body, she thought she heard the sounds of a human demanding to be let out. She ignored it. Discarded spirits usually gave up the fight after a few days.

She frowned. "I will have to steal a slave."

"Good." He helped her stand. "I don't think I could fuck you like this."

Balban laughed. "Everyone knows you'll fuck anything." She scanned the agent's memories for useful information, quite pleased and somewhat terrified with what she saw. Her jaw dropped when she realized this human knew the wolf shifters. Not only did he know what they were, he knew their secrets.

"What is it?" Aosoth asked.

"This agent's memories are interesting." She thoughtfully rubbed her jaw. "The pretty virgin is a shifter. Her mother was human."

Aosoth's eyes widened. "I thought you said shifters didn't mate with humans."

"I did," Balban snarled. "Her fathers are their gods." The same gods, she wanted to add, who'd killed her beloved Sitri. "They bred with humans to create fresh blood."

"So the virgin is a wolf?" He stepped back, his muscular arms visibly shaking. "Then we shouldn't pursue her."

"Of course we should." Balban laughed as a plan formulated in her mind that involved infiltrating the shifter race and finally enacting revenge for Sitri's demise.

"But our magic can't penetrate their defenses." Aosoth threw the tire iron, sweat dripping down his brow. "We have no way of defeating them."

"We do now." She rubbed her hands together. "I know their kryptonite."

Red flashed in his eyes. "What is it?"

"Amethysts."

He scratched his head. "Amethysts? The gemstones?"

"Exactly. They are used to prevent shifting. This human has them in case of an emergency."

Balban stumbled to the human's truck on shaky legs, then lifted the backseat. Beneath it was a long black box titled "emergency supplies." Maniacal laughter rose in her throat when she saw what was inside it: a long black dart gun and several amethyst-tipped darts, plus several handcuffs with locks on the cuffs and little amethysts embedded in the black leather. There was also a vial of sleeping medicine, the kind that could knock out an elephant, and enough weapons to take down several packs of shifters.

Why would the human need these when he was friends with the shifter race? Then she uncovered in his memories a juicy bit of information. The shifters were at war with one another because the old chieftain had gone mad. Balban would use their inner turmoil to her advantage, stealing the girl while they were distracted. Not only would she claim this virgin's blood, she would take her body and become a shifter succubus. With such power Balban could infiltrate the shifters and teach other demons how to do the same, taking over their race so they no longer posed a threat to demons. Most importantly, she would enact her revenge on this she-wolf's fathers for killing her beloved, for after she stole this she-wolf's body, she would send her soul to the abyss, a cold void of loneliness and pain, not hot like hell but equally maddening.

A strange howl sounded in the distance, followed by another, and another, each one louder than the last, indicating whatever was out there was closing in on them.

Aosoth froze. "What is that?"

"Sounds like a wolf. We need to go."

She searched the agent's memories, dismayed when she saw images of a mutant wolf who ate humans.

"But the body," Aosoth cried.

"Leave it." Jumping in the agent's truck, she tore off down the road, not bothering to see if Aosoth had followed her. Only when his truck caught up to hers did she heave a sigh of relief.

Mutant wolves? Ancients mating with humans? What was happening to the shifter race? This madness was almost enough to make her give up on the delicious virgin. Almost.

WITH MOONLIGHT LIGHTING their way, Annie got out of Cesar Coyotechasers' truck and followed him, his brother Ben, and Tor along the side of the dirt road. Even though the sun had set, it was still too hot for her liking. Her feet were sweating in her borrowed boots and even more sweat dripped down her cleavage. About twenty yards from the truck was the drape, presumably covering the demon who'd wanted to kidnap Annie. If this demon was dead, was she safe, or did that mean the other one would pursue her?

Tor watched the road while Cesar uncovered the body with a stony face. Rigor mortis had already set in, and the stink of decay was strong as flies buzzed around the corpse.

"Annie," he asked, "is this her?"

Releasing a shaky breath, she scanned the familiar thick band of red hair and knit dress with the matching belt. She looked pretty much the same, except for the pool of blood under her back, soaking into the dirt.

"Yes." Annie clutched her gut when the smell of death hit her like a brick to the head. "What happened?"

"Bullet wound. We found her dead at the side of the road."

Annie didn't know if she should feel relief or shock that Balban was dead. "Who killed her?"

Cesar pulled the blanket back over the body. "We're not sure."

"Did you call Roy?" Annie asked.

"Yes. He said to leave the body until he could send reinforcements. Said he's handling something bigger at the moment."

Weird. She waved at the corpse. "What could be bigger than this?"

Cesar shrugged. "Probably that chucacabra."

She cringed and hoped the strange animal hadn't killed any more humans.

Cesar's tracker brother, Ben, knelt beside the body, his nostrils flaring. "You sure she was a demon, Annie?"

She vehemently nodded. "I saw her eyes. I heard her thoughts. Why?"

He stared at the corpse. "She smells entirely human."

"What do demons smell like?" she asked.

"Like dark magic."

Annie didn't remember any dark magic, just awfully strong perfume.

She knelt next to the body, noting how that the overpowering fragrance was gone. "Huh. I don't smell the lavender anymore." But she did smell Roy. She sniffed her shirt, which had his scent on it, too. Was Roy's smell coming from her?

Ben arched a brow. "She smelled like lavender?"

"Yes." Annie made a face. "It was so strong, I wanted to puke."

Ben looked at Cesar. "Dark magic usually smells like old blood."

Tor cleared his throat. "The perfume is meant to lure her victims."

Ben blinked at him. "What does that mean?"

Tor crossed his arms, his eyes shifting from yellow to brown. "It means she was most likely a succubus."

"Any idea why the scent would be gone?" Cesar asked.

Tor gestured at the ground. "The demon has gone back to her pit."

Annie's throat suddenly felt as parched as the Sahara Desert. "What about the other demon? The big, bald guy?"

"Our trackers are looking for him," Cesar answered, looking away.

She slowly stood, clenching her fists. "There's something you're not telling me."

"We scented Roy on her. His smell was stronger earlier, but it's fading," Cesar said. "The tire tracks next to her body match his truck."

Roy had been here? These demons could've killed him. Bile rose in the back of her throat. "D-did you ask him what happened?"

"Yeah," Cesar answered. "He said they waved him down because they had a flat tire, but when he stopped, she tried to seduce him, so he got back in his truck."

"So he didn't see who killed her?" Cesar crossed his arms, looking out across the horizon at the moon as it dipped behind the clouds.

Tor dragged a hand through his peppered hair with a growl. "None of this makes sense."

"Maybe the two demons had a fight," Ben said.

Tor said, "Why would he leave the evidence?"

"I don't know." Cesar straightened. "They shouldn't have been on tribal land to begin with."

Tor scowled. "No, they shouldn't. Something definitely isn't adding up."

"What should we do with the body?" Cesar asked him.

Annie wondered why Cesar kept looking to Tor for advice. Wasn't Cesar the chieftain of the Texas tribe? Shouldn't he have been making the decisions? This didn't bode well for the Texas tribe if none of their leaders had a backbone. Or maybe Cesar relied on Tor's advice because he was older.

Tor shrugged. "Leave her, like Roy said, but set trackers to watch from a safe distance and follow the feds when they take her."

Cesar arched a brow. "Don't you trust Roy?"

Tor patted Cesar on the back. "At this point, I don't trust any damn human, and neither should you."

Annie's breath hitched when he gave her a look as he brushed past her. Was Tor insinuating that Roy was mixed up with demons? Impossible. He would never betray the Amaroki.

Unless he was under a demon's spell. Her heartbeat faltered at the thought.

ANNIE LAY IN BED, BLINKING up at the stars painted on the ceiling. This bedroom belonged to the Coyotechasers' little girl. A pack of howling little cartoon wolves were painted along one wall, overlooking a canyon with a full moon overhead. The scene reminded her of the night her fathers had taken her to run the canyon, a night she'd always cherish. If only they could come back tonight. She had so many questions and concerns about these demons, and she needed reassurance.

She jumped at a tap on the window. "Fathers!" she squealed, throwing open the curtain.

Her heart plummeted and then soared with a mixture of sorrow and apprehension when she saw her mates. Well, all of them save for Magnus. And they were all naked, which meant they'd traveled to her as wolves.

She opened the window, scowling at Raine before looking away, embarrassment flushing her cheeks. She'd only gotten a brief glance of his nude body, but she liked what she'd seen. Very much. Especially that tanned, corded muscle working its way down to his navel.

Brushing her hair back, she feigned disinterest. "What do you want?"

He gave her a crooked smile. "To talk to you. There's a nearly full moon tonight. Will you run with us?"

A thrill zinged through her. Maybe they would visit the canyon with the beautiful waterfall? She sure hoped so. Warning sirens sounded in her head when she remembered another demon was still out there. But he hadn't been the one who wanted her, at least not like the redhead wanted her. Besides, she'd be with her mates. They wouldn't let anything happen to her. But she'd feel safer if there were two alphas with them.

She shot Raine a look. "Where's Magnus?" Didn't he want to be with her?

Raine cupped his dangly bits, looking out of sorts as he shifted from foot to foot. "We didn't bring him."

"Why?"

Raine grinned ruefully. "We didn't think you'd want him here."

She jerked back. "I-I never said that."

Granted, Magnus had pissed her off on more than one occasion with either his indifference toward Vidar's treatment of her or his obvious lack of manners. But did she never want to see him? She knew if she had any chance of bringing him out of his shell, she'd have to spend time with him, something she was both anticipating and dreading.

"Well," Raine said, looking far too adorable and sweet for an alpha. "You coming?"

When he waggled his brows, she wondered if he'd intended a double meaning. No way would she have sex with Raine and his brothers before their bonding ceremony, and she wasn't bonding with them until the climate in their community changed. But a little run with them wouldn't hurt.

Against her better judgment, she threw off her pajamas and crawled out the window, landing smack in Raine's lap. She gasped when her bare breasts brushed against his hard chest, the sparse hairs tickling her nipples. Her pussy swelled and then dripped like a leaky faucet. He growled his approval, his eyes shifting to brilliant gold, his fingers searing her skin while he stroked her back, then cupped her bare bottom.

She traced the scar across his cheek. "How did you get this?"

"How do you think?" He chuckled. "A fight with our father."

"Oh," she breathed, worried. "Do you fight often?"

He shrugged. "Sometimes, when he's in a mood."

She bit her tongue. As far as she could tell, Vidar was always in a mood. She realized their household would always be filled with violence and drama as long as they had Vidar in their lives. She couldn't risk subjecting children to that.

"But enough about me," he purred, tracing her lip with his thumb. He reached down with his other hand and boldly squeezed her butt. "I've been wanting to do that ever since I first saw your sweet round ass in those jeans."

She scooted away from the fleshy rod poking her side. Great Ancients, she was naked and entwined in the arms of a dangerous shifter. What the hell had she been thinking?

Though she didn't want to break free of his touch, she knew no good would come from it. She couldn't mate with them. Not now, maybe not ever. She shuddered when he stroked her inner thigh, turning her insides to jelly, and all the while keeping her transfixed with his molten eyes. Great goddess, he was wicked, and hot damn, she wanted nothing more than to spread her legs for him.

His younger brothers whimpered. Too shy to come up to her, they gawked from a distance. That was fine. All she wanted at the moment was Raine and his magic fingers. When his fingertips came dangerously close to her wet, puckered button, she tensed, then pulled away. Despite wanting him badly, he was trouble.

He smiled. "Didn't you like what I was doing?"

She pulled her hair over her breasts, then covered her mound with both hands. "You know I did." She looked away as heat flamed her face.

He reached for her. "Then why stop?"

She heaved a groan as she asked herself that same question. She wanted him to finish what he'd started. "You know why. Are we going to run or not?"

Before he could answer, she shifted into wolf form and sprinted away, laughing when she heard their pounding paws behind her.

They ran until Annie's throat was parched and her paws ached, but they made it to the canyon, which was all that mattered. They jumped from rock to rock until they reached the bottom, then ran some more until they ended up where the water splashed into the lagoon. She dipped her paws in the water. Three furry creatures flew over her head into the lagoon, landing with large splashes. When they came up, they'd transformed into three handsome, laughing brothers.

"Come in, Annie," Raine said. "The water's refreshing."

She shifted and leaped in, shocked by the cold. She sank like a stone, a little panicked by the inky water that surrounded her like the black of night while she fought her way up to the surface.

Raine was beside her, his hand snaking around her waist. "You okay?"

She wrapped her arms around his neck, a shiver coursing through her. She looked into his luminous golden eyes. "It's dark down there."

He laughed, shaking water from his shoulder-length hair. "It's spooky, but you get used to it."

She clung to him, the feel of his bare skin searing her flesh like bands of liquid fire. She knew she should let go, but her traitorous body refused to release him. The cradle of his arms was perfect, like their bodies were meant to be entwined. She searched his eyes as a thought occurred to her. "Isn't it forbidden to run the canyon?"

He laughed again, his throaty chuckle as sensual as a touch. "It is, which is what makes it so fun."

She locked eyes with him, trying, and failing miserably, to block out all sexual thoughts of Raine and how easy it would be to straddle that hard thing between them. He wanted her as badly as she wanted him. She could tell by the way his fingers branded her flesh when he dug them into her skin.

Shaking her head, she tried again to clear all sexual thoughts and focus on the conversation at hand. "You'd defy your father's orders?" He was more of a rebel than she'd realized, which made her reluctantly want him even more, dammit. She didn't want another reason to mate with him or his brothers.

"We do it all the time," someone said at her back. Still clinging to Raine, she turned and looked into Jax's eyes. Because of his feral look, it was easy to tell he was the beta.

"Magnus, too?" she asked.

"No, not him." Jax said and glanced at Raine.

She turned back to him and could tell they were speaking telepathically. How she wanted to pop into their heads. Though she'd used her mind-reading powers on countless others, she didn't feel right invading her mates' privacy.

"Do you know how Magnus lost his hand?" Raine asked her.

As difficult as it was to release him, she let go of him and kicked back, a little disappointed when he let her go. Treading water, she faced the three brothers, their yellow eyes glowing in the moonlight. "I heard about it."

"But you didn't hear the whole story," Frey, the gamma, said.

Even in the dark, she saw his cheeks flush. Gammas were usually the shyest in any pack, and Frey was no exception. She couldn't deny she was attracted to his baby face and big, sad eyes. Gammas were the shifters who stayed home and helped with the kids and housework. They also had crazy libidos. Even though he was floating several feet away from her, she could feel his desire for her rippling the currents between them, as if his lust had electrified the water.

She licked her lips, trying hard to focus on the conversation. Damn, these guys made her horny.

"What's the whole story?" she asked, desperately needing a distraction.

Raine leveled her with a look that made her insides churn. "Our family stumbled on a caravan of drugs and sex slaves crossing the border. Wrong place, wrong time."

"Sex slaves?" Annie gasped. "I was told it was a drug deal."

Raine's expression was grim. "There were women, too. Some were just little girls."

Annie felt sick.

"Our fathers wanted to turn back," Raine continued, "but our mother insisted they follow, so they could report back to the trackers." Raine paused, his face screwed up tight.

"They were caught," Jax whispered. "And the cartel began firing." Jax choked up.

Raine continued the story. "Magnus tried to shield our mother from the barrage of bullets, but there were too many. Instead of celebrating his ability to shift, Magnus returned home with our mother's body in his arms, his mangled hand hanging from his wrist like a limp sock."

"Great Ancients," Annie cried, her heart breaking.

"He refused medical attention and returned to the canyon with our fathers, but the smugglers were gone," Raine said. "They could've tracked them and enacted their revenge, but they found our youngest father, Sami, missing an eye and still clinging to life despite being shot seven times."

Annie wiped away tears. "So they returned home with Sami?"

Raine nodded. "Vidar wanted to leave Sami and go after the drug smugglers, but our beta father, Tyr, convinced him to take Sami and Magnus to the hospital instead."

"I'm so sorry," Annie said, too choked up to say more.

Raine ducked under the water. She watched, waiting for him to resurface.

"Physical recovery for Magnus and Sami took months," Jax said, his eyes simmering with cold rage, "but the damage to their souls has never been repaired, and now the rest of our family is paying for it."

She was at a loss for words. She'd known the story was tragic, but she hadn't expected the heart-wrenchingly painful details. Raine resurfaced with a roar, shaking water droplets from his hair.

"She barely managed to speak through a constricted throat. "Guys, I'm so sorry about your family."

Raine swam to her, reaching her in a few strokes. "You don't need to be sorry." He cupped her cheek, his eyes glossy in the moonlight. "It wasn't your fault."

"I know." Her skin lit on fire at his touch. "I just feel so bad."

The hard angles of Raine's face softened. "We don't want pity, Annie. We just want you to understand why Magnus is the way he is."

"What can I do to help him?" she asked, suddenly feeling an overwhelming urge to leave them and run to Magnus.

"We've been fighting for him the past twelve years." Jax swam over, treading water while his eyes seared holes through her skin. "You can join the fight. Make him believe he's worthy of love."

She swallowed a knot in her throat. "I will try, but I don't know if I'll be good at it." What if she couldn't bring Magnus out of his funk? Would they be able to make their pack whole without Magnus?

"Of course you will." Raine snaked an arm around her waist again, pulling her against his hard chest. "Your smile lights up our world."

His wicked, fanged grin seared her insides, making her want to go limp in his arms and wantonly spread her legs. What the hell was happening to her? She'd never felt the urge to surrender to any man, but just one look from Raine, and she was melting like a scoop of ice cream on hot pavement.

She placed a palm on his chest, her vision tunneling on his perfectly sculpted face, made even sexier by the scar that cut across his cheek. When he bent his head to hers, she didn't stop him, and she loathed herself for it. Wasn't she supposed to put up a fight?

When he brushed his lips across hers ever so softly, she threaded her fingers through his hair and opened her mouth to his. Cupping her chin, he claimed her more intimately, their tongues melding as he deepened the kiss.

She gasped when the tip of his thick cock slid across her slippery barrier. How easily it would be for him to slide into her, taking Magnus's place as head alpha by claiming her virginity. Her ribbon pulsed while he probed her swollen button.

Even though the more sensible part of her was yelling at her to swim away, she surrendered to her mounting passion and sank against him, needing him to enter her.

"Enough, you two," Jax warned behind them.

Raine pulled away, releasing her like she was a hot potato. She reached for him in a lustful stupor. "Come back."

He put more distance between them. "I have to stop."

As the reality of what they had almost done settled in the pit of her stomach, she was overcome with a wave of shame. What the hell was the matter with her? She wasn't ready to mate with them, not until Magnus put their father in his place and helped heal the rift in the tribe. Why had she caved so readily?

Humiliation burning her cheeks, she swam back to the rock, wishing that sensitive spot between her thighs would quit throbbing.

"Where are you going?" Jax swam up behind her, his voice a heated whisper, his mouth dangerously close to that sensitive spot beneath her ear.

She turned halfway toward him, avoiding eye contact, knowing the possessive look in his eyes would be her undoing. "We should go back."

"Why?" He caressed her shoulder.

She shivered and grabbed hold of the rock. "You know why. I can't control my stupid lust."

He shoved a firm erection into her buttocks. "You have nothing to be ashamed of. It's natural to want us."

"Jax," she said with a gasp, "you shouldn't." But her body betrayed her words as she pressed into his erection.

"I just want to touch you." He boldly slid a hand between her legs, cupping her crotch and resting one fidgety finger on her nub.

Her eyelids involuntarily shut as he stroked her. Falling back against him, she spread her legs, giving him easier access. He had one hand on her breast, squeezing and pinching her nipple while he fucked her with the other hand, banging against her tender button until she thought she'd expire. As his tempo increased, the sound of water splashing around them and her labored breaths were drowned out by his ominous growls as he clamped down on her neck with his teeth. She spread her legs wider, a prisoner to her lust as he continued his assault on her weeping pussy. Her euphoria rose to a feverish pitch as he stroked her harder, faster, stopping only to dip his fingers into her well and spread creamy moisture across her swollen bud. She climaxed without warning, her button rebelling against his fingers with angry thuds. She groaned his name when he shoved his fingers inside her, holding her while she convulsed around him. This intimate touch was the best feeling in the world, more beautiful than a dozen sunsets and more euphoric than a thousand tender kisses.

He cradled her in his arms, kissing her forehead. Wow. She could definitely get used to this. Sex with Jax almost made up for the asshole father-in-law. He carried her to the shallow end of the pond and laid her on a bed of grass. With a giggle she laid back and stretched out while his brothers swarmed her, their cocks jutting toward their chins. She heaved a satisfactory sigh when Jax and Frey trailed hot kisses down her neck and breasts, stopping to suckle her nipples like newborn babes. She felt like a goddess as they worshipped her nude body with their hands and tongues.

When Raine trailed kisses from the crook of her knee to her thigh, she willingly spread her legs for him without giving her virginity another thought. She was doomed, but at the moment, she didn't care. Her giggles turned to gasps when Raine swirled his tongue across her tender bud. Her dripping pussy bloomed like a flower, opening to him. Circling her swollen nub with his thumb, he gently fucked her pussy with his long tongue, probing and thrusting until another orgasm claimed her, this one rolling through her like a wave. By the time Raine released her, they were both breathless.

His face was smeared with her juices. "You taste delicious."

Too exhausted and spent to speak, she stretched her arms over her head while her mates continued to shower her with kisses, rubbing their swollen cocks against her. She languidly sat up and cupped Raine's heavy balls. His eyes rolled back while she circled the base of his thick cock. She moved her hand up and down, pumping him, fascinated at the way his balls tightened and his cockhead swelled before he let out a roar, spurting creamy liquid all over her breasts and neck.

Raine's eyes lit like twin suns as he rubbed his essence into her breasts, then smeared it across her tender pussy. "You're ours," he growled in her ear.

She nodded, then took Frey and Jax in hand and stroked them. Frey came quickly, spurting a prodigious amount of fluid across her chest. Jax jutted his cock at her mouth. She took the hint and kissed up and down the shaft, gasping when he spurted down her neck. Jax nudged her onto her back and rubbed sperm into her pussy until she swelled and burst like a balloon.

They lay together in the grass, watching the clouds part across the moon and listening to crickets buzzing nearby. Raine and Jax held her hands, kissing her fingers, while Frey clung to her leg, resting his head on her thigh. She'd never felt more content, more happy in all her life than at that moment. But her bliss fizzled as guilt drove a wedge into her happiness. Magnus should've been here with them, marking her, too, but they'd left him out, and she hadn't even thought about him until they'd finished.

She looked at Raine, who was drunk with satisfaction. "Will Magnus be angry?"

"Hope so." He chuckled. "Maybe he'll fight for you if he smells your fluids on us."

She turned back to the night sky. "Oh, okay." That was one way of looking at it.

"Did you enjoy it?" Raine asked her.

She couldn't help but smile. Cupping his cheek, she leaned over and planted a kiss on the tip of his nose. "Very much."

"You seem upset," Frey said.

"I'm sorry. Just worried about Magnus."

"Don't be," Jax said. "He'll come around once he sees what he's missing."

Raine sat up, lazily stroking her breast. "The sun will rise soon. We need to get you home."

She bit her lip as her nipple peaked. "Okay." She wasn't ready to go. Her pussy still throbbed with need, and she wanted them to touch her again.

They washed off in the pond, playfully splashing and teasing each other, until she found herself groaning into their mouths. They climbed onshore, kissing and toying with each other. She had three more orgasms, and they ejaculated in her hair and on her tits. After another bath, they made the long trek home, sated and spent, their tails dragging.

Day was breaking by the time she reluctantly climbed inside her bedroom.

Leaning out the window, she gave them each long, languid kisses, groaning when they pulled back.

"May we come to you tomorrow night?" Raine asked.

She eagerly nodded. "Yes, please."

Raine paused. "May we bring Magnus?"

"Of course," she answered without hesitation. A small voice in the back of her mind told her she was being a lovesick fool. That she'd capitulated too easily.

But another voice argued she hadn't capitulated at all, that the struggle wasn't with her mates but for her mates, and the fight had just begun.

Raine held her hands, his eyes darkening as he desperately searched her eyes. "Annie, I swear to you we will do everything in our power to make you happy. We will not let him ruin us."

Without realizing she'd been holding her breath, she released a shaky sigh. "Thank you."

"I'm damn sick of the sorrow," he continued, "but now that you are in our lives, the Ancients have blessed us with a new start. I'm not about to let my father or Magnus blow it."

When his brothers voiced their agreement, she smiled. "That's good, because I'm in this fight now, too, and I'm not going to let them blow it either."

She blew them kisses, then closed the window, not even cringing over behaving like a lovestruck pup. Feeling like a gutted fish, she fell into bed, surrendering to exhaustion and thanking her fathers for her mates. Now that she'd gotten to know them, they were actually amazing, and she couldn't wait to see them again.

Chapter Eight

BALBAN WOKE FROM A much-needed nap and stretched, saddened to find that cumbersome set of testicles sticking to her thigh. She hated male bodies, even though they were generally stronger. She identified with women more. Their soft curves and sensitive nipples brought her great pleasure, and Aosoth liked touching them, too, which meant he was always in the mood to fuck. And Balban loved to fuck. So far Aosoth had not expressed interest in fucking her new body. This made Balban sad. Though she could never replace her long-dead mate, her beautiful and brave Sitri, who'd been the demon to rescue her from the fiery pit, she thought of Aosoth like a mate. She would never admit it, but she found comfort in his presence. She couldn't risk losing him. She needed him to want her, so she needed a different body.

Speak of the devil. Aosoth was waiting for her in the hall with a lineup of dirty, chained girls.

She looked over their dejected, frightened faces with derision. None of them spoke English. What had they been expecting when they crossed the border? Did they really expect their bleak lives to get any better?

Aosoth's white smile was a contrast to skin that shone like onyx. "Balban, I have picked several fresh bodies for you."

She folded muscular arms against a flat chest, frowning at her lack of curves. "Why?"

"You don't wish to remain in this man's body, do you?" he said with a sneer.

She stiffened, not wishing him to see how much his rejection stung. "Of course not."

"This is my first choice." He yanked on a chain, pulling the girl forward.

The girl stumbled, then hung her head.

Balban shot him an accusatory glare. "I knew you'd pick her."

She had the largest tits of the bunch, plus she had a pleasing, wide mouth and thick, pretty lashes.

When a sickeningly familiar smell wafted toward Balban, she backed up with a hiss. "I can smell her venereal disease."

He shrugged. "She's on antibiotics." He licked his lips and stared down her deep cleavage.

She rolled her eyes. "You really need to get over your obsession with tits, Aosoth."

"I can't help it." He pulled the girl to him, grabbing her tit so hard, she cried out. "You know I like squeezing them."

The girl turned away, cringing when he licked her cheek.

A blade of jealousy stabbed Balban's gut. He was going to fuck the girl, and she wouldn't get to partake in the pleasure.

"Don't worry," she said. "I will not be in this body for more than a day."

Lines of his bald forehead scrunched. "Do you have a new body in mind?"

"Yes," she said casually. "The half-human she-wolf."

His mouth fell open. "You still think the amethyst darts will work?"

She tapped her head. "According to this human's research, they are very effective."

He latched onto her arm. "What if he's wrong?"

She stiffened. "He's not." How dare he question her judgment? She had been in this agent's body for more than twelve hours. She knew his deepest secrets and his darkest desires, and she planned on exploiting every juicy piece of information.

Aosoth's eyes flashed red. "It's dangerous."

"Listen to me." She wagged a finger in his face as if she were scolding a child. "If this works, we will be able to steal any shifter's body, even the mighty protectors. Think of what we could do if we controlled the shifter race."

"They will know." His eyes darkened to the color of old blood. Clasping his hands together, he fell to one knee "They will wage a war against us. We haven't been on their radar for a hundred years. They will hunt us down when they discover our existence, just like their ancestors slaughtered our kind in the medieval ages."

What did he know of the dark slaughter? He'd still been in hell. Unable to stare at his pitiful face another moment, she turned from him. "I'm sickened by your cowardice, Aosoth."

"And I'm sickened by the thought of burning in hell's fiery pit for another ten thousand years." His voice rose as he jumped to his feet.

"You forget, we know their weakness now." She broke into a slow, seductive smile and fingered the large amethyst stone around her neck. "We know how to penetrate their magical barriers."

A thudding door, followed by thunderous footsteps, echoed down the hall.

"Señor." Their armed guard, a big Mexican named Miguel, with arms covered in skull tattoos, stood at attention while addressing Aosoth. He did not recognize Balban, which was good, as she wouldn't be in her current body much longer.

"What is it?" Aosoth snapped.

"You told us to tell you if we saw any *lobos*."

She stifled a gasp. The wolves were here? They must have followed her men when they picked up the body, which meant they no longer trusted the Agent Roy Miller.

Aosoth's eyes bulged. "How many? Where?"

"About three dozen a quarter mile from the compound." Miguel pointed at the small window at the end of the hall.

"Shoot them," Aosoth said.

"We can't." Miguel looked at his dusty boots. "They're gone."

Shaking a fist at Miguel, Aosoth roared, a sign of the wild, horned beast that lurked beneath his stolen mortal skin. "Hunt them down."

The girls behind him whimpered, their chains rattling.

Miguel's jaw slackened. "In broad daylight?"

"Bring me the guards who were watching the perimeter." Aosoth's voice dropped to an ominous baritone.

The color drained from Miguel's face. "They're dead."

Balban's knees weakened, but she refused to make a sound. Aosoth couldn't know she was afraid.

"Dead?" Aosoth's voice cracked.

Miguel frowned. "Mauled."

"Double the watch," he ordered. "And shoot anything that moves."

Miguel nodded and hurried back down the hall.

Aosoth turned to her, eyes wide with fear. "They're onto us. What do we do?"

She feigned indifference. "We relocate."

"You need to get out of that body."

Crossing her arms, she leveled him with a smirk. "You have no faith in me, do you?"

"I have no faith at all, Balban," he said over his shoulder as he dragged his slaves back down the hall. "You should know that."

ANNIE WOKE UP WITH a groan and stretched while rolling onto her side. Slowly she remembered last night's events. Great Ancients! What had her mates done to her? What had she *let* them do? Crossing one leg over the other, she did her best to quell her growing desire as she recalled Raine's intimate kisses. Whatever they'd done to her, she was determined they do it again and again.

After a much needed cold shower, she trudged into the kitchen, weary and sore. Ioana and Cesar were there, along with Tor. Judging by the sly look Cesar gave her, she had a feeling he knew what she'd been up to last night.

"Have a good rest?" Ioana gave Annie an exaggerated wink, a humorous lilt to her voice.

Cheeks flushed, she slumped in a seat at the kitchen bar and set her phone in front of her. "Yes."

Tor looked up from his coffee. "You slept in late."

"Did I?" She feigned innocence, thanking Ioana as she handed her a glass of orange juice. She drank and greedily ate a double serving of pancakes and sausage.

She was so consumed with breakfast, she hadn't noticed they were sitting stoically, backs stiff as they watched the front window.

"What's wrong?" she asked.

Ioana turned to her. "Our trackers haven't returned." She sat on a stool beside Annie. "They've been gone all night."

Annie tensed. "Where did they go?"

"They followed the feds who took the redhead's body," Tor said gruffly.

"Oh." Annie felt ten shades of selfish for forgetting all about the fact that demons had invaded their reservation. She'd been so consumed with her mates, she hardly thought of anything else.

Ioana jumped off her seat and ran to the door. "They're back!"

Annie watched with envy as Ioana threw herself into Ben's arms, plastering his face with kisses. Realization dawned that the Texas trackers had gone from tracking humans to a demon who could smell them, and she'd no idea what else it was capable of.

When Van gave Annie a sympathetic look, a nagging feeling told her that something had happened to Roy. Her knees gave out, and her limbs went numb with fear.

"Well, brother," Cesar asked after taking Ben in a fierce hug. "What did you find out?"

Ben thanked Ioana when she handed him a tall glass of water. After drinking it all in a few gulps, he set it down and wiped his mouth. "The men who took her weren't feds. The body was taken to a heavily armed ranch about halfway to San Antonio."

Alarm bells went off in Annie's head. Roy had said the feds were coming for the body. "This doesn't sound right."

Cesar turned to her. "Have you spoken to him?"

She checked her phone. No missed calls and no messages. "No." She'd sent him one last night before bed, asking him to call and let her know he was okay. Panic and dread turned her veins to sludge. She'd been so consumed with her mates, she had totally forgotten about Roy.

She swiped the screen with a trembling hand. "Let me try again."

Cesar latched onto her wrist. "No."

She looked up at him. "Why?"

"Annie." His gruff voice softened. "Something's wrong."

"W-what do you mean?" she stammered, though deep down inside, she knew what he meant. Roy was in danger, and it had something to do with the demons. Why hadn't she warned him about them?

"We think the demon is holding him hostage," Ben said.

Annie's world tipped and then spun. Luckily, she was sitting, because she would've hit the ground had she been standing. She was so filled with fear and dread, she couldn't think about crying. "Omigod, what do we do?"

"I'm calling a tribal meeting," Cesar said.

"When?" she asked.

Cesar picked up his phone. "Now."

She nodded absently, burying her face in her hands. When Ioana sat beside her and put an arm around her shoulders, her eyes exploded like busted water pipes. To think, she'd been running the canyon with her mates and enjoying amazing foreplay while Roy was in danger. She felt like the world's worst sister, but her feelings didn't matter. All she cared about was getting her brother back.

MAGNUS FURIOUSLY WHITTLED a piece of wood in the barn and tried not to think of the nightmare that had woken him, the same nightmare he'd been having several times a month for the past twelve years. Each time he'd tried to jump in front of the gunfire, and each time he couldn't move fast enough, as if his legs were stuck in quicksand. The bullets had sliced through his hand and pierced his mother's head. She'd crumbled to the ground without so much as a whimper, spasmed once, then shifted from wolf to human, her brains leaking out into the dirt. Magnus had scooped her up and run, tears streaming down his face as he howled for help while attempting to hold her brains in place with his one good hand. Fool that he was, he'd thought he could still save her, but her spirit had already passed. And just like all the other times, he'd awakened in a pool of sweat, crying to the Ancients to take him instead of his mother.

But they never did let her come back, though he'd have given anything to trade places with her. Because of his incompetence, his younger siblings had grown up without a mother, and his remaining alpha father had reminded him daily that her death was his fault. His baby sister had gone to live with their Romanian uncles at age eight, preferring to grow up in a third-world country rather than spend another day in their miserable house. Not that he'd blamed her, but he hadn't seen her in eleven years, and he missed her almost as much as he missed Mother. She'd had her kind smile and gentle heart. His family had badly needed a woman's soft touch. For too long they'd lived with their father's abrasive cruelty.

He sniffled, willing the tears to subside while he whittled the piece of wood into oblivion. Damn. He'd been trying to carve a wolf. Cursing, he threw the mangled wood into the fire and picked up another. Usually his brothers soothed him after a nightmare, but they were nowhere to be found. Dawn had already broken, yet where were they? Their absence made his heart hurt even more, so much that he could hardly bear it. They'd gone to Annie without him.

He jumped when he heard footsteps outside. Throwing his tools on the bench, he stomped to the barn doors, throwing them open and blinking against the blinding glare of the morning sun. His brothers, naked and in human form, wiped dirt off their hands, their satisfied smirks shooting a thousand tiny bullets into his heart.

"Where have you been?"

Raine shrugged, sporting a smug smile. "Out with Annie."

A drum pounded so wildly in his head, he could hardly hear his own thoughts. "With Annie? And you didn't think to include me?"

Raine looked away, his cheeks coloring. "We didn't think she'd want you there."

Magnus's world imploded, and he let out an ear-splitting howl.

Jax and Frey were smart enough to back up, but Raine had the nerve to hold his ground, looking Magnus in the eye. That's when he knew Raine was trying to assert himself as first alpha, maybe even the only alpha. Would his brothers really abandon him? Leave him to the desolate life of a lone wolf?

His throat was so tight, he could only speak with a strained whisper. "Where did you go?"

"We ran the canyon."

Magnus's head swelled with rage. "Are you trying to get her killed?"

"We're not fools. *We* kept her safe."

Magnus heard the censure in his brother's voice. Even though Raine had always asserted their mother's death hadn't been Magnus's fault, it was clear Raine blamed him now.

Magnus ignored the throbbing from phantom blade wounds in his back. "As opposed to me?"

"This has nothing to do with you, Magnus." Raine chuckled. "The world doesn't revolve around your insecurities."

He released a low warning growl, standing toe-to-toe with Raine, and the smell hit him hard. No, it couldn't be. His brothers wouldn't betray him like that.

His lips pulled back in a feral snarl. "Why do I smell her fluids?"

Raine's eyes held no hint of regret. "We marked her."

Magnus gulped air, hardly realizing he'd been holding his breath. All this time his brothers had stood by him, defending him while their father blamed him for their mother's death. Never had their support wavered until this night. Why? He clutched his chest, his heart feeling buried beneath an avalanche. "And she let you?"

Raine licked his lips. "She begged for it."

Clenching his fists tight, Magnus fought the urge to pummel Raine's face into oblivion. Instinct took over, and he shifted into a giant, hulking protector, panting like a wounded animal while bearing down on Raine. He'd expected his brother to shift, too, but he only blinked at him, unmoved.

A roar erupted from his chest so powerful, the ground shook under their feet and the barn doors rattled. "What's next? You'll take her virginity without including me? You'll vote me out of the pack?"

Raine was impassive. "I never said that."

"Why not?" Magnus pounded his chest, anger clouding his vision. "Then you could be head alpha."

Raine went up on his toes. "I already am head alpha!"

Magnus stumbled back, his jaw going slack as he gaped at his brother. "N-no," he stammered.

Still in human form, Raine advanced on him. "I am as long as you refuse to stand up to Father and continue to blame yourself for our mother's death." He sucked in a breath. In an instant he transformed into a giant hulking beast eye-level with Magnus. "I. Am. Head. Alpha."

Magnus could scarcely hear anything above the torrid beating of his heart and his shallow breaths as he stared into his brother's golden eyes. He'd expected to see the usual pity there, but this time he saw only revulsion. Something deep inside Magnus snapped, and he let out a deep, dark roar, feeling as if he was expunging not just his breath but his very soul. Panting heavily, he grabbed the barn door and ripped it off its hinges. The door had his mother's name carved on it inside a heart and was surrounded by the names of her mates and sons. His heart plummeted. Gently leaning the door against the wall, he turned from Raine, unable to meet his eyes.

Raine was right. He'd never have a future unless he let go of the past. He thought of carving Annie's name into the other side of the door and how much he wanted his name to be joined with hers. He wanted to find a little piece of happiness in his bleak existence, even if he was only half a man and hardly a protector.

A familiar roar cut through the silence, and he spun around, exchanging a apprehensive look with Raine.

"Where are those goddamn boys?" Father slurred drunkenly.

Their father stormed into the barn in human form, not even noticing that the door had been pulled off its hinges. "We have to go," he said, buckling his belt.

Magnus frowned at him. "Where to?"

Father looked at him through a scowl. "The Coyotechasers called a tribal meeting."

"You've never followed their orders before," Magnus said.

"Cesar says it's urgent." Father threw up his hands. "We have to hear him out."

How odd that he was suddenly taking commands from the Coyotechasers. This was not like him, which made Magnus suspicious.

"And if it's not urgent?"

Father rubbed his hands together, flashing a fanged grin. "Then we kick Coyotechaser ass."

JAX RELUCTANTLY LOADED his shotgun in the back of the truck he shared with his brothers. He didn't want to bring guns to the meeting, but Father had insisted. He glanced at Raine. "We'd better not need to use these."

Raine grimaced. "Annie wasn't happy last time she saw us with guns."

"I'm tired of the tribal fighting." Hanging his head, Jax leaned against the truck. "I want a fulfilling life. I want to serve in the Army." Jax was hardly aware he'd revealed his deepest desire until the words were out. His blood ran cold as he looked over his shoulder for any sign of Father.

Raine clasped Jax's shoulder. "You would've made a good tracker."

"It's not too late," Frey said, grunting as he threw a bag of ammo in back of the truck. Holy cowshit! Was Father preparing for WWIII?

Magnus was heading their way with more guns, and his heart sank. No way would Annie agree to this lifestyle, not that he blamed her. Heck, he didn't want to bring a mate into the middle of this turmoil.

"Annie's not going to mate with us until he's gone," Jax said, making sure his voice carried far enough for Magnus to hear.

"I know," Magnus said, adding the case to the weaponry.

Jax shared hopeful looks with Raine. *Do you think he's coming around?*

Raine nodded. *About damn time.*

Their gamma father, Sami, approached, dragging his bad leg behind him. He carried a cooler, no doubt stocked with Vidar's beer. Jax elbowed Raine when he saw the splatter of blood under Sami's nose and the bruise darkening his only eye.

"Do you need help, Sami?" Raine asked.

"No," Sami mumbled. "I've got it."

The weird thing about Sami was that they never called him father. Probably because he never acted like one. Usually he was no more noticeable than the old beaded lamp in a corner of the living room that nobody used for fear it would burn down the house. After their mother and alpha father were murdered, Sami had withdrawn from everyone, claiming his injuries prevented him from shifting. Jax and his brothers agreed it was probably a mental thing, and they'd never pressed him. They'd always been afraid of hurting him by dredging up old demons he was trying to drink away.

Magnus folded his arms. "What happened to your eye?"

Sami tried to heave the cooler into the truck. Frey quickly raced to his side, taking it from him and sliding it in the backseat with one hand.

"Did Father hit you?" Magnus pressed.

Jax wondered why Magnus was so concerned. Was he finally sick of Father's shit, too?

When he dragged himself back to the house without answering, Magnus stopped him, searching his eyes with concern.

A hopeful seed began to take root in Jax's chest. If they had Magnus on their side, there would be no stopping them. Father would finally be forced to back down.

Sami sniffled, wiping his nose with the back of his hand. "I haven't been doing a good job keeping house." As if that was an excuse for Father to hit him and risk injuring his remaining eye.

Magnus was pissed. "There's no reason for him to hit you."

"He's under a lot of pressure," Sami answered, looking away.

Magnus shook his head. "Great Ancients, is this how I sound?"

Raine smirked. "Exactly."

"You're not well, Sami." Magnus clutched Sami's shoulder with his one hand. "That bully knows it, too."

A tear slipped down Sami's cheek. "I'm well enough to make dinner and clean the floors."

Magnus released Sami like he had the plague. "That monster needs to go."

Sami's shoulders fell. "Where do you propose he go?"

"This house belongs to all of us. If we all stand firm, he'll have no choice but to leave."

Sami looked at Jax and Raine in alarm. "He won't go peacefully."

Jax again looked over his shoulder to make sure Vidar wasn't nearby, hating himself for his cowardice. "We lost our sister because of him. We won't be able to bring a mate here until he's gone."

To Jax's delight, his brothers, including Magnus, voiced their agreement.

"You still haven't told me where he'll go." Sami's voice shook like a sapling in a thunderstorm.

Magnus's face reddened, making him look like a volcano ready to explode. Removing the case of guns from the back of their father's truck, he threw it into the horse trough, laughing. "He can go to hell for all I care."

Chapter Nine

CESAR STOOD AT THE pulpit like a preacher ministering to his flock, frowning at his tribe. They were in the old barn that had been converted into a meeting hall. Magnus leaned against a wall in a darkened corner, eyeing Annie, who sat on a bale of hay in the front row, legs crossed at the ankles. Her lower lip trembled as she wiped a tear from her eye. What had upset her? If his brothers had hurt her during their marking, he'd pummel them. She scanned the room and stopped on Magnus. His world came to a grinding halt at the hopeless look in her eyes. He ached with the need to protect her.

"Brothers and sisters, please be seated," Cesar said from his podium, waving at the bales of hay circling him.

Shifters took their seats in an orderly fashion, which was strange. He didn't remember Amaroki speeding to their seats when Father was in charge. Usually Father had been forced to break a beer bottle over the side of the podium to get their attention. He also noted how those tribal members who'd supposedly been on Vidar's side wouldn't make eye contact with any of the Wolfstalkers, which meant they'd all turned on Vidar.

"Thank you for coming at such short notice," Cesar continued grimly. "We have no time for formalities. Our tribe has faced many trials these past twelve years, but never have we faced a crisis of this magnitude. As many of you know, Annie Thunderfoot and her uncles are visiting from Alaska." He nodded at her with a tight smile. "Blessed by the Ancients, Annie has the gift of telepathy. Not the kind that we all share within our packs, but she can listen to anyone's thoughts, even humans and demons."

The crowed broke into gasps and murmurs.

Magnus straightened and glanced at his brothers. "Did you know this?" he asked Raine.

"First I'm hearing of it."

"Yesterday she heard the thoughts of two demons," Cesar continued. "They are sex traffickers, and they know about the Amaroki."

The gasps and murmurs grew louder, accompanied by whimpers and cries.

Raine stiffened, his face a mask of stone.

She didn't tell you that either? Magnus projected into his mind.

No, brother, Raine answered solemnly. *She didn't.*

Magnus jerked when Cesar banged on the podium. "Quiet, please." He held his hands out, trying to control the crowd with a calm voice. "Their magic can't harm us. One of the demons was found dead yesterday, but the other is still at large." He held up a picture of a large black man with ripped jeans and a bald head that shone like marble. "This is what he looks like. We have strong reason to believe this demon killed his partner and kidnapped Agent Roy Miller, Annie's brother. The trackers traced them to a heavily guarded ranch. We think that's where they're keeping Agent Miller hostage."

Pushing off from the wall with a curse, Magnus shared dark looks with his brothers.

Father let out an ominous, deep chuckle while smacking his open palm with a fist. "Why is that our concern?"

Cesar looked at Vidar like he was a wayward toddler who'd been caught stealing cookies. "Agent Miller may be in trouble."

"Let me guess," Father said with a sneer. "You want Amaroki to risk their lives for a human."

Annie jumped to her feet, hands fisted by her sides. "He's my brother!"

"So?" Father chuckled. "No good can come of this," he warned the others, his gaze sweeping the room. "When we risk our lives for humans, we risk everything."

Cesar gave him a long look of derision. "I need every available tracker. I will also need protectors. Breaking into this compound will get ugly."

Jax pushed off from the wall and stuck a hand in the air. "I'll go."

"Like hell you will," Father roared, facing down Jax.

Surprisingly, Jax stood his ground, snarling at Father.

Raine held up a hand, smirking at Father. "I'll go, too. We're not sitting on our asses while our mate's brother is in danger."

Father threw back his head with a roar, his brothers ducking behind him while he swung his fists. "You goddamn worthless pussies."

"Worthless?" Raine chuckled. "You're slap-ass drunk every day by noon, and you call us worthless? Look around." Raine gestured at the rest of the tribe, that had gone eerily silent. "Your tribe has abandoned you. Nobody respects you, least of all your sons."

"I'll kill you!" Father shifted, bursting through his clothes and pounding his chest like an ape. With a roar, he launched at Raine, who shifted and matched Father's blows, letting out a howl when Father raked long nails down his face. Jax and Frey shifted into angry wolves, nipping at Father's feet and crying out when he kicked them. Magnus's other fathers slunk into the shadows, saying nothing.

Tor Thunderfoot and Cesar Coyotechaser transformed into protectors, too, roaring as they tried to pull Father and Raine apart.

"Stop!" Annie cried, racing toward them.

Magnus's vision tunneled on Annie, and he ran toward her. Time seemed to slow, and he felt as if his feet were once again stuck in quicksand, just like in his dream, as he dodged flying bales of hay to reach her. He couldn't let anything happen to her.

Scooping her up in his arms and then draping her across his back, he ignored her protests, taking a glancing blow to the head when he ducked under his father and carried her to the exit.

"Go help your brothers, you goddamn coward!" she cried, punching him.

He winced, his heart splitting in two at her admonition, but he refused to release her until she was safe.

"Let me go!" she screamed. "Raine! Jax! Frey!"

Magnus's cracked heart shattered in a million pieces when she called for his brothers. Couldn't she see he was helping them by keeping her safe? Didn't she understand his job was to protect her from harm? That he'd failed before, and he was determined not to fail again?

Once they were safely outside and sheltered inside a nearby set of old stalls, he lowered her to the ground, painfully aware of her tempting smell and the feel of her soft skin, and especially of her denim-clad leg grazing his groin when she slid down the length of his body. He smelled something else on her, too: his brothers. Their trace was all over her, from her hair to her feet. It seemed they'd left no part of her untouched. Bastards.

"You're not leaving my side until the fighting is over." He sat on a hay bale and forced her to sit beside him.

The sound of women and children screaming, wood splintering, and bodies slamming into one another made him cringe. He hoped his father didn't kill anyone. Other shifters ran out of the barn, women clutching babes to their chests and alphas shielding them. They fled in the other direction when they saw him. He wondered if they ran because they feared or loathed him. He supposed it didn't make much difference. The Wolfstakers had become the tribe pariahs, thanks to Father.

"Magnus, let go." Her lower lip quivered. "Your grip is too tight."

He instantly released her, feeling like a ten-pound bucket of dogshit for upsetting her. "Sorry. I didn't want you to get hurt."

"I'm not hurt." She touched his forehead. "You're bleeding."

Her gentle caress electrified him. He looked into her eyes, a beautiful mixture of silver, violet, and blue.

"I'm fine," he breathed.

He wasn't lying. Pain was irrelevant when he was so near this tempting woman. He badly wanted to kiss her soft, plump lips and wondered how it would feel to have them wrapped around his cock. He wanted to mark her as his brothers had done. He hardened at the thought and then hardened even more when she released a wave of pheromones.

Angry with himself for his lust, he stood, turning from her, and adjusted himself.

When he turned back to her, she was looking away. Crossing one leg over the other, she toyed with a loose thread on her top. Was she turned on as much as he was? She had to be. That's why she smelled so good.

"Sit down." She frowned. "Let me take a look."

Magnus was about to protest, but treating him would keep her busy and away from the violence. Besides, he longed to feel her fingers on his skin again.

"Will Vidar really kill Raine?" she asked, fingering the injury on his head.

He winced when she touched him, then swore at a sharp pain that felt like she was removing a nail from his scalp.

Removing a shard of wood as long as her index finger, she showed it to him. "What the hell, Magnus?"

He remembered being struck by his father's glancing blow. Had Vidar hit him with a board or stick? "Guess my father fights dirty." Blood dripped into his eye, and he wiped it away.

Pulling a pretty scarf from her hair, she wrapped it around his head. "This will have to do until we can get you to a hospital."

"I don't need a hospital," he said, feeling bad that she'd ruined her scarf for him. "It will stop."

"You're going." She looked around in alarm when a thunderous roar shook the ground. "Do you think your brothers are okay?"

"They're faster than Vidar, and they'll be able to focus without worrying about you getting hurt," he said.

"I hope you're right." She chewed her lower lip and winced when they heard another boom.

Magnus knew it was wrong to be envious of his brothers, but he couldn't help the wave of jealousy flowing through him. "You care about them?"

"Of course."

When the slightest of smiles tugged at her lips, a fire lighting in her eyes, he knew she was thinking sexual thoughts. She was probably remembering their wicked night of pleasure without him.

"Did you have fun with them last night?" he asked, unable to keep the note of accusation from his voice.

Cheeks flushing, she looked away. "Yes."

"I smell them all over you," he said, unable to stop himself.

She flashed a provocative and bold smile. "Jealous?"

"What do you think?"

She cocked her head with a laugh. "Then you should've come."

"I wasn't invited," he said, hating himself for picking an inopportune time to get a boner. Her lilting voice should've frustrated him, but it only made him harder.

"You're the alpha." She jabbed him, spitting out the words like they were made of venom. "You don't wait for an invite."

He arched away from her. "Would you want me there?"

She shrugged, picking grime out of her fingernails and acting as if his heart wasn't on the chopping block. "That depends."

"On what?" He suspected he didn't want to know the answer.

She gave him a pointed look. "On if you're willing to stop feeling sorry for yourself and stand up to Vidar."

He shrank back, indignation flushing his face. "I don't feel sorry for myself."

"No?" She chuckled.

Her laughter was like nails on a chalkboard. She had no respect for him.

"There's a difference between self-pity and self-loathing," he said.

"From where I'm standing, it's all the same."

"Look at me, Annie." He held up his prosthetic hand, dismayed to see one of his fingers had broken off. "I'm half a man, a worthless protector."

She snorted. "You're annoying is what you are."

When another roar shook the air, she got up, turned on her heel, and marched back toward the barn.

He jumped up, blinking back a wave of dizziness. "Where are you going?"

"To stop the fight."

"Like hell you are!" He lunged forward and spun her around, dragging her back into the stables. "You're staying with me."

"Why are we out here, Magnus?" She threw up her hands. "Is it to keep me safe, or are you hiding from Vidar?"

He couldn't stand the accusation in her eyes, the loathing in her tone. The damn of anger burst, spilling through him. "Damn you! You're as bad as he is with the taunts."

"The difference is he's trying to pull you down, and I'm trying to lift you up."

His breath hitched as he gaped at her. She was trying to lift him up? Did that mean she cared about him? That she wanted to be his mate? The thought both excited and depressed him. What if he wasn't a good mate to her? What if he failed to protect her, like he'd done with his mother?

"I don't want you to go back inside." The pain in his chest was so severe, it felt as if he'd run a marathon. "I don't want you getting hurt." Voice cracking with emotion, he hung his head.

"Magnus, I've battled werewolves." She gently cupped his cheek. "I can handle one douchebag father-in-law."

He was overwhelmed by her sincerity while reveling in her touch. He wished they could stay like this forever. "Your courage humbles me." He placed a hand on his heart, bowing to her. This woman was more than just his future mate, she was the daughter of the gods, a goddess in her own right, and he intended to treat her like one.

Her eyes softened. "I'm not trying to humble you. I'm trying to free you. Your soul has been chained long enough."

The last threads of his sanity snapped when he saw the pity in her eyes. He was a fucking alpha protector, capable of ripping full-grown trees from the ground. He wasn't supposed to be pitied. He was supposed to be revered and feared. He clenched his hair by the roots and let out a primal roar, screaming until he was out of breath. Falling to his knees, he looked up at the warped wooden ceiling. He was damned sick of people pitying him and of being ashamed of something that had happened to him as a boy. Most of all, he was fucking sick and tired of the way Father treated everyone around him. Enough was enough. He was ready to make a change, and not just for himself. She deserved no less.

"Magnus." She knelt beside him, clutching his arm. "Are you okay?"

Though he refused to let any tears fall, he looked at her through a watery film. Cupping her chin in his one good hand, he said, "What did I do to deserve a mate like you?"

She grabbed his forearm and squeezed, her strength flooding into him like a raging river. "The real question is what will you *do* to deserve a mate like me?"

"Anything," He said without hesitation.

She moved closer to him, so close he could smell her minty breath. Her eyes shut and her lips parted. Though he was terrified, his heart pounding a thousand beats a minute, he had to take the chance and kiss her. When he moved his lips across hers, she cupped the back of his neck, moving into him like they were two interlocking puzzle pieces. He hugged her tightly, pleased when she sighed into his mouth, deepening the kiss. His cock was harder than steel, throbbing with painful need, straining toward her touch. He wanted to strip off her clothes and make love to her. Fuck the mating ritual. Fuck his brothers. He'd never wanted anything so badly in his life than to claim her. The only thing stopping him was his respect for Annie. He would not turn into a monster like his father and force himself on her.

When they finally came up for air, the violent sounds inside the barn had died down.

She pulled away. "We should see if they're okay."

He felt as if the sun had disappeared, casting a gloom over his heart. "No," he said. "I need to make sure it's safe first." Though he didn't want to leave her alone, he wouldn't risk bringing her into the barn if Vidar was still unhinged. "Do not leave this spot, okay?"

"Okay, but don't take too long."

"Believe me, I won't." Kissing her forehead, he gave her one last forlorn look before hurrying to the barn. Ancients save Vidar if he hadn't been subdued. It was well past time he stood up to Father and became the protector Annie needed him to be.

ANNIE SAT DOWN ON THE bale of hay, wrapping her arms around herself and praying to the ancients her mates were okay. Vidar was a major asshole, but he wouldn't kill his sons, would he? She turned at the sound of footsteps behind her, startled to see Roy.

She ran to him and threw her arms around him.

He hugged her back. "Annie. You don't know how happy I am to see you." He kissed her forehead, his lips lingering a little longer than she was used to, his hands sliding down to her ass.

She jerked away, shocked and disturbed. Was he drunk? Her nostrils flared. He smelled like that redheaded demon's awful lavender perfume, but she was dead. "Where have you been?" she asked suspiciously. "Why didn't you answer my calls?"

"Long story. I was captured and escaped." He nodded at the barn. "What's going on?"

"Vidar." She grimaced. "That's what's going on." Why did he put his hands on her ass? He'd never done that before. "Why do you smell like her?"

"Like who?"

The hairs on the back of her neck stood on end. "The redheaded demon."

His eyes bulged. "You know she's a demon?"

She took a step back. "What were you doing with them?" Her heart rate quickened, drowning out all other thoughts when she thought she saw red embers flash in his eyes. She quickly scanned his mind.

I need to act now. She's onto me.

He splayed his hands in a gesture of surrender. "I already told you I was captured."

"You're not my brother," she said, the wolf inside clawing at her skin. But how had the demon turned into Roy? Had it shifted into his image or somehow managed to steal his skin? If so, was he lost to her forever?

"What are you talking about, Annie?" He cocked his head, bewildered.

She hesitated, not knowing how to act. What if Roy's soul was trapped inside his body? If she killed the imposter, would she kill him, too?

She advanced on him, rage threatening to split her skull in two while her inner-wolf howled. "What did you do with my brother?"

"I-I can explain," he stammered, then glanced at something over her shoulder. She turned and winced when a sharp pain pierced her neck.

She yanked a dart out of her skin, then fell to her knees when her legs gave way. Her veins turned to sludge and she fell on her back, blinking up at the demon in Roy's skin.

He flashed an evil smile and laughed. "Goodnight, little wolf. When you wake, your shifter skin will have a new owner."

A scream died on Annie's lips as she succumbed to darkness.

MAGNUS BURST INTO THE barn in protector form. He wasn't taking any chances with Vidar. So what, that he was missing a hand? He could still take on an old, stumbling drunk. He pushed his way through a circle of protectors, all beating their chests and hurling insults at Vidar, who'd been pinned to the ground by Raine and Tor Thunderfoot.

Raine looked up at him, his nose bleeding and swollen to twice its size. "Where's Annie?"

"She's safe," he said, feeling bad that Raine had taken the brunt of their father's abuse. Magnus puffed up his chest, resolved that this would be the last time.

Vidar gaped at Magnus and let out a primal roar. "Tell them to release me!"

Raine dug his furry knee into Vidar's throat. "Not until you promise you'll calm down."

Vidar roared again. "Let me go, you son of a bitch!"

Raine threw back his head with a deep bellow. "You do realize you're calling my mother a bitch, don't you?"

Vidar thrashed beneath him. "You damn worthless piece of coyote dung."

"Tell us how you really feel, Father." Raine chuckled.

Tor grunted, nearly falling over when Vidar managed a good kick between his legs. Cesar helped Tor up, and Magnus took his place, sitting on Vidar's heavy legs and wedging an elbow above his groin.

Magnus pressed his elbow deeper until his father grunted in pain. "Here's what's going to happen," he said in a surprisingly steady voice. "You will promise to behave yourself and then Raine will let you go. Then your brothers will take you home, where you will sober up."

Vidar lifted his head and spit at Magnus. "Fuck you."

"Wrong answer." Magnus was sorely tempted to slam his elbow down hard enough to make Vidar's nutsack black and blue for a month, but he refused to stoop to his father's level. Instead he stood, holding his one hand down to him. "Let him go," he said to Raine.

"You sure?"

Magnus solemnly nodded. Raine jumped back as if Vidar had the plague.

Their father stumbled to his feet and roared at Raine.

Magnus pounded his broad chest. "Over here, Father. One on one."

Turning back toward Magnus, Vidar let out a demonic chuckle. "You?" He sneered at Magnus's prosthetic. "I'm not fighting a cripple."

Of all the insults Vidar hurled at him, Magnus hated "cripple" the most, and Vidar damn well knew it. Flexing his arms, Magnus locked gazes with him, knowing exactly what to say to get him riled up. "Tell the truth, Father. You're not afraid of hurting a cripple. You're afraid of *losing* to one."

Father charged like an angry bull, falling into Raine with the grace of an armored vehicle plowing through a wall before pushing him aside and rushing Magnus.

He sidestepped his father, knocking him to the ground with his crippled arm, not even caring when the prosthetic flew from his wrist and shattered against the wall.

Father hit the ground so hard, he shattered the wood under him and landed in the crawlspace below in a plume of dust. Growling and cursing, he climbed back out, slapping his hands together before charging again.

This time Magnus stuck out a leg, tripping his drunken father, who barreled into a mound of hay.

Father kept on coming, spitting hay and dirt. He charged again and again, until he finally fell to his knees, gasping for breath.

Embarrassed for him, Magnus shook his head.

He addressed his two other fathers, who stood in the shadows like frightened mice. "Take him home and sober him up, then pack his bags. He's moving out."

"Y-you can't do that," Sami said, voice trembling. "He's your father."

"I can and I will, and if you have a problem with it, you can go with him."

Sami's eyes watered, then he ran from the barn.

Every protector in the room backed up several steps, eyes locked on Vidar.

Father got to his feet once more with a growl. "That's my damn house."

"No," Magnus said, bracing himself for another attack. "That house belongs to all the Wolfstakers, and we don't want you there anymore. Majority rules. We will not subject our new mate to your drunken tantrums."

Voicing their agreement, Magnus's brothers stood beside him in a show of solidarity.

Vidar threw back his head with a howl. "You ungrateful, worthless, piece of crap." He charged Magnus one last time, fell over his own feet, and landed smack into Magnus's fist. He crumbled to the floor with a heavy *thud*, blood pouring from his nose. He let loose a loud snort and passed out.

"Get him out of here," Magnus said to Tyr, his last remaining father, and usually the least drunk of the three.

Tor and Cesar helped, dragging Father to the other end of the barn.

Cesar returned, wiping dirt off his big paws. "We can't take him outside like this. He'll have to sleep it off in the barn."

Magnus shrugged. "Fine by me."

Clapping him on the back, Cesar flashed a fanged grin. "I'm glad to see you finally stand up to him, son."

"Me, too." He grimaced. "Sorry it took me so long."

"No need to be sorry. I know you had your own demons to face before dealing with him."

Magnus gazed at the trail of destruction left by their father's tantrum. Hay bales had been ripped apart, beams pulled from the rafters, and a gigantic smoker with a full hog had been overturned. The blackened animal lay in the dirt. "I'm afraid my feud with him has just begun."

"If there's anything I can do...." Cesar said.

"Keep Annie safe until our home is ready for her."

"Of course," he answered.

Magnus shook Cesar's outstretched hand. "I appreciate it."

Cesar stepped aside and Raine was there, holding out a hand to Magnus. When Magnus took his hand, Raine pulled him into a fierce hug.

"You okay?" Raine asked.

"Never been better." Magnus had a much longer answer, as well as an apology to his brothers for his brooding behavior, but it would have to wait. "Come on. I don't like leaving Annie alone."

As Magnus strode toward the door, a lead weight settled in his gut as the scents of stale blood and lavender hit him. Something was wrong. "Annie!" He took off at a run, his brothers howling behind him.

FOLLOWING THE STRANGE scents, the trail went cold fast in one direction, so they followed it back to the stables, where Magnus had left her, but Annie wasn't there either.

Clenching his hair by the roots, Raine roared at the rafters. "Where is she?"

"It's all my fault." Magnus hung his head, weeping into the dirt. "I shouldn't have left her."

Raine was in no mood to offer him comfort. What he'd said was true, but what was done was done. All that mattered was getting her back.

Raine sniffed. "Smell that?" He turned to the tracker. "Ben? What do you think?"

Ben Coyotechaser stalked to the spot where she'd been left. Falling to all fours next to a hay bale, he sniffed the ground, then looked up. "I smell Agent Roy Miller and something else." He sniffed again. "I recognize that smell."

Raine's nostrils flared as he belatedly recognized the agent's familiar scent. "So do I. I also smell lavender."

"The dead demon's perfume," Ben said.

Had a woman abducted Annie? If so, why hadn't Annie fought back? Did the woman have Roy with her, maybe as a hostage? He scratched his head, trying to make sense of the situation.

They did a quick but thorough perimeter search but found nothing. Annie was gone.

Raine and his brothers howled in grief and anger. No force in heaven or hell could save that demon if it hurt Annie, and Ancients save Magnus for letting her get captured. Raine had forgiven him for losing their mother, but he would not forgive him this time.

Chapter Ten

BALBAN DROPPED THE limp she-wolf into the cab of Aosoth's borrowed truck. "Drive!" she commanded.

Aosoth gaped at the girl.

"Did you not hear me?" Balban snapped. "Drive!"

He put the truck in gear and tore off down the road. "I don't like this."

She folded her arms across her ugly, flat chest. "I don't give a damn what you like." She smugly smiled to herself, looking down at the pretty sleeping girl sandwiched between them. Over a hundred years she'd waited to seek vengeance on these wolves, and she was about to achieve the impossible. Sitri would've been so proud. If only he were here to see what she'd done to avenge his cruel murder, bringing her more satisfaction than the time she'd ambushed that pack of shifters twelve years ago, killing the female and her alpha mate.

"But if we bring attention to ourselves, they might figure out we're demons," Aosoth whined.

An odd feeling came over Balban as she looked at the demon who'd been her mate for over a decade. She realized she didn't like him. Though he'd been on this plane for less than a century, he was always second-guessing her decisions and complaining. She was growing tired of him.

Another thought occurred to her. Once she took this female shifter's body, she would have four mates, for she recalled from Agent Roy Miller's thoughts that the shifter named Annie would soon give her virginity to four brothers, as was the way with the shifter race. She knew Aosoth would try to claim her virginity and keep the pretty shifter to himself. Was that what she wanted? To run off with this whining demon and let him claim her first blood? Or did she want to give herself to four strong, young shifters? Hopefully, horny men who'd want to fuck all night? She'd never had four brothers at once before. The thought made her dangly parts harden. The choice was clear. She would have to get rid of Aosoth, but would he let her?

"They know we're demons," she said, eyeing him sideways to gauge his reaction.

"What?" He slammed on the brakes, nearly running into the ditch.

"Keep your eyes on the road!" she snapped. She looked behind them, pleased when she saw they weren't being followed, but their luck would soon run out. She had to get the she-wolf to a secure location, so she could switch bodies.

"You're a fool, Balban," he growled, his eyes turning blood red as he steered back onto the road, "and you're going to get us both killed."

"Shut the hell up!" She turned away, anger making her blood boil.

"They will follow her scent," he continued. "What will we do when a whole tribe of shifters comes for us?"

When they come for us, Balban thought, *I will be in the she-wolf's body, and they will take me back as one of their own.* Balban chose not to voice her thought aloud, her anger rising while he continued to nag her.

She cringed and grabbed onto the dashboard when he slammed on the brakes again, pulling over with such violence, her seatbelt pinched and the she-wolf tumbled to the floor with a groan.

"Kick the shifter bitch out of the truck." He jutted a finger toward the door. "I will not let you send us to hell!"

She took off her seatbelt and pulled the girl back onto the bench seat, dismayed when she saw a bloody gash on her forehead.

"Look what you've done," she hissed. "You're going to ruin this body!"

"If you won't get rid of her, I will." He unlatched his seatbelt, opened the door, and yanked the shifter off the seat by her wrist.

Balban was left with no other choice. Pulling out Agent Miller's gun, she shot Aosoth in the forehead, then jerked the girl away from him and kicked him away before he could switch bodies. He fell to the road with a heavy *thump*, mouth hanging open and eyes wide with shock.

With no time to mourn her dead lover, Balban climbed over the moaning shifter and sat in the driver's seat. Aosoth's winged spirit broke free of his mortal skin, howling to the heavens while the embers of his dragon's breath shone through his throat like hot coals. She pulled the door shut and locked it, mouthing an apology to the demon as he released his fire, melting the glass.

She put the truck into gear and drove over Aosoth's body with sickening thumps. With no nearby body to occupy, it was only a matter of seconds before hell's portal opened and sucked him through, trapping him for at least another ten thousand years while he clawed his way back to freedom. A rumble sounded behind her, followed by a thunderous crack that rent the air. She dare not look, because she knew the portal had opened and Aosoth was no more. She mourned his loss, for he had been useful and such a gifted lover. She'd have to train her four young lovers how to do the things Aosoth had, especially the rough anal foreplay. Though the prospect should've excited her, she felt a twisting in her gut. What if the amethysts didn't work, and she wasn't able to steal the she-wolf's body?

When the shifter moaned, her hand rising to her forehead, Balban took out her dart gun and fired another shot into the girl's leg, hating having to drug her again. She wouldn't be able to steal the shifter's body until she woke up; stealing a sleeping skin would make her too vulnerable, and she had no idea how long two doses of sleeping medicine would last.

She glowered at the girl. "You'd better be worth it. I lost a perfectly good fuck, thanks to you."

MAGNUS CAUTIOUSLY APPROACHED the crushed and blood-splattered body of a huge human. "Who is this?" he asked Van Thunderfoot.

Van grimaced and kicked the lifeless corpse until it lay on its backside, mouth agape and eyes staring blankly at the sky. "The other demon."

A swarm of hornets raced through Magnus's veins. "If both demons are dead, what happened to Annie?"

Van frowned at the corpse. "Something's not making sense." He pointed his nose in the air, inhaling deeply. "There's that lavender perfume again."

Magnus crouched down, scenting the corpse. "It's not on him."

"It's wherever that redheaded demon has been. I smelled it on her at the bar last night."

"There must be more demons," Raine said, circling the body, searching for clues.

"Who all wear the same perfume?" Van asked.

Magnus had run out of ideas. "Who all wear the same perfume and keep killing each other."

Van shook his head. "That makes no sense."

"They are succubi."

Magnus looked at Tor's grim expression and stony eyes. "What?"

"Annie said the redheaded demon was four hundred years old. How do you think she's lived so long?"

Magnus froze, his mind reeling. "I-I don't know."

Tor looked horrified. "Switching bodies."

All moisture evaporated from Magnus's mouth, making it feel like he'd swallowed a mouthful of sand. "Y-you mean stealing them?"

Tor's features hardened. "Yes."

"Do you think she took Roy's body?" Van asked.

"That would make sense," Tor answered. "Then she used Roy's body to lure Annie away."

Fuck! Fuck! Fuck!

Magnus felt as if the earth was about to open up and swallow him whole. "So then what about this demon? Whose body did he take?" Somewhere in his subconscious, he already knew the answer.

Tor didn't respond, but his dark look softened to one of pity.

"The demon took Annie's body," Raine said, storming up to Magnus and giving him a look that could melt steel.

At that moment, Magnus wished the earth would open up and swallow him whole. He ripped off the blood-splattered scarf that Annie had given him, letting it fall to the ground. It had been the last thing she'd given him—the only thing. He didn't deserve it. He'd failed his mother, and now he'd failed his mate. Father was right. He was a worthless protector.

BALBAN PULLED UP IN front of the unassuming two-story farmhouse with faded white planks at the end of the road. This place was one of their many exchange posts and had worked well for them the past several years. It wasn't as big as their fortress near San Antonio, but that house was no longer an option after the wolves found it. The wolves would soon locate their other hideout, which was why it was urgent she switch bodies. Hoisting Annie into her arms, she walked around to the back of the house. The old wooden stairs creaked as she climbed to the porch.

A guard let her in, exhibiting a wicked grin as he looked over Annie.

Balban glared at him. "Touch her, and I slice off your dick."

The guy visibly swallowed, then nodded. Though most of her guards were native Spanish speakers, they knew enough English to understand the meaning of her threats.

She carried Annie upstairs and laid her on top of a large crate they used to house their sex slaves. Frightened eyes blinked at her, like curious forest animals watching her through underbrush. Only these animals were girls in cages, each one with the potential to make them a profit of four thousand dollars a day. Balban thought about the money she and Aosoth had saved over the years. It was enough to ditch the stress and drama of running a sex trafficking operation and live comfortably in another country for a century. Someplace tropical, where the waiters brought drinks in coconut shells. She wondered if she'd fucked up by killing Aosoth. He would've brought her much sexual pleasure on that tropical beach, but he was at the bottom of hell's pit now. No use mourning what she could no longer have.

After securing Annie in a cage, her rumbling stomach reminded her she needed to feed her mortal skin. One thing she hated about this body was his constant need for nourishment. According to the agent's thoughts, he'd been starving himself for months to financially support his invalid father. Humans were so foolish. He should've put a bullet between his useless wheelchair-bound father's eyes instead of sacrificing his own pleasure and well-being to keep him alive. If Balban had been forced to remain in Agent Miller's human shell much longer, she would've put the old man out of his misery herself.

She went to the kitchen, pleased when she found a bag of tacos in the fridge. She ate three of them straight from the bag, too hungry to care they were cold. When her stomach rumbled again, she decided to eat three more, though this time she wanted them warm. After setting them on a paper plate, she zapped them in the microwave.

"Where's Señor?"

It was the foreman named Miguel. Either he'd snuck up on her or she'd been too focused on food to hear him come in. As head foreman, Miguel had been following Aosoth's orders the past three years. Aosoth had paid and treated him well only because he'd planned to use him should he need to switch bodies. Now that Aosoth and the beautiful redhead were gone, she didn't expect Miguel to take orders from Roy. That left her with only one choice. She'd have to take Miguel's body just long enough to give instructions to the second in command. After that, she'd kill Miguel.

"Dead," she answered, wishing she was in the redhead's body so she could use her cleavage to distract him. "I'm in charge now."

Miguel shook his head. "Señor left me in charge, not you."

"Fine." She threw up her hands. "You're in charge. Here." She reached into her pocket and pulled out a wad of bills. "Señor told me to give this to you."

He greedily held out his hand, making it too easy for Balban. Latching onto his wrist, her soul easily slipped into his skin like water flowing from a jug into a glass. Miguel's terrified scream was quickly silenced as she squeezed his soul, sending him to the abyss. She gave herself a minute to adjust to her new body. Agent Roy Miller fell to the floor in a motionless heap, looking as lifeless as a corpse. She didn't think she'd occupied his body long enough for his soul to be permanently stuck in the abyss, but she'd been wrong before.

Miguel was easily twice Agent Miller's size, and she found lifting him to be no effort at all. Though she hated male bodies, she valued their strength. After depositing Roy in a cage across from Annie, she sneered at the trembling girls, hating them for their weakness.

Balban talked to Miguel's second in command next, a scrawny Mexican kid named Jose. He couldn't have been more than twenty. Not only was he a man with unwelcome dangly parts, he was skinny and sickly, but he made a decent guard, and they needed all the guards they could get.

"Order all men to stand guard," she rattled off to him in Spanish, pleased with herself for knowing the language so well. "Shoot anyone who comes near. Notify me when the girl wakes."

"Sí," Jose answered and marching out with purpose in his stride.

She sat at the table and ate, her appetite significantly decreased in the new body. She only managed two tacos before a twisting in her gut warned her to stop. What the hell was in those things? Oh, well. It made no difference. She'd be out of this body soon enough.

MAGNUS STOOD WITH HIS brothers, facing Tor and Cesar while several other alphas and trackers circled the map of Texas Cesar had laid out on his kitchen table.

"If we leave at sunset, we can get to Cotulla by truck in an hour." Cesar pointed to the south Texas town. "We leave our vehicles outside Cotulla and shift, then follow the trackers to the ranch."

Magnus already saw holes in Cesar's plan. "What makes you think they'd go back there again?"

"Our trackers scented Roy's truck going in that direction."

"That makes no sense." Jax rubbed his chin. "They have to be aware we know about their compound. They shot at our trackers last night."

"Our trackers have much more experience than you." Cesar gave Jax a condescending look. "They said they were headed there, and I believe them."

Jax bristled, and Raine laid a hand on his arm. "Easy."

Magnus didn't appreciate the slight. Cesar meant to insult Jax because he hadn't served in the Army, but now was not the time for rivalry. Annie needed them. They could kick Cesar's ass later.

"Did you send trackers to the compound?" Magnus asked Cesar.

He shook his head. "I made them come back."

Magnus gritted his teeth. "Why?"

Cesar gave him a blank look. "Because I didn't want them getting shot at again. We'll wait until nightfall."

Magnus threw up his hands. "That makes no damn sense. How can we be sure she's there?"

"Tor," Cesar asked the senior alpha. "What do you think?"

Tor shot Cesar a withering look. "If I'd known you ordered the trackers to come back, I'd have followed them myself."

"If she's not at that compound," Cesar said, "we'll make them tell us where she is."

"Curse the Ancients!" Jax hollered, his eyes shifting to blinding gold. "Our father might have been a belligerent drunk, but he was a hell of a lot smarter than you."

Magnus balled his hands into fists, expecting Cesar to strike out, but the alpha hung his head.

"It's not easy being chieftain," he muttered. "I never asked for this damned job."

Jax backed away from the table, waving to his brothers. "We're wasting time here."

"Where are you going?" Tor asked.

Jax's features hardened. "To find Annie."

Chapter Eleven

JAX KNELT AT THE SIDE of the lonely dirt road, checking the tire tracks and inhaling the faint scent of lavender perfume. "Well, what do you think?" he asked Van Thunderfoot, a far more experienced tracker.

Van tasted the dirt, then gazed east. "I think you were right to lead us here, Jax. You're a natural tracker."

Van's praise would've gone to his head if he hadn't been so worried about Annie. "Thanks."

"Look at this." Raine held out his phone, showing them an aerial map of the area. Jax's eyes honed in on an old farmhouse, protected by a high fence. Beside it was a red barn and four newer trucks. "What does your instinct tell you?" Van asked.

"That Annie's in that house."

Van stood, eyes narrowed on the horizon and the distant setting sun. "I agree. There's a ridge on either side. We split up and each take a ridge."

Jax froze at that. The Thunderfoots were leaving them? He would have to rely on his tracking skills without Van? He released a slow exhale. He'd gotten them this far. He could do it. He had to. Annie was counting on him.

"And then what?" Raine asked.

Van gave Jax an assessing look. "What would you do?"

A plan quickly unfolded in his mind. "I'd set fire to the barn to create a diversion."

Van smiled. "Good idea."

"And while they're putting it out, we get inside the house and free Annie. We don't attack unless we need to," Jax added, worried she would get caught in the crossfire if the guards started shooting. "Our main goal should be getting her to safety."

"Excellent." Van rubbed his hands together. "Who starts the fire?"

Jax stepped up. "I will," he barely rasped the words. He'd never been trained in reconnaissance, and now the entire operation relied on his ability to sneak into the compound and set fire to a barn that no doubt contained weapons or drugs.

"Good, good," Van said. "Let's get started."

ANNIE WOKE, HER HEAD feeling like a cracked egg. She rubbed an aching temple, not surprised to find a crusty cut and a massive bump. What had happened? Where was she? She sat up and found herself looking through the bars of a cage into several other cages. Each one held a sleeping person, mostly slender girls from the looks of it. They were illuminated by pale moonlight shining through a narrow window on one wall. A lone man was caged across from her, his chest rising and falling with erratic breathing while he thrashed in his sleep. Her nostrils flared as she inhaled his familiar scent.

"Roy?" She poked her fingers through the bars, then pulled back when she recalled he had attacked her in the barn. He was probably the reason she was in a cage. No, wait. That wasn't Roy. It was a demon who looked like him. Roy would never harm her. But why was he in a cage?

She probed his mind, listening to his thoughts as he woke up. *Where am I? What the fuck happened?*

His eyes flew open, and he blinked and rolled onto his side.

"Roy!" she whispered.

"Annie?" Hunched over, he clasped the bars and gazed at her.

"Do you remember anything?" She rubbed her sore neck, recalling the pain and pulling out a dart. It had to have been laced with a sleeping drug. Had they drugged him, too?

"The last thing I remember was this redheaded woman touching me and then I went to a dark place."

Had Balban possessed him? She berated herself for not warning Roy about the demons. She'd had no idea they would involve him. "We have to get out of here."

He straightened, then slouched when his head hit the top of the cage. "Do you have anything that can pick the locks? A hairpin or an earring?"

"No."

"What about your claws?"

"Good idea," she said, then closed her eyes and summoned the change. Nothing happened. She cursed the demon who'd shot her. Something was preventing her from shifting. "I can't shift."

"Why?"

"I don't know." Glaring at the bloody hole in her jeans, she pulled them down and saw a red, inflamed wound on her leg. "My skin itches."

Roy shook his head in dismay. "Amethyst darts."

"What?"

"I had amethyst darts in my trunk." Fuck! No wonder she couldn't shift. Amethysts were a shifter's weakness. "Why?" She couldn't deny she was hurt that her brother would carry weapons that could cause her and the Amaroki harm.

"For Vidar," he said and laughed hoarsely. "Why else?"

Damn Vidar! She couldn't blame Roy for wanting to protect himself after Vidar had attacked him.

She heard footsteps. "Someone's coming. Pretend you're sleeping." She laid down, praying to her fathers for help when someone poked her with a stick.

"Get her out," a gruff voice said.

Strong hands dug into her arms and dragged her out of the cage, depositing her on the floor.

Roy rattled his bars. "Leave her alone!"

She kicked and punched, smacking a few shins before a big man threw her on her stomach and pinned her down.

"You son of a bitch!" she yelled, panic making her heart pump overtime. "My mates will kill you." Or she would if she could just get those darts out of her body.

"You hurt her, and *I'll* kill you," Roy hollered.

The man laughed.

She screamed and thrashed like a fish out of water when the man threw her over his shoulder and carried her out the door. *Fathers, save me,* she thought, fearing she was about to be raped or worse.

JAX FRANTICALLY DUG under the fence until his paws bled. He'd learned the hard way the fence was electrified, which meant he had to dig even deeper to avoid being shocked again.

Luckily he'd found a section that wasn't well lit and covered by a thick bush which had a burrow made by some animal, so he didn't have to dig for long. He picked up the lighter in his mouth and crawled into the hole.

Once he was through, he froze when he saw how bright the area was. Lights were hung everywhere. He'd never make it to the barn without being seen. A tall shadow fell over the place, blocking the overhead lights. Squinting at it, he could've sworn it was in the shape of a protector.

A sudden gust of wind ruffled his fur.

Go, an ethereal voice directed.

Who was helping him? Could it have been the Ancients? Knowing he needed to hurry, he crawled to the back of the barn and nudged open a rotting plank with his snout. After he barely squeezed inside, he found himself behind several wooden crates. The smell—almost like a blend of window cleaners and rotten eggs—was not one he recognized, but he knew it wasn't natural.

Common sense told him he was in a meth lab, and as it was highly flammable, he'd just need a bit of kindling to start the fire. He only hoped it didn't lead to a deadly explosion, or if it did, that it didn't injure Annie. The house was a good two hundred yards away. Any explosion shouldn't go that far. He didn't know how he knew it, but Annie was inside the house.

When he heard voices outside the barn, he cursed himself for his indecision. Shifting into human form, he pulled the lighter out of his mouth and gathered stray pieces of hay, tied them together with discarded pieces of twine, and set it alight. He dropped it into a stall laid with old, dry straw. It quickly caught fire.

He did the same in the other three stalls. When the barn filled with smoke, he shifted and went back outside, barely getting out before an explosion rattled the barn and the whole thing lit up like a flaming inferno, singing the fur off his back. With a yelp, he scurried toward the hole as more explosions rocked the ground, his backside still on fire. Shots rang out. He yelped when a bullet hit his back paw. After crawling into the hole, he limped out the other side and rolled to put out the fire. Another shot struck his ass, and he yelped again, dodging bullets while racing up the ridge. By the time he limped to his brothers, he was physically and mentally exhausted. Shifting, he looked at his injured foot with concern, crying out when Frey touched the wound on his ass. His entire backside felt raw and exposed, as if his skin had melted.

Jax cried and thrashed when Frey tried to apply ointment.

"Jax." Frey cupped his face. "Look at me. You need to stay still. You're bleeding everywhere."

Jax tried to speak, but all that came out was a gasp, and then his world dimmed, his brother's worried eyes fading into darkness.

ANNIE SCREAMED WHEN the man carried her to a room, slamming the door behind them and dropping her on a squeaky bed with a crusty bedspread. Her nose wrinkled as she inhaled the familiar lavender perfume, which overlaid a musty urine smell. Muscles too big to be natural, he was a 'roided Latino covered in tattoos and had several earrings on his ears and face. So why did he smell like Balban, who was dead? Then she remembered Roy, or whoever that was, had smelled of lavender when he'd abducted her.

A sickening feeling twisted her stomach when the man looked at her with red in his eyes.

"Don't you dare touch me, you demon fuck!"

"How'd you know I was a demon?"

"I can smell it."

He looked at her in surprise. "Can all the shifters smell it?"

"How'd you know I'm a shifter?"

"I'm not stupid, that's why." He snorted, then chewed on his nails, a surprisingly feminine gesture for a buff guy covered in tattoos. "What is the smell like?"

Annie put off telling him. She didn't want to give away too many of her secrets. Not that he probably didn't know them all already. "You don't know your own smell?" She laughed.

His eyes blackened to two lumps of coal. "To you."

"Like the most noxious gas imaginable," she lied, then discreetly rubbed her leg against the side of the bed. If she could break open her wounds and get the amethysts to fall out, she might stand a chance at defeating this demon.

"That will never do." Her captor rocked on his heels. "It looks like we will have a change in plans. Your mates will never accept me if I smell."

Annie gasped. "You were going to steal my mates?"

"And your body." He gave her a pointed look. "I think I'll still take the body, but I'll hold off on the mates."

A terror unlike Annie had ever known made her temporarily see spots before her eyes. She fought him when he latched onto her arm, his eyes glowing red.

His face screwed up tight, he grunted and groaned and his cheeks flushed bright red. Finally he let go of her with a curse, shaking his hand as if he'd been burned.

"I don't understand. Your magical defenses are down. I should be able to get through."

So this was why Roy had tricked her. He'd been possessed by this demon, who had tried and failed to steal Annie's body.

She forced a smile, though she felt anything but happy. "Aw, tough luck." Why was she taunting him? Was she nuts? But maybe she could buy some time. Her mates had to come for her soon. If not, then her fathers had to have heard her prayers.

The demon's eyes pulsed red like a strobe light. "I have too much on my mind, that's why."

"Uh-huh." She laughed, hoping he didn't hear her nervousness. "Or maybe you're just an incompetent demon."

He slapped her so hard, she thought she saw stars. The sound of his large hand striking her cheek ricocheted through the room. She blinked at the dizzying pain and then felt something fall from the back of her neck. The amethyst! Her face would probably be bruised and swollen by morning, but at least it had fallen out. One more to go. If she could just get at the one stuck in her leg, she could shift and bite the demon's face off.

He grabbed her again, this time circling her neck with his meaty fingers. "Stay still," he commanded.

As if she could go anywhere with his gigantic hand around her throat. She coughed and sputtered when he pressed against her windpipe, veins popping out of his forehead and neck.

"You might as well give up," she rasped. "You're not getting in, and even if you do, my mates will not let you get away with it."

"Of course they will." He flashed a feral smile. "They won't harm your body."

She could barely breathe. "My mates will," she sputtered, wanting to add that they'd hunt him to the ends of the earth, but he tightened his hold, and she couldn't speak anymore.

"I will claim your body or kill you trying, and then I will switch bodies so they never find me."

Annie's vision tunneled while the demon swore and squeezed harder, sweat dripping down his brow.

Fathers! she cried.

The bed suddenly shook so hard, she thought it was possessed. The demon let go and fell back against the wall, crying out when a section of the ceiling fell on top of him. Annie rolled off the bed, gasping for breath while crawling underneath the frame, waiting for the tremors to stop.

She didn't know if the earthquakes had been a freak of nature or her fathers sent them, but she was grateful for the chance to regroup. She needed to free Roy and get out of here.

As soon as the tremors stopped, she crawled out from under the bed and scrambled on top of the debris crushing the demon. Choking on smoke and dust, she found her way in the dark to the basement with the cages, which appeared to be intact after the earthquake, made from impenetrable steel to keep the prisoners secure.

Several girls were screaming and crying while a guard lay in the center of the room, bleeding out, the pointy tip of a chandelier stuck through his chest. Annie dug through his pockets and found the cage keys.

"I'm here, Roy," she said, fumbling with the keys. There were too many, and her hands were trembling.

"Are you okay?" he asked, gripping the bars with whitened knuckles. "The explosions didn't hurt you?"

Explosions? She thought they had been earthquakes.

She coughed on drywall fumes. Her throat was already sore from being choked, but now it felt like it was on fire.

He held out his hands, waggling his fingers. "Let me do it."

She gladly handed him the keys, and he was out of his cage in a matter of moments, taking her in a fierce hug. She cried and clung to him, relieved they were both still alive.

Pulling away, he clutched her shoulders, desperately searching her face. "Did he rape you?"

"No. He was trying to steal my body."

Roy frowned. "Where is he now?"

"Buried under rubble."

Roy heaved a shaky breath. "We have to get out of here now."

She swallowed back a lump of emotion, silently nodding as tears of relief streamed down her face.

He opened the rest of the cages, encouraging the girls to escape, but they refused to leave, trembling and cowering with their arms wrapped around themselves.

"Por favor," Annie pleaded, trying to recall what little Spanish she remembered from high school. "We won't hurt you. It's not safe here."

Still the girls refused to budge.

"Leave them." Roy took Annie's hand. "We'll come back for them after we get backup." He kicked the dead guy onto his side and pulled a set of car keys from his pocket. Then he took the man's gun.

Holding onto Roy like he was a lifeline, she followed him down a darkened hallway. They stopped, hearing panicked voices. Looking out the window, she saw the reason for their alarm. A large barn was on fire, and the guards were trying to put it out with garden hoses and buckets.

"Probably their meth lab," Roy grumbled. "Drugs and slavery go hand in hand."

After carefully making their way down a crumbling set of stairs, they found themselves in the kitchen. She grabbed two water bottles off the counter, relieved to have something to soothe her parched throat. Another explosion rocked the house. Annie screamed, ducking while Roy shielded her from falling debris.

They tiptoed out the back, relieved to see all of the guards were too preoccupied with the fire to notice them. When Roy clicked a key that he pulled out of his pocket, a newer King Cab's lights came on. They climbed into the truck, and Roy drove off, forcing Annie to lie down in case a guard saw her. He didn't turn on the headlights until they were a safe distance away from the house.

She clutched the water bottles, peeking above the seat at the fire as it shrank in the distance. Only when it had completely disappeared from view did she sit up and breathe a sigh of relief. But that relief was short-lived. Though the demon was buried under rubble, what if he'd survived? Or worse, what if he'd found a new human body and chased her again?

MAGNUS SAT BEHIND A bush, his tail tucked between his legs, alternating between watching the rise and fall of Jax's chest as he erratically strained for breath to scanning the horizon for threats below the ridge. A nearly full moon made it possible to see what was going on. Most of the guards were busy putting out the inferno Jax had created. Now was the time to strike.

The plan was simple. Get Annie out as quickly and stealthily as possible, which meant he couldn't go full-on protector no matter how badly he wanted to crush her captors' skulls, especially after what had happened to Jax. If he survived, he'd be scarred for life, and all because Magnus had let Annie out of his sight.

As much as he hated having to leave Jax, that's exactly what they had to do, praying to the Ancients he'd be okay until they returned.

They would sneak into the back of the house as wolves, shift, and break down every door until they found her.

You ready? he asked Frey and Raine.

They answered with growls, still too angry with him to look him in the eye. Not that he blamed them. He'd been a fool for leaving her for even a minute.

Ears pinned against their skulls, they crept down the ridge toward the house, their coppery fur muted by the darkness, as clouds moved in, blocking out the moon's light.

Suddenly violent tremors shook the ground when another explosion lit up the night sky. No doubt they were having difficulty containing the fire. Good. The more distracted the guards were, the better.

Magnus howled when a large stone hit his head, bouncing off his skull and smacking Raine's backside. Yelping, Magnus and his brothers scurried down the hill, an avalanche of rocks and debris following in their wake. Once they reached the bottom, Magnus shifted into a protector, shielding his two brothers and taking the brunt of the avalanche until the dust settled.

Choking on dust, Magnus sat up and wiped blood and sweat from his eyes, then quickly shifted back into wolf form. Raine and Frey got up, shaking dust out of their fur. Nobody thanked him for acting as a shield. He didn't deserve any praise, since he was the reason they were in this mess in the first place. He started off again, and his world spun. Dizzy, he whimpered, waiting for his four dancing brothers to turn back into two.

Magnus, Raine projected. *Are you too injured to go on?*

No, no. Give me a moment.

We don't have a moment, Raine growled.

Magnus stood, and then sat back down. Maintaining balance on three legs was hard enough. Now with an added head injury, it was nearly impossible.

You are too injured. You'll slow us down, Raine said without a hint of sympathy.

The world steadied long enough for Magnus to see a truck drive off down the dirt road behind the house, its headlights off. It disappeared like a phantom in the night. Though he saw only one silhouette inside, a man with cropped hair, instinct told him Annie was with him.

She's leaving, an unfamiliar voice echoed in his skull.

We need to follow that truck, he blurted. *She's in it.*

Raine's ears twitched. *I see only a man inside.*

She's with him, Magnus said firmly. *We need to go after her.*

No! Raine was unyielding, his upper lip turning back in a snarl. *We attack the house as planned.*

Are you more interested in vengeance or saving our mate? Magnus snapped. *My instincts are telling me she's in the truck.*

The fur on the back of Raine's neck stood on end as he bared his fangs. *And we're supposed to trust your instincts after you let Annie get captured in the first place?*

Look, Magnus whimpered, *I don't blame you for being mad at me.*

Raine advanced on him, snapping. *You don't blame us? You're lucky we're letting you come along.*

Magnus stepped back, not wishing to get into a fight. Annie needed them, and they were wasting time. *What do you want me to do?*

Nothing, Raine snarled. *You've done enough. If you want to chase the truck, then go. We're going to that house.* He turned and ran, Frey trailing him.

Tail drooping, he watched them go, then circled the burning barn and trotted along the dirt road behind the house. Though the truck was long gone, and he was still dizzy, he would not fail. He would find his Annie and bring her to safety or die trying.

Chapter Twelve

BALBAN KNEW HER TIME in the stolen body was almost up. She could scarcely breathe because of the pain in her chest and her lifeblood was slipping away after something had pierced her side. If someone didn't come for her soon, she'd be forced to join Aosoth at the bottom dimension of hell. She trembled at the thought. The Prince of Darkness would certainly punish her for her escape, and she shuddered to think what Aosoth would do to her.

"Miguel!" Jose shouted.

She listened to a distant chorus of girls screaming, followed by the slamming of metal cage doors. Footsteps finally thudded into the room, and she heaved a groan of relief when a heavy weight was lifted from her chest.

Jose frowned down at her, clucking his tongue. "*Lo siento.*"

She tried to give commands, but blood poured from her mouth when she tried to talk. Jose knelt beside her, removing a rosary from his neck and placing it on her chest. That one touch was all she needed to slip inside Jose, squeezing out his soul and taking over his body.

From her new position, she witnessed Miguel take his last breath, a look of pure shock in his eyes. She imagined Miguel wasn't too happy, waking up from a demonic possession only to find out he was dying. She didn't feel empathy for others, and she certainly didn't feel pity for her hired slaver. He would most likely be escorted to the lowest dimension of hell after his sins of imprisoning and raping girls. Miguel would have an eternity to regret the time he spent on Earth.

She stood, pleased with the elasticity and strength of her new legs. Kicking the rosary off Miguel's chest, she watched with distain as it slid to the ground. Resolution hardened her spine when she stood and looked out the window. The barn was on fire. A sneaky suspicion told her the wolves had created it as a diversion, which meant they'd be in the house soon, tearing it apart while searching for the virgin. Swearing, she punched the wall. She'd come so close to avenging the loss of her lover. Though she couldn't take over their bodies, she could still enact her revenge.

She knew the Amaroki's secrets. She knew their strengths and weaknesses. With that knowledge, she could destroy them.

RAINE SWORE WHEN HE found the chaos had been diverted from the barn to the house. One young, wiry guard argued with the others, waving a gun in their direction from the porch. After an intense standoff, the guard finally jumped in an old red truck with orange flames and tore off.

Good. Less guards for them to fight, but there were still at least a dozen, all heavily armed. When they dragged two bodies out of the house and laid them on the dirt, Raine became alarmed. Though he didn't recognize the men, it was clear the compound was falling apart. He just prayed Annie hadn't gotten caught in the crossfire.

Raine's nostrils flared. Annie's scent was strong here. He hoped he was right, and she was still in the house.

Most of the guards returned to the barn fire, leaving only two to watch the back of the house. Two armed men to three shifters was a much fairer fight.

Be safe, brother, Raine projected, praying to the Ancients that Frey wasn't injured or worse. After watching Jax crawl back with burns all over him, he didn't think he could stand having another brother fall.

You, too, brother, Frey answered.

When Tor and Van showed up, giving Raine questioning looks, Raine nodded at the house. Tor nodded his approval.

Wait for me to clear the way, Raine projected to Frey. Under cover of darkness, he skirted the house, hiding behind bushes, barrels, and rusty old cars. He ended up behind a stack of heavy tractor tires, the perfect cover and the perfect weapons. He quickly shifted into his behemoth protector form, a ten-foot tall, two-legged beast with two tusks curling out of his mouth and a barrel chest. He picked up the tires as if they weighed no more than footballs and deftly threw them at the guards, knocking them down like bowling pins. Then he whistled to the others, who slunk into the house.

Once inside, Raine changed into a man and sped through the house, following Annie's scent. He raced up a set of crumbling stairs two at a time until he reached a shaky landing. The others darted ahead of him, still in wolf form. They saw the cages. It smelled like piss and mold and something else he couldn't identify.

What the hell? Frey howled.

Raine searched each cage, despondent when he saw young girls no older than fifteen in each one. He became even more upset when he couldn't find Annie.

Frey shifted into human form and offered a girl his hand. She turned away, pressing into a corner of the cage.

We can't help them now, Raine projected. *We'll come back and free them after we find Annie.*

Frey nodded. It's not like they'd trust a naked man who'd been a wolf a few seconds earlier.

Magnus had been right. Annie wasn't here. What if she really was in that truck? That meant Magnus was her only hope of escape. Would he be capable of saving Annie?

"Come on," he said to the others, waving them downstairs. "We're wasting time here."

Frey slunk past him, his tail between his legs.

They ran out the back door while the guards still struggled to put out the fire.

Does that mean Magnus was right? Frey asked as they raced down the dirt road as wolves.

Yes. Raine grimaced. *Ancients save him if he loses her again.*

"HOW LONG BEFORE WE reach the reservation?" Annie asked Roy as they drove down the darkened highway.

"About forty-five minutes."

She looked over her shoulder again, fearing the demon wasn't dead. Or maybe it had died but then managed to steal another body. With Annie's luck, that's exactly what had happened, which meant she'd have no idea what the demon looked like.

She probed Roy's mind for at least the tenth time, hating herself for invading his privacy, but she had to be sure. At the moment the only things on his mind were his desire to get Annie to safety and the strong need for a toilet, and not in that order. His stomach burned like demon hounds were playing fetch with his guts.

"My mates are probably looking for me," she said. "I wish we had our phones." Or at least a pocket knife, so she could dig the amethyst out of her thigh.

"No telling what the demons did with them," he answered.

And it's not like they could stop to call them. What if a demon was following them and stole Roy's body again? No, they couldn't pull over until they were safe among the Amaroki.

Annie's heart clenched when Roy gripped the wheel more tightly, his face screwed up and tension radiating off him in waves.

"What was it like?" she asked. "When the demon possessed you?"

"It was hell," he answered solemnly, his voice hollow. "My soul was lost in darkness."

"I'm sorry." Just knowing her brother had been subjected to such hell—that she could've lost him forever—twisted her up inside.

"What matters is you're safe," he said. "I'm sorry the demon used me to get to you."

"It's not your fault, Roy." She leaned against him, grasping his arm, hating how he jerked from her touch. "It's my fault I didn't warn you about the demon. I never thought it would go after you."

Roy glanced down at her hand. "We'll probably need a lot of therapy after this is over."

"Therapy never helped me." A bitter laugh escaped her. "They tried it when we were in foster care, remember?"

"Yeah. We've been through some shit."

All thanks to their deadbeat parents. Their mom was a selfish whore, but their dad's—correction, Roy's dad—his apathy was even worse. After the accident, he hadn't just given up on himself. He'd given up on his children.

"We have." Emotion colored her words as she swallowed back a knot of sorrow. "I'm glad I still have you, though." She squeezed his arm again, pleased when he didn't jump.

"Me, too." He took one hand off the wheel and laced his fingers through hers, holding tight. "We'll get through this, Annie."

Yes, they'd get through this. She always found a way to overcome her challenges. She just wished life would throw her a few less curve balls. It would be nice to enjoy living for once.

MAGNUS HAD BEEN RUNNING across rough terrain for what felt like hours, staying parallel to the road the truck had taken. He had more cacti needles stuck in his legs than he could count, and his calves were in knots. But he wouldn't give up. He'd shifted into protector form, hoping nobody would see him in the darkness, knowing he could run better on two feet than three paws. All the while he prayed to the Ancients, Annie's fathers, that he wouldn't be too late and his brothers had survived their confrontation with the guards. He'd never forgive himself if anything happened to his family.

Regardless of the outcome, he'd already decided he wasn't worthy of having a family. Once Annie was rescued and he was assured Vidar wouldn't be a threat, he would leave Texas and set out as a lone wolf. His brothers didn't want him around anyway.

When the terrain changed from rough dirt to softer soil, he knew he was getting closer to the reservation. He hoped that was a good sign. Why would the truck driver take Annie home unless he meant to free her?

An eerie howl sliced through the air, making Magnus halt, heart thumping hard while he strained to hear it again. Another howl practically pierced his ears. What was that? It sounded like a wolf, only darker. Perhaps it was an old, sick Amaroki. It made his blood run cold. Whatever it was, it was on the hunt.

Chapter Thirteen

ROY HUNCHED OVER THE steering wheel, his cheeks as red as volcanic lava while pained sounds escaped him.

"Roy!" Annie cried. "What's wrong?"

"That demon fed me poison," he said and groaned, his stomach grumbling so loudly it sounded like there was a pack of coyotes under his belt. "I need to stop."

Annie spied a large brick building just ahead.

"Pull over there." She pointed. "That looks like a hospital."

Roy nodded and sped into the parking lot, slamming the vehicle in park. "Stay here."

"Nope." No way was she letting him out of her sight. She jumped out and helped him to the front door. It was locked, but he seemed to know the code to get in.

"How did you know that?" she asked.

He hunched over like a feeble, old man. "I don't know if I'm going to make it." He punched more codes to get through more doors, then raced to a nearby restroom.

She sat on a sofa, eyes fixed on the bathroom door, wishing for once she didn't have wolf-touched hearing... or smell.

She waited in a room that looked like the parlor of an old lady's house, with old-fashioned furniture and paintings, and even an old record player on a sideboard. The check-in area looked more like something that would be staffed by a concierge, with a sign-in station, a complimentary juice and snack bar, and guest badges lined up neatly on the counter. Was this a hospital or a hotel for the elderly?

By the time he finally came out, he was as white as a sheet.

"Better?" she asked.

He smiled. "Much better."

Roy went directly to the juice and drank several cups. Annie helped herself to pink lemonade. The two water bottles had done little to quench her thirst.

"What is this place?" she asked, wiping her mouth with the back of her hand before putting two complimentary glazed donuts on a paper plate. They were stale, but she was too hungry to care.

Roy gave her a blank look. "It's where they're keeping Dad."

She nearly choked on a stale donut. "He's not *my* dad, Roy."

"He thinks he's your dad."

"Let's go." She dragged him toward the front door. "We're wasting time."

"Wait." Roy dug in his heels. "I want to get Dad first."

She gaped at him. Had he lost his mind? As if being chased by a body-snatching demon was the best time to haul around a quadriplegic!

"Annie," he said, "the demon knows every single one of my thoughts. She knows our dad's here. He's not safe."

"*Your* dad," she reiterated, feeling thousands of tiny needles pricking her skin.

Roy threw up his hands. "Jesus, Annie!"

She cocked a hand on her hip. "Have you forgotten how he treated Amara?"

"No." Roy shook his head. "But don't you think he's paid for his sins?"

How could he be so flippant about this? As if their father abandoning Amara and them was no big deal? "He didn't try to get better. He just sat in that wheelchair like a corpse while they took us away. He didn't even put up a fight. When you love someone, you fight for them." Her voice broke, and she was forced to turn away, biting on her knuckles to keep from crying out. Couldn't he see that just talking about that man was torturing her? She did not want to see him.

"Look at me, Annie." He grasped her shoulders. "We have a bigger fight at the moment. We don't have time to deal with our repressed teenage emotions. We have a body-snatching demon chasing us."

"Don't you think I know that?" She jerked away, ready to punch him or the wall until she saw a nurse coming their way.

"Hi, Roy." The nurse, a pretty Latina woman, glanced at Annie dismissively and then looked over Roy's dirty, torn clothes with concern. "Are you okay? Looks like you've been through something."

"Our tire had a flat, and we got dirty changing it. We came to see Dad."

"Your father's asleep. Visiting hours are over."

"I'm sorry, Gloria, but I'm afraid this can't wait," Roy pleaded.

Gloria clucked her tongue. "You know how he gets when we wake him."

"He'll want to wake for this." Roy wrapped an arm around Annie's shoulder. "My sister is visiting from out of town."

Gloria smiled warmly, and that's when she knew this woman had a crush on Roy and had probably initially thought she was his girlfriend. "Annie? Your father talks about you nonstop." She held out a hand.

She probed Gloria's mind, searching for any sign of deceit. The only thought she heard was *It's about time she visits that poor man.* She shook the woman's hand, surprised by her firm grip.

"Oh." She didn't know what else to say. She hadn't expected Roy Senior to remember her. Sure, Roy had said his father talked about her, but she figured he was exaggerating.

"He'll be so happy to see you." Gloria clasped her hands together, her attention settling on Roy. "It's very hard for him here." She smiled at Annie again. "Everyone else has dementia, and he gets easily frustrated. Thank god your brother lives nearby. He seems to be the only one who can soothe him."

Annie flashed a smile so forced, her face felt ready to crack. "That's good."

When Gloria turned and beckoned them forward, she felt as if she was walking into the pit of hell. She almost thought she'd rather face the demon than see the man who'd ruined her childhood.

IT TOOK FREY AND THE others far too long to trek back to their truck. Deciding it would be best if they stuck together, Tor and Van followed them instead of going back to their vehicle. The explosions had left wide chasms and dangerously slippery slopes. He'd wanted to chase after Magnus and Annie on foot, but Raine insisted driving would be faster. Besides, they had to get Jax.

The treacherous journey gave Frey ample time to dwell on his insecurities and failures.

Yesterday he'd been dreading mating with Annie and being responsible for her and their pack's offspring. It wasn't that Frey wasn't attracted to Annie as a mate. She was perfect in every way. He just didn't know how to be a good mate, and he was terrified he'd disappoint her and his brothers. He'd had no positive role models growing up. When his mother died, he'd been barely ten years old, not old enough for Sami, his birth father, to teach him how to be a good gamma. After losing his mate, Sami had become a depressed drunk. He'd never taught Frey how to cook or what was expected of him. He was usually off somewhere, leaving the rest of the family to fend for themselves when it came to meals.

Frey had prayed to the Ancients for a way to delay their mating until he'd practiced cooking and cleaning, and it had been answered, because Annie was kidnapped. He felt like a ten-pound bucket of dog shit for the inconsiderate prayer. He'd give anything to have Annie back, even if it meant he had to disgrace himself by feeding his family macaroni and cheese and ham sandwiches.

They were chasing after a mate he didn't deserve, a mate who might already be dead, leaving Frey and his brothers to suffer as their fathers had mourned for their mother and alpha father.

They found Jax where they'd left him, his skin on fire and his eyes sunk in the back of his head. Frey checked his pulse. It was steady, but his breathing was too ragged for Frey's liking. He may have damaged his lungs in that fire.

By the time they made it to the truck, Raine was in such a foul mood, Frey knew to keep his distance. Frey had never seen him this angry. The look in Raine's eyes frightened him, for he feared one wrong move would set him off. Frey was not a fighter. He didn't have a confrontational bone in his body. As the gamma, his instinct was to be a lover and peacekeeper. Keeping the peace in this family had been no easy task, and he had failed more times than he'd succeeded.

Frey climbed into the back of the truck, Jax's head in his lap, and waited for Raine to start the engine. Rubbing his tongue across his parched mouth, he got a bottled water out of the cooler beside him. After opening it, he realized the others would be thirsty, too. He handed bottles to Tor, Van, and Raine, feeling a small measure of comfort when Van thanked him. Then he offered them each one of the sandwiches he'd packed, but they refused. He was too upset to eat, too, so he threw the sandwiches in the cooler and stared out the window, watching tumbleweeds fly by while Raine tore off down the road.

Jax's pitiful cries startled Frey. He was burning up, and his back was oozing all over the bench seat.

Sending a silent prayer to the Ancients, he promised not to sulk over his lack of culinary skills as long as they returned Annie safely to him and Jax recovered from his injuries.

AS THEY WERE WALKING toward Roy's dad's room, Annie spied a kitchen behind a tall counter, blocked off by a gate. Inside was a chopping block and several knives.

Annie tugged on Roy's sleeve, nodding to the restroom sign across from the kitchen. "I need to go. I'll meet you there."

"You don't even know where to go," Roy said.

"I'll figure it out." Annie could easily find his room. She remembered his smell, but she didn't want to say that in front of Nurse Gloria.

"Dad has a bathroom in his room."

"Ew," Annie answered, as if that was explanation enough.

She waited until Roy and the nurse turned the corner, then jumped over the gate and pulled each knife from the block. Settling on a paring knife, she stuck it in her pocket, then jumped back over the gate, whistling a cheerful tune and pretending she wasn't a thief.

She obviously hadn't been gone long enough, because Roy Senior was still asleep, though sitting up in bed, his hair sticking up in all directions. Machine wires hooked up to his arm and chest made bleeping noises. Seeing him like that brought back too many childhood nightmares and filled her with dread. He looked so sick and helpless, just like the first day their mother had brought him home from the hospital. Their insurance didn't provide for a nurse, so Annie's mother had parked him in front of the television and gone upstairs to cry. Annie ended up looking after him, though she didn't know what to do.

Nurse Gloria tapped her cellphone, then shoved it in her pocket with a curse. "I have to go. A patient fell out of bed."

She heaved a sigh of relief when the nurse left. Something about the way she stared at Annie made her feel like she was being judged.

Roy leaned over the hospital bed and gently shook him. "Dad, wake up."

"W-what is it?" The older man's eyes flew open.

"Annie's here," Roy said, motioning at her.

"Annie?" His father gasped.

She turned away, unable to look at him another moment. "Why doesn't he have a phone in his room?" She had Tor's cell number memorized and needed to call for help. What if the demon had survived and was pursuing them?

"None of the rooms have them," Roy answered. "Say hi to Dad."

She stiffened, feeling like she was trapped in a noose, and Roy was her executioner. "I'll go up front and ask the nurse." She didn't want to say hi. She didn't even want to look at the man.

"Annie?" Roy Senior rasped, a strong rattle in his chest.

Her veins turned to sludge as she slowly spun around, forcing a smile. "Hi."

"Look at you." He flashed a wide grin, revealing several missing teeth. "A beautiful grown woman."

"I'll go make the call." Roy nudged her toward the bed. "You stay here."

No way was she sitting by him. She latched onto Roy's arm. "It's not safe for you out there." She dropped her voice to a heated whisper. "She can't take my body, Roy. Only humans."

"What the hell is going on?" Roy Senior demanded.

"Nothing, Dad." Roy shot Annie a warning look.

She refused to back down. "If we're taking him with us, he needs to know."

Roy Senior banged his head against the headboard. "Know what?"

Roy groaned into his hands. "I don't even know where to begin."

"I need to call for help." Annie went to the door. "Lock it and don't let anyone in."

"Fine," Roy relented, his shoulders falling. "But you're not off the hook."

She made a spluttering noise and rolled her eyes.

And that's when the power went out, engulfing their room in darkness, with the exception of Roy Senior's bleeping machine, which obviously had backup power.

"What the hell?" Roy Senior grumbled.

"The demon is here." Annie pulled Roy close and hissed in his ear. "She's doing this to create confusion."

"Will someone explain what the hell is going on?"

Roy groaned. "I know it sounds crazy, Dad, but you're not safe here, so we're relocating you."

"Annie." Roy Senior shot her a questioning look. "You said you're not human?"

Annie froze, feeling like she was caught in a hunter's crosshairs. "I'm not evil, and I'm not going to hurt you, if that's what you're worried about."

She kept her distance as Roy loaded his father into a wheelchair, knowing Roy Senior was probably freaked out by her. Not that she cared. Now he knew how she felt.

"Where are we going?" the old man feebly asked.

"Someplace safe," she answered. At least she sure as hell hoped so.

Chapter Fourteen

"ROY, WHERE ARE YOU going?" Nurse Gloria hollered, chasing after them.

Annie's intuition told her she needed to protect her brother. "Go!" she said to him, pushing him toward the front doors. "I'll handle her."

"We're taking him out for a bit." She stood in front of the door, blocking the nurse's path. "We'll bring him back."

The nurse tried to peek around Annie's shoulder. "We don't let our patients go out this late."

"He's not a memory patient," Annie said stiffly, her stance unwavering. "He'll be fine."

The nurse made a lot of huffing and puffing noises, but Annie refused to be intimidated. She walked out, shutting the door in the nurse's face.

The moment Annie was outside, she felt as if she'd run into a brick wall. Parked next to Roy's vehicle was a familiar classic truck with flames stenciled down the sides.

Roy stood behind a pillar, gun drawn, while he scanned the area.

"Do you sense anything?" he asked Annie.

She scented the air. "I think we're alone." She looked over her shoulder at the front door. The nurse was gone. She didn't know if that was a good or bad sign.

"Stay here," Roy said to her.

Before she could stop him, he raced to their stolen truck.

Roy jumped in and tore out of the parking space, hopping the curb and parking next to them. "Come on!" He waved his gun in the air.

Annie pushed the wheelchair toward the vehicle.

Roy was about to scoop up his dad when the front door opened and Nurse Gloria ran out.

"Mr. Miller!" She waved a red jacket over her head. "You forgot your jacket."

The old man looked confused. "That isn't mine."

"Of course it is." Skirting the wheelchair, she lunged at Roy. "You hold it for your father." *Come a little closer, my pet.*

Annie jumped between them just in time, hackles raised, growling like a rabid wolf.

"No!" she screamed when she saw red flash in the nurse's eyes. "I'll kill you!" With a howl, she wrapped her hands around the nurse's throat, knocking her to the ground.

"Annie, no!" Roy cried, trying to pull her off.

"What in god's green earth is going on?" Roy Senior hollered.

"Don't touch her," Annie warned. "It's the demon, Roy."

"If you kill her, you kill Nurse Gloria, too!" Roy said.

Annie released Gloria's throat, then grabbed her wrists and pinned them above her head.

"Roy, my darling," Gloria rasped, trying and failing to buck Annie off. "Don't let her hurt me."

Annie gazed into Gloria's red eyes. Releasing her wrists, she wrapped her fingers around Gloria's throat again. "If we don't kill her, she'll go on terrorizing us and selling girls into slavery."

"No," Roy begged. "There has to be another way."

Annie pretended not to notice when the nurse reached for Roy Senior's foot. Yes, it was cruel of her to want the demon to go into a disabled man's body, but at least she could control her if she was incapacitated, and she knew a witch who could banish the demon's soul to hell.

"Sorry, Roy. The only way is death."

When the nurse's eyes rolled back, Annie let her go, then looked at Roy Senior. She saw a flash of red in his eyes and dug into his mind.

She'll never suspect I'm in here. Roy Senior cried, "Roy, get me away from this crazy woman."

"Don't touch him!" Annie warned Roy. Jumping to her feet, she wagged a finger at the demon in Roy Senior's skin. "Stupid demon. You'd really go into a paralyzed man's body?"

Roy Senior gaped at her, then looked to Roy with pleading eyes. "I don't know what she's talking about. I think she's gone mad."

"Don't give him that look." Annie laughed. "I know it's you, Balban."

Roy Senior glared at her. "How do you know my demon name?"

Annie chuckled. "That's for me to know."

Chest heaving, Roy looked like a bull ready to charge, but he wisely stayed a safe distance from the wheelchair. "What the hell did you do with my dad?" His voice was too calm, too even, which frightened Annie. She knew he was teetering on the edge of insanity.

"What choice did I have?" Roy Senior snarled. "Your sister was going to kill the nurse, and I know she won't kill her father."

"That's where you're wrong." Annie clenched her hands so tight, nails broke skin. "He's *not* my father."

Roy Senior's laughter was low and sibilant, sounding like a snake slithering across her senses. "Ah, yes. Your gods are your fathers, but this cripple thinks you're his spawn."

Roy fell to his knees, looking at his father with watery eyes. "Why are you doing this?"

Roy Senior's face twisted. "They killed my lover."

"Who?" Annie asked.

When Roy Senior looked at her, she thought she saw the devil himself in his eyes. "Your fathers."

Annie clutched her throat. "My fathers killed your lover?"

"Over a century ago, and I have not forgotten." Roy Senior's face morphed into something that didn't resemble him. "If anything, my rage has only intensified over the years. He was the best lover I've ever had."

Roy let out a strangled sob, turning his back on him. "What do we do with him?"

"You can't touch him," Annie said. "I'll put him in the van."

"The Amaroki will kill the demon and my father with him."

"Roy, we don't have a choice." She tried to project a calm she didn't feel. "Besides, we know a witch who might be able to banish the demon's soul. We can get Agent Johnson to fly her out from Romania."

Roy Senior's eyes narrowed. "She lies, Roy. They will kill your father. Let me take your body."

Roy shook his head. "I'm not falling for that again."

Roy Senior let out a wail. "You would let your father suffer in the abyss? What a selfish son you are."

Nurse Gloria let out a groan as she began to wake. Annie had forgotten about the poor nurse.

"Carry her back into the hospital," she said to Roy. "I'll put your dad in the van."

"But he's too heavy," Roy argued.

Annie braced herself, determined to see this through. "I'm not a weakling, Roy."

"No, you're not." Roy Senior looked at her, licking his thin lips. "And yet you have soft, round tits."

"Disgusting." Annie repressed a shudder. "I'm gagging him."

Roy Senior let out a yowl that could wake the dead. "Help! Help!"

Nurse Gloria rolled over, rubbing her eyes. "What's going on?" Annie's finger marks were around her neck. Uh oh. Roy would have a hard time explaining that later.

Roy scooped up Gloria, apologizing profusely as he rushed her inside. Annie gagged Roy Senior. Roy was right. He was heavy. She had to drag him into the truck and cringed when she banged his legs. Her one solace was that he couldn't feel it. Roy returned, and they lifted the wheelchair into the truck bed.

Annie thought about going back into the hospital and calling for help, but she feared Gloria would call the cops soon, and they should be gone before they arrived. They got into the cab, and Roy cast a furtive glance at the demon behind them, who was banging his head against the window.

"Drive!" she said, praying he wasn't having second thoughts. Their only option was to take Balban to the Amaroki. She hoped she was right, and they would fly Dr. Eilea Lupescu from Romania to help them.

Chapter Fifteen

MAGNUS BECAME MORE hopeful as Annie's scent grew stronger. His feet were bleeding, and his legs were so cramped each step was torture, but his mate was near, and that's all that mattered. His heart plummeted when he heard police sirens. He quickly shifted into wolf form and limped on three legs toward a big brick building that looked like a hospital.

Circling the place, he read several signs referring to it as "respite care."

Sitting on the curb was a woman in a nurse's uniform, waving her hands and yelling at the police. "They took him!"

"But if the son is his power of attorney, there's nothing we can do," a police officer said, looking at her with a patronizing smile. "Is there anything else you want to say?" The nurse bit her nails, and Magnus knew she was holding back. She'd seen something else, but she was too terrified to tell the cop.

He was wasting time at the respite center. He ran around the building to avoid being seen and back to the road, picking up Annie's scent again. She wasn't far ahead. If he pushed harder, he could catch up to her.

ANNIE SWORE WHILE TRYING to dig the amethyst out of her leg. It was dangerously close to the artery, but it needed to come out. Just because one demon had been captured, that didn't mean there wouldn't be others, and they were still a good fifteen minutes from the reservation. The highway cut through a swath of endless desert, marked only by a few tumbleweeds and the moon and stars.

Roy gripped the steering wheel like a lifeline. "Should you be doing that here?"

She hissed when blood spurted her hand. "Where else am I going to do it?"

"Wait until we get you to a doctor."

"And what if more demons come after us?" she asked. "I can fight better as a wolf." Her human form was far more vulnerable than her wolf, which had gone eerily silent since she'd been struck by the darts, making her feel panicked and alone. She'd grown so used to having the wolf always with her, it felt as if that part of her had died. The silence was deafening and soul-crushing.

She was about to dive back into her leg when Roy screamed and slammed on the brakes. Her knife fell to the floor as she flew forward, stopped by the seatbelt which dug into her chest. She saw a flash of gray fur and screamed when the truck hit it before coming to a violent halt.

Dazed, she lay back against the seat, rubbing her pounding head. "What the hell happened?"

Roy reached for her, blood dripping down his face. "Are you all right?"

"I-I don't know."

She looked at her ripped jeans and the bloody hole on her leg, then looked up at a long, gray snout sticking up from the grill guard of Roy's truck.

"Roy," she cried. "I think you hit a shifter!" *Please, Ancients, don't let it be one of my mates.*

Roy Senior laughed. "One down. Several more to go."

Annie undid the seatbelt and stumbled out of the truck, then turned at the clanking sound of the knife hitting the pavement. She pocketed the knife and walked around to the front of the truck, vaguely aware of another door slamming and Roy calling to her.

"Don't get too close, Annie."

Her hands flew to her mouth when she saw the creature hanging from the grill. What the hell was it? Because it sure wasn't a wolf.

When it let out a heart-wrenching cry, Annie lunged for it.

"Stop, Annie!" Roy yelled.

The beast snapped at her with its long snout, nearly biting off her hand. She jumped back.

"That's it!" Roy pulled his gun. "It's the chupacabra."

"The what?"

"It's already eaten five humans."

Annie held out her hands. "It's dying, Roy. You can't shoot it." The beast's back leg was bent at an awkward angle, and it was missing an eye. Blood poured from its mouth.

With a resigned sigh, Roy lowered his weapon. There was a howl in the distance. The chupacabra howled back.

"There are more." Roy raised his pistol again. "They're talking to each other. Let's go."

"No, no!" Annie protested. "That's not a chupacabra howl. I know a protector when I hear one."

The chupacabra howled again and was met with a distant answer.

Roy's hand trembled as he centered the site on the beast. "You're wrong. Get back in the truck."

The chupacabra suddenly untangled itself from the grill, letting out an ominous roar. Roy fired two shots, and the beast lurched. After releasing an ear-piercing yowl, it turned on its heel and ran into the desert, leaving a trail of blood in its wake.

Annie screamed when a protector jumped on top of Roy's truck, caving in the driver's side of the cab. She looked into a pair of familiar, menacing eyes and breathed in Vidar's scent.

"Run!" she said to Roy, her heart pounding wildly when Vidar leaped from the truck, straight toward her brother.

Roy fired several shots into Vidar, but it didn't slow him down. When Vidar lifted her screaming brother over his head, Annie barreled into his legs, but it was like running into a brick wall. He didn't budge. Just as Vidar was about to toss Roy, she jabbed the knife in his leg, right in the tender spot behind his knee.

Howling, he released Roy, who fell to the ground with a sickening *thud*. Rolling onto his side, he moaned and went eerily still.

"You sick son of a bitch!" she screamed.

Roaring, Vidar threw back his head and pounded his chest like an ape. The rust-colored fur on his torso was matted with blood. She tried to stab him again when he reached for her, but he knocked the knife out of her hand and threw her over his shoulder like a sack of potatoes.

Furious, she pounded his back, but he ran into the desert, bouncing her around until her brain felt like a jar of marbles. What the hell was he doing? She probed his thoughts and froze in fear when she learned his objective.

Now Magnus will know the pain of losing a mate.

MAGNUS COULD HARDLY believe it. The front of Roy's truck had been crushed, and the highway was painted with blood and fur. There was no sign of Annie.

He found Roy lying motionless on his side. Turning him over, he felt his fading pulse. "Roy," he called, gently shaking him.

Roy groaned, his eyes fluttering open. When he looked at Magnus, he let out an unholy, phlegmy wail.

Magnus feared Roy's lungs had been punctured, but there was nothing he could do for him.

"Roy, it's Magnus." He shifted back into a naked human, offering a weak smile. "I'm not going to hurt you. What happened? Where's Annie?"

Roy lifted a hand and pointed east. "V-Vidar," he said, wheezing.

Every muscle in Magnus's body tensed, and his vision clouded red. "Did he take her?"

Roy nodded, then cried out, his hand flying to his side, his breathing becoming more labored.

Magnus hung his head. "I'm sorry I have to leave you, Roy. Help will be along soon," he promised, praying to the Ancients his brothers and the Thunderfoots were right behind him.

Roy winced, releasing a shaky breath. "Doesn't matter. Find Annie."

Urgency fueled his movements as he jumped to his feet, determined to save Annie from his lunatic father. "Don't worry, I will." He shifted back into protector form and raced into the desert, forcing his legs to pump faster despite the screaming pain that shot through his calves. He'd not fail another woman he cared about. He'd save Annie from Vidar's clutches, and then he'd do what he should've done a long time ago—kill Vidar.

Chapter Sixteen

RAINE SLOWED DOWN WHEN he saw the carnage on the road. Putting the truck in park, he jumped out. His brothers remained behind but the Thunderfoots followed him.

"Annie!" Raine screamed, going rigid when he was answered by a distant, unholy howl.

"What was that?" he asked Tor.

"It almost sounds like a wolf."

Van scented the air. "It smells unnatural. I bet it's that chupacabra."

"Annie!" Raine called again, his heart beating double-time. Shifting into protector form, he tore through the truck's wreckage for clues, dismayed when he found a human lying immobile on his back. He quickly shifted back into his human form. "Are you okay?" The man blinked at him, eyes wide with shock.

"He's a demon," someone nearby said.

Raine raced toward the sound of the voice, disheartened to find Roy lying on his back, covered in blood and breathing laboriously.

"What happened? Where's Annie?" he asked.

Lifting a shaky finger, Roy pointed at his mangled truck. "D-don't let the demon touch humans."

Raine narrowed his eyes at the disabled man as Tor and Van pulled him and his wheelchair from the wreckage. "Just humans?"

"Y-yes. He can't steal Amaroki bodies." Roy coughed a prodigious amount of blood.

"Where's Annie?" Raine asked again.

"Vidar took her."

Raine thought only one thing. *I'll kill the bastard.*

"Magnus is chasing them."

Raine patted Roy's shoulder, worried he wouldn't survive much longer. "Thank you. No more talking. Save your strength." Knowing Magnus had gone after them brought Raine a small measure of comfort. He only hoped his brother would reach them in time and he wouldn't fuck it up.

"B-but," Roy stuttered. "Don't kill him." Again he pointed at the wrecked truck. "He's in my dad's body."

"I understand," Raine said, fearing there wasn't much hope for the disabled human.

Jumping up, he strode over to the others. He scowled down at the human, who Tor had put in his wheelchair. "My father took Annie. Magnus has gone after them. Roy needs to get to a hospital immediately."

Tor nodded. "Van and I will take him and Jax. You and Frey go after Annie."

"But him," Raine said, glowering at the pathetic demon in his human skin. "Inside is the demon who's been stealing human bodies. This one belongs to Roy's father. We need to figure out how to get the demon out, and for the love of the Ancients, keep him away from other humans."

A wicked grin split Tor's face in two. "Don't worry." He shared a dark look with his brother. "We'll handle it."

Raine was tempted to kick the old man when he whimpered, but he decided to save his aggression for Vidar. He was going to kill the bastard if Magnus didn't kill him first.

VIDAR JOSTLED ANNIE so much, she vomited down his back. She hoped he would release her, but he only grunted and jostled her more. He ran so fast, the terrain passed in a blur, but the scent was familiar. They were heading to the canyon. Annie probed his mind, throwing up again when she saw images of him throwing her off the cliff and laughing as she fell to her death. What a sick fuck. The wolf inside her howled in anger.

Wait a minute! Her wolf was back? All that bouncing around must have dislodged the amethyst. With a roar, she shifted, ripping through her jeans and digging her claws into his back. She clamped her jaws down hard on his neck, shaking with all her might, then scrambled off his shoulders when he released her with an ear-splitting yowl.

She landed hard, yelping and coughing up dirt. Ignoring the lancing pain in her shoulder, she took off at a run, howling for help. Vidar chased after her. A cyclone spun in her head after being jostled by Vidar, making her disoriented. She had no idea where she was going. She just ran, praying she could outpace Vidar.

She ran until her legs nearly buckled, and the thunderous thudding of Vidar's heavy feet grew ever more distant. Her chest heaved so badly, she thought she'd pass out. She was beyond thirsty, her tongue so swollen and heavy, she could barely pant. She had to find water before she collapsed.

Recognizing the edge of the canyon, she tumbled down the incline, landing on her ass with a thud. The pain in her shoulder returning with a vengeance, she forced herself to her paws and hobbled toward the pool. Not much farther, and she'd be at the waterfall.

MAGNUS BARELY HAD THE energy to stand, much less walk. His feet were so badly worn that he left a trail of blood as he dragged himself across the desert. But he wouldn't give up. He would keep pushing himself to save his Annie.

He jerked when he saw his father standing at the edge of the canyon, his eyes downcast.

He let out a roar, crying to the heavens, "Please, Ancients, don't let me be too late!"

His father spun around growling, the golden glow in his eyes dulled to a soft yellow. His furry chest was coated in blood, and he had a big, oozing gash on his neck. It was clear Vidar was dying.

Magnus charged his father like a bull, stopping short when Vidar refused to put up a fight. "Where is she?" he demanded.

Vidar shrugged. "Down there."

"Did you kill her?"

"No, but she is injured. Let's hope the chupacabra finishes her."

"No!" Magnus hollered, crashing hard into Vidar.

His father was amazingly fast for a drunk. He gripped Magnus in a headlock, squeezing his skull until Magnus thought it would be crushed. When

Magnus throat-punched him, the old man released him, hunching over and clutching his neck while coughing and sputtering. Then he straightened, eyes blazing like twin suns, and charged.

He sidestepped Vidar, wincing when the old man ploughed into a cactus. He jumped on Vidar, pummeling him with his fist. He had to end this fight soon and get to Annie before the chupacabra found her.

Vidar threw Magnus off. He landed on his ass precariously close to a drop that had to be at least two hundred feet. He rolled away when Father flew at him and scrambled to his knees.

Vidar spit out a mouthful of dirt, turning to Magnus with the vehemence of a thousand dust storms swirling in his eyes. "You let them kill her!"

"I was not responsible for my mother's death, and you know it." A renewed sense of determination pushed him forward. He couldn't lose this battle. Annie needed him.

When Vidar raised claws curved like talons, he didn't waste any time. He ran over Vidar like a steamroller, watching with a feeling of detachment as his father screamed and tumbled over the edge, flailing through the air like a ragdoll and hitting the earth with a soft *thud*.

His heart sank. What an anticlimactic ending to a man who'd made his life a living hell. There were so many things he'd wanted to tell his father, but it wouldn't have done any good. Vidar's lack of compassion would've only caused Magnus more heartache.

He'd grieve later for what could have been, but now he had to find Annie.

LACKING THE ENERGY to go any farther, Annie tumbled into the pond, greedily lapping up water, then gently paddling to shore. Collapsing on the pebbled beach, she continued to drink, listening to the sounds around her. If Vidar tried to sneak up on her, she'd hear it. At least she hoped she would, but what if she didn't? She was too weak to fight, and he could easily rip her in two. She could find a place to hide, but he'd just follow her scent.

Fathers, she cried. *What do I do?*

A shard of moonlight struck her cheek, then cast a glow across the pond to the waterfall.

Go there.

Thank you, Fathers.

Annie climbed back into the pond and swam to the waterfall. Once she reached it, another shard of moonlight pointed the way to a tunnel behind the curtain. Holding her breath, she fought the current in an effort to get behind the curtain of water and yelped when she was dragged under. Too tired to fight, she gave up.

Just when she thought she might drown, she bobbed to the surface on the back side of the waterfall, spitting water and gulping air. A shallow set of stairs led to a cave. Careful not to slip on the moss, she managed to drag herself up the stairs and into the cave one slow step at a time. The thunderous sound of falling water drowned out her grunts as she collapsed to the ground. She had finally found sanctuary.

Resting her head on her paws, she shut her eyes, going boneless against the cool stones.

A loud clacking sound resonated from deep within the cave. Her eyes flew open.

One glowing, gold eye gazed at her from atop a mountain of human skulls.

Chapter Seventeen

WHEN THE CHUPACABRA jumped off his mountain of bones, Annie let out a low whimper and strained to stand. So much for him only killing five humans. There must have been hundreds of skulls there. She retreated when it advanced, her paws slipping on the slick, mossy cave floor.

The creature was odd looking, like a mutant wolf with a wide ribcage, a missing eye, and a scraggly tail. Too tired and terrified to fight, her legs wobbled when the chupacabra approached and sniffed her neck. Surprisingly, it backed away with a whimper. Grabbing a skull from the pile with its long, pointy maw, it dropped it at her feet.

Well, shit. He was trying to share his dinner? Did this mean it had accepted her as part of its pack? She certainly hoped not. No way was she eating people. When it limped back to the pile of bones, she noticed the blood it left behind and wondered if the accident and gunshots had proven fatal.

When she heard a roar beyond the waterfall, the chupacabra turned, snarling. A one-handed protector burst through the wall of water. Pounding his chest, he growled at the injured animal. Annie's tail thumped in relief. Limping over to Magnus, she nuzzled his leg.

The chupacabra looked at Magnus, whined, fell over, and shifted into the form of a man. Annie's heart caught in her throat when she recognized Magnus's gamma father, Sami.

MAGNUS SHIFTED INTO his mortal form and took Annie in his arms. She shifted, too, revealing a dislocated shoulder. Seeing her covered in cuts and bruises made Magnus hate himself even more. How could he have let this happen?

He kissed her forehead. "I'm so sorry, Annie."

She wrapped her arms around him, nuzzling his neck. "Don't be. None of this is your fault."

Emotion weighed on his chest like he was being crushed by a bull. "But I left you alone."

She trembled in his arms. "I should've told you about the demon."

Magnus froze, sick to his stomach as horrible thoughts of Annie being tortured or raped ran through his mind. He traced that large gash on her forehead. "Did the demon hurt you?"

"She tried to." She pulled back. "She was going to possess me and destroy our race."

He cupped her cheek, relieved when he saw no internal pain reflecting in her eyes. "I'm not letting you out of my sight again."

"Magnus, it's not your responsibility to watch me every second of every day. I survived the demon and Vidar." She pushed his hand away and entwined her fingers with his. "I'm not helpless."

"No, you're not." He kissed the tip of her nose. "You're a perfect mate."

They heard a groan. Annie scooted off Magnus's lap and nudged him toward Sami. Magnus didn't know how to process what he was seeing. Sami was the chupacabra their tribe had been talking about? There had been sightings for years but only recently had it come to light that the chupacabra was killing humans. He was shocked at the sight of all those human skulls. He'd likely been killing humans for quite a while.

He crawled over to his dying father.

"Magnus." Sami lifted a shaking hand.

Magnus took Sami in his arms, trying to make sense of how and why Sami had become the chupacabra. "Why?" he asked.

Sami cupped Magnus's cheek. "Her death was not your fault. I'm sorry we weren't good fathers to you." His eyelid drooped. His other eye socket was an empty hole, filled in by angry scar tissue.

Magnus fought to speak around the lump in his throat. "But why?"

Sami exhaled slowly, sounding like a deflating balloon. "Vidar had discovered black magic."

As if that explained anything. It only left him with more questions. "How?"

"That's not important now." Sami sighed. "We tried to bring your mother back to life. Tyr warned us not to experiment with dark magic, but we were desperate." He winced and held his side. Blood seeped through his fingers. "We failed, and as a result, the black magic tainted us, me worse than Vidar. It made him an angry drunk, but look at what it did to me."

"How did I not know this?"

"Vidar helped me conceal it. I've been turning into this thing almost every night."

Magnus thought about how Vidar had always treated Sami like a second-class brother, forcing him to sleep in the shed behind the barn. No wonder. Becoming the chupacabra had given him a means of escape.

"When I'm the chupacabra," Sami continued, "I can't control myself. I go on a rampage, killing innocents."

All moisture evaporated from Magnus's mouth. "And Vidar knew this?"

Sami hung his head. "Yes. I've lived a miserable existence, waking up each morning to discover I've killed another human. Vidar celebrated their deaths. He said it was a gift from the gods."

As much as Magnus wanted to hate Vidar for his part in it, he couldn't. He vaguely remembered his father had once been kind, but his mate's death had changed him. Now he knew why. Dark magic had blackened his soul.

"I'm dying." Sami emitted a weak smile. "No more innocents will be slaughtered, and I can finally go to your mother. I should've ended my life years ago, but every time I worked up the nerve to pull the trigger, Vidar stopped me."

"Please tell Mother and Father I miss and love them," Magnus said, rocking Sami in his arms.

When Sami's eye fell shut, Magnus hunched over his lifeless body, releasing a pitiful howl.

"Magnus," Annie whispered, placing a hand on his shoulder.

Releasing Sami, he turned to her, burying his head against her uninjured shoulder, unable to stop the flow of tears. For once he didn't feel like less of a man for showing his emotions. She rocked and soothed him, encouraging him to cry. It felt good to rely on her strength.

MAGNUS SHIFTED INTO protector form and carried Annie back under the waterfall. Now that she was safe, his main priority was getting her to a hospital. He wasn't surprised to find Raine and Frey circling the pond as wolves, frantically sniffing the ground.

As soon as he saw them, Raine shifted into human form, jumped into the pond, and swam toward them. "Annie, thank the Ancients you're okay." He spoke with a nasally pitch, his broken nose looking even more swollen than before.

Without even acknowledging Magnus, he took her from him and turned toward shore.

"I am." Draping an arm around Raine, she looked over his shoulder, smiling at him. "Thanks to Magnus." She cupped his face, frowning. "What happened to your nose?"

"Never mind me." Raine shrugged. "Look at your shoulder." Raine waded through the water with a stiff back, then gently deposited her on shore. Frey, also in human form, sat behind her, reaching for her injured shoulder.

She jerked back with a hiss. "Don't touch it."

Frey's lips turned down. "Sorry."

Magnus hesitated, waist-deep in the pond, not wanting to intrude on Raine's time with her. Then he thought better of it. To hell with Raine. He was tired of feeling worthless and undeserving. Annie didn't blame him, and that's all that mattered. He walked over to them and sat beside her, not caring if Raine had a problem with it.

"Who did this?" Raine demanded, gesturing at Annie's shoulder.

"Vidar," she answered. "Who do you think?"

Magnus growled, thinking how close Vidar had come to killing his mate.

Raine eyed him for a long moment. "We found him at the bottom of the canyon."

Magnus swallowed. Knowing that Vidar had been cursed, he felt guilty for pushing him, but he'd do it again to keep him from harming Annie. "Did he survive the fall?"

"No." Raine's face was a mask of stone. "Did you push him?"

Magnus locked eyes with his brother's. "I had no choice."

"Thank you." Raine clasped Magnus's shoulder in a surprising gesture, his features softening.

Raine's praise took him off guard, and it took all his willpower not to tear up.

Frey clasped his other shoulder. "I know that wasn't easy. You did what was right."

Magnus nodded, then looked away, unable to speak as emotion clogged his throat.

Raine motioned toward the pond. "Where were you?"

Magnus pointed at the waterfall. "There's a cave behind it." He was concerned about Jax's safety. Last he'd seen him, he'd had burns all over his back. "Is Jax okay?"

"Tor took him to the hospital, along with Roy," Raine answered.

Annie shot up. "How hurt is he?"

Raine grimaced. "Bad. I think Vidar broke his ribs."

She let out a strangled cry. "And the demon?"

Raine flashed a fanged grin. "Tor said he'd take care of it."

She nodded.

Magnus leaned into her, wiping her tears with his knuckles, wishing he had two hands but still grateful for the one. He gazed at his brothers stonily. "Sami is dead."

"Wh-what?" Frey cried, his eyes filling with tears.

"He was the chupacabra."

Frey jumped to his feet. "How can that be?"

"Vidar and Sami used dark magic to try to bring our mother back. It tainted their souls." Sami hadn't been much of a parent to any of them, but he was still Frey's birth father.

"He wanted to die," he told Frey, leaving out the part about how he was killed and the mountain of human skulls. "He wanted to be free of the monster and go to our mother."

Raine's jaw dropped. "Where did they get this magic?"

"Sami didn't tell me." He'd sure like to know, so he could make sure it never happened to another wolf. He hoped Tyr, their last living father, could tell them.

"He and Vidar have not been good fathers for a long time." Raine tightened his hold on Annie. "Now we know why."

When Frey fell to his knees, sobbing, she untangled herself from Raine and climbed into Frey's lap. "Please don't cry."

"I never even learned how to be a gamma," he sobbed, burying his face in his hands, "or how to take care of you and our children."

"It's okay." She peeled his fingers back and kissed his tear-stained cheeks. "We'll figure it out together."

Magnus was struck with a pang of jealousy when she showered Frey with kisses. It was then he became fully aware that Annie wasn't clothed. None of them were. Despite the night's heartbreak, he couldn't deny his primal desire and how much he wanted to lay Annie on the grass and make love to her.

"We should get going." He coughed, trying to quell his growing desire. "Jax needs us."

"You and Annie are injured," Raine said. "I don't think you can make it back."

"I'll make it back." Magnus stood, ignoring the cramps in his calves and summoning energy from deep within his reserves. He was the head alpha, after all. He was determined to lead his family home.

"Are you sure, brother?" Raine said, brow furrowing. "I could carry you."

His chest warmed at the thought. Though Raine wasn't always good with words, his offer meant Raine had forgiven him. "Thank you, but no." Magnus clapped his brother's back, feeling a renewed sense of purpose. "You've carried me long enough."

Chapter Eighteen

AFTER THANKING IOANA Coyotechaser for bringing everyone clothes and blankets, Annie was relieved to see Amara Thunderfoot waiting on the long front porch at the Coyotechaser house.

"Amara!" She left her mates behind and raced up to her cousin, giving her a one-armed hug, as her dislocated shoulder hurt to touch. "How did you know we'd need you?"

Amara pushed back a strand of blonde hair. "Hrod told me." She motioned to her preschool-aged son, who was playing with his toddler brother on the porch under a light. "It's not bedtime yet in Alaska." She rolled her eyes. "This was their first plane ride, and they're wired on juice boxes."

The wooden floorboards creaked when Annie knelt beside Hrod and ruffled his mop of black hair. "Aren't you going to say hello?"

He held up a toy rattlesnake. "Papa is going to catch a real one for me." His brows creased. "You okay, Annie?"

She couldn't help but smile. "I am now."

Amara held a hand down to Annie. "Let's fix that shoulder."

"But I need to see Roy."

"He's already healed," Amara said with a wink. "So is your beta."

"You healed Jax?" She clasped a hand over her heart, relief washing through her. "Thank you! You've been busy."

"Your tribe needs its own healer." Amara chuckled. "I can't fly out here every time you're attacked by demons."

She winced, but was glad someone thought it was funny.

"Annie," Magnus said behind her.

She turned and wound a possessive arm around his waist. "Amara, these are Magnus, Raine, and Frey."

"Nice to meet you all. This is Rone." She nodded at her gamma. He was a big guy with squeezable cheeks, who reminded Annie of Frey. He waved from his spot on the floor, where he pretended to be bitten by Hrod's pet snake. "And Drasko." Amara pointed at the stoic sentinel watching from the shadows. He'd been so quiet, Annie hadn't even noticed him.

Drasko gave the slightest of nods before turning back to the pasture. No doubt he was keeping an eye out for more demons. She hoped they'd all been banished to hell.

"My other mates are inside, talking with the Coyotechasers and their fathers," Amara continued.

Annie felt apprehensive. "And Roy's dad?"

As if on cue, she heard a set of violent thumps coming from inside a nearby shed.

Amara cocked a brow. "My deadbeat uncle? Locked up over there. They don't want me healing him until Eilea arrives and casts out the demon."

She wanted to tell Amara that she didn't have to heal him, even after the demon was cast out. Not after all he'd done to Amara. She chose not to say anything, though, because Roy cared for his father, and hurting Roy Senior meant hurting Roy Junior. No grudge was worth putting her brother through more hell. He'd suffered enough.

"So the doctor's coming?" Annie asked, shifting the subject to Dr. Eilea Lupescu, once an esteemed surgeon and now a witch doctor living in Romania with her four mates.

"Oh, yes." A shaky burst of laughter erupted from Amara. "Tor insisted. She's the only one who can cast out the demon."

Annie wrapped her borrowed blanket tightly around her shoulders, sharing worried looks with her mates. "I hope it works."

"Of course it will. Eilea has been practicing her spells. She knows even more now."

She heaved a sigh of relief, thinking how happy Roy would be to have his father back. Roy Senior had better damn well appreciate the sacrifices the wolves were making for him. He'd also better not tell a soul about the Amaroki, or she'd never forgive him.

Amara scowled at Raine, and without waiting for an invite, leaned into him, grasping his nose. He cried out and then stilled, letting out a satisfied groan when she pulled back. His nose had shrunk back to normal size. The only reminder of the breakage had been the dried blood coating his nostrils.

"Wow!" His hand flew to his nose. "Thanks!"

"Don't mention it." Amara shrugged, acting as if healing his swollen nose had been no bid deal.

She reached for Magnus's stump. "Magnus, right?"

His horrified look when she examined the angry, puckered skin would've been comical if Annie hadn't listened to his mortified thoughts.

Why would she touch it? What does Annie think about it?

"Yes," he said and pulled away.

Amara impatiently waggled her fingers. "I wasn't done with you. Let me see it."

Hiding the amputation behind his back, he gave her a look that suggested he'd just sucked on a lemon. "Why?"

"She's a healer, Magnus," Annie said.

He scowled at Amara. "You need to heal Annie first."

Amara snorted, waving him off. "I'll get to her." She impatiently tapped her foot. "Now let me see it!"

"Do what she says, brother," Raine chided.

There was horror in his eyes. "She can't grow back a hand."

"Magnus," Annie huffed. "She's healed werewolves and stage four cancer."

Cursing and grumbling, he held his truncated arm out to her, looking away as if repulsed by it.

"Wait!" Annie cried. Rubbing the angry scars against her cheek, she blinked back tears. "I just want you to know I don't care what you look like. I love you for you."

"Us, too, brother," Raine said.

Frey agreed with him.

Magnus's jaw dropped.

"Aw, how sweet," Amara cooed, then latched onto him again.

Magnus shifted from foot to foot, turning ten shades of red while she rubbed her hands over his skin.

Annie watched in amazement as little branches grew off the stump, then formed into a palm and five fingers.

Amara released his hand with a gasp. Drasko was by her side in an instant, leading her to a chair.

Annie couldn't help the tears that spilled over as she smiled at her alpha. "Well?"

He gaped at his new hand, flexing his fingers. "Bless the Ancients," he said and pulled Annie close, kissing the top of her head.

His brothers joined in the hug, and they alternated between kissing and crying. Annie winced a few times when they banged her shoulder, but she didn't complain. It was worth it to see Magnus so happy.

ANNIE SAT ON A STIFF chair in the Coyotechaser's den, rubbing her shoulder, though it no longer pained her after Amara had healed it. The room, which appeared to have been a converted garage, didn't have good ventilation and the weak portable air conditioner barely kept her cool. Still, she refused to complain. She supposed she was going to have to get used to the Texas heat. She held Roy's hand, peering over Magnus's shoulder. Dr. Eilea Lupescu hovered over Roy Senior in his special wheelchair and conducted the spell that would send Balban back to hell. Dr. Lupescu needed the demon's name to conduct the ceremony, and Annie had been happy to provide it.

After pouring salt around the room, lighting sage, and whispering the incantations, commanding Balban to abandon her mortal body and return to hell, Dr. Lupescu said she was finally ready for the extraction.

Balban screeched, thrashing her head so hard, Magnus had to restrain her.

The demon gaped up at Magnus, breaking into a wicked grin. "I remember you. I recognize your scent."

Magnus's brows furrowed. "I've never met you, demon."

Wicked laughter bubbled up from Roy Senior's throat. "I blew the bitch's brains out. Her mate, too. I shot your hand." The demon inside Roy Senior squealed like a stuck pig.

Annie's heart slammed against her ribcage when Magnus let out a roar, shifting into a giant protector while raising his fists.

"Wait, Magnus!" Annie lunged forward. "You hurt the demon, you kill an innocent human, too." She held out staying hands, nodding toward the doctor. "Let Dr. Lupescu banish the demon."

With her alphas, each of whom resembled a blond Viking warrior, by her side, and both placing a possessive hand on her very pregnant belly, Dr. Lupescu wiped a bead of sweat off her brow before pointing a wand at Roy Senior and pulling what looked like a long string of snot out of his nose. As the strand grew in length, it also expanded in size until her wand held the tail end of a translucent dragon with a wingspan of twelve feet and a jagged, spiny ridge going down its back. The dragon howled and blew smoke. Dr. Lupescu seemed unfazed.

She held her wand out to Magnus. "Would you like to do the honors?"

"With pleasure." Magnus took the wand from her, waving the dragon around like a sparkler.

Annie nearly crapped her pants when a giant hole resembling a fleshy throat opened in the center of the room. Magnus pointed the wand toward the hole, and it sucked the squealing dragon in and then shut with a snap, leaving behind the stink of Sulphur.

Dr. Lupescu slapped her hands together as if she was dusting flour. "All finished," she said with a grin, her ebony skin glowing under the sage lanterns strategically placed around the room. Dr. Lupescu took the wand back from Magnus and she and her mates shuffled out of the room.

Magnus remained by Annie's side, refusing to leave her without a protector. When his brothers filed in, Magnus told them he'd just banished the demon who'd killed their parents. Annie was surprised at how calm he spoke, though his rigid spine belied his pent-up emotions.

Magnus sat on the edge of a chair, back still stiff, waiting with Annie, Roy, and his brothers for Roy Senior to wake. Annie threaded her hands through his, giving him a squeeze. He said nothing as he squeezed back. She didn't expect him to speak. She knew he was still processing what had just happened.

The only sounds in the room was the breathing machine hooked up to Roy Senior. Where it had come from, Annie had no idea, but she supposed he couldn't breathe without it. That would soon change after Amara healed him. She looked over at Roy, who was as stoic as her mates.

Threading her hand through his, she forced a smile. How she wished she could be anywhere but here, but Roy needed her, and he'd sacrificed so much already to help rescue her, even coming close to dying.

He gave her a funny look. "How did you know the demon's name?"

She froze at that, her mind reeling. In the end, she decided it was time to fess up. No more secrets. "Uh...I can read minds."

His jaw dropped. "You can?"

Heat flamed her face. "Yeah." She turned into Roy, releasing Magnus's hand, unable to look at her mates. Cesar had already told the entire tribe she could read minds, but she still wasn't sure how they felt about it, and she couldn't bear accusatory looks from them. The look Roy gave her was bad enough.

Both of Roy's brows shot up. "When were you going to tell me?"

"I'm sorry." She slouched in her seat. "I was waiting for the right time."

His eyes narrowed. "You're not using it on me, are you?"

"I try not to." A discomforting feeling came over her, and she wished so badly she had the power to turn invisible instead. "Sometimes your thoughts just pop into my head."

"Like when?"

Annie cringed. "Like the other night at the bar when you were worried about paying for drinks."

His face flushed bright crimson. "Dad's care has been expensive."

"I know it has."

"Any more secrets?"

"None."

He heaved a sigh. "Good."

"So..." She paused, a tightness in her chest making it hard for her to speak. "Are we cool?"

"You're my sister." He gave her hand a good squeeze, his eyes misting over. "And I love you no matter what."

Annie swallowed back a lump of emotion, too choked up to answer. Instead, she rested her head on his shoulder, focusing on the bleeping lights by Roy Senior's chair.

When Magnus rested a hand on her knee, she slipped her fingers through his, pleased when he squeezed her tight.

"Don't worry," he whispered in her ear. "We'll be reading your mind soon enough."

She shivered at that. Yeah, after they took her virginity. Though she was looking forward to their night of bonding, she did her best to push thoughts of fucking her four virile mates out of her mind. Last thing she needed was to cream her panties while keeping vigil over her disabled step-dad.

After nearly an hour, Roy Senior began mumbling in his sleep, his head moving from side to side. "It's dark! So dark!"

Annie stifled a cry, her heart twisting in a knot. She hadn't expected to get emotional over this, but listening to his pitiful voice brought back too many painful memories. When Magnus put an arm around her shoulders, kissing the top of her head, she felt his strength surge through her. How fortunate she was to have him.

"Dad!" Roy fell beside his father's chair, clutching his hands. "You're okay now. I'm so sorry."

Roy Senior's eyes shot open, and he looked at his son a long while. "What happened?"

"I don't know how else to put this," Roy said. "You were possessed by a demon."

Roy Senior looked at his son in amazement, then gestured at Annie's younger mates in the corner. He hadn't noticed Annie yet. "Who are these people?"

"They are my friends," Roy said. "They helped cast the demon out of you, but Dr. Lupescu did most of the work."

Raine cleared his throat. "Should I get Amara?"

Roy Senior's eyes widened. "Amara?"

"Not yet." Roy patted his father's hand. "We need some time."

"Amara, your cousin?" his father said.

"Yes." The color drained from Roy's face, and Annie knew he was dreading telling his dad about their magical world, especially since he couldn't tell him too much.

Roy Senior looked at his son in alarm. "What's she doing here?"

Roy heaved a shaky breath. "Dad, there's something you don't know about my job. If I tell you, I need your promise that you won't tell another soul."

His dad blinked. "I promise."

"I'm a government liaison for a magical race." Roy spoke so fast, his words sounded as if they were tripping over each other.

His father blanched. "Shifters."

Roy jerked. "How did you know?"

"My sister accused Amara of being a wolf," his father said. "I never believed her, but I didn't believe in demonic possessions either."

"Yes, she's a wolf," Roy said. "She's also a healer. She and the other shifters are my friends. Annie is a shifter, too."

"Annie?" His lower lip trembled. "Is she here? Can I see her?"

Annie struggled to speak around the knot in her chest. "I'm here."

He tried to turn his head toward her. "My Annie? Is that you?"

She inwardly cringed. She didn't like being called 'his Annie.' If she belonged to anyone, it was her mates. When Roy gave her a pleading look and held out his hand, she had no choice but to go to him. She missed Magnus's touch and scent the moment she left his side.

She sat beside Roy. "Yes."

"Oh, Annie!" Roy Senior's eyes teared, and his voice sounded thick with emotion. "I'm so, so happy to see you."

She thought it strange that he didn't seem frightened of her, how he brushed aside the knowledge of her shifter status and took pleasure in seeing her. She couldn't respond to him, though. Unlike him, she wasn't happy to be here and couldn't wait for their meeting to be over.

"Does our family have a gene?" he asked her.

Annie shared a look with Roy, then shrugged. "Something like that."

"Anyway," Roy continued, "I can't give you too much information. I've said enough already. Just know that they are good people, and they mean you no harm. Some of them can do more than shift. Amara can heal injuries and sickness with her touch."

Roy Senior searched his son's face. "Can... can Amara heal me?"

Roy nodded.

When Roy Senior let out a low wail, Annie sat back, hugging herself. How many nights had she tried to fall asleep, listening to that pitiful cry? "I don't deserve to walk. I didn't treat her well. I didn't treat any of you kids well."

"Dad," Roy said, "that's all in the past."

Annie wasn't too pleased that Roy let his father off the hook.

A single tear slipped down Roy Senior's cheek. "No, it's not. I know it's why Annie never visits." He looked at her with an unnerving stare. "And I don't blame you."

"Gee, thanks," Annie huffed, unable to keep the sarcasm out of her voice. How generous of him to absolve her of blame.

"I should've done more when they took you." He hung his head. "I thought you kids would be better off without me."

"You took Amara's inheritance and sent her packing," Annie said through clenched teeth, barely restraining her anger.

Roy Senior blinked and more tears cascaded down his face. "Your mom—"

Annie jumped to her feet. "I don't give a damn whose idea it was," she spat, unable to keep the hurt and anger from her voice. He had a lot of nerve placing all the blame on her mother. He could've said no.

"You're right." He stared at his lap. "She was my niece. I should've never let her go."

"You owe her money."

"I fully intend to pay her back, with interest if I'm able to walk again, and if there's anything I can do for you—"

She cut him off. "Don't squander this second chance. Be a decent person."

"I will. I promise. I'm going to work to pay off Amara and you, Roy," he said, "for all the money you spent for my care."

Roy flushed. "Dad, I don't expect you to—"

"No," his father said, "I'm paying you back."

Annie probed the old man's thoughts, pleased when she didn't sense any deception.

"Okay," Roy relented.

Annie took that as her cue to finally make her escape. "I'll go get Amara." When she abruptly stood, her mates stood, too.

"Annie, wait," Roy Senior said as she reached the door.

With a stiff spine, she stopped and slowly turned to him, tightening her face muscles lest he sense any weakness.

"I'm sorry," he said.

She didn't know how to answer him. "Okay." She made her escape, relieved to finally get away from him.

Her mates followed her into the kitchen, where they were distracted by a platter of tamales.

She tugged Magnus's arm. "Hey, you okay?"

"My mate is safe, my hand is healed, and my parent's death is avenged." Magnus beamed. "Never been better."

She studied him a long moment. Shadows that had once plagued his eyes seemed to have been lifted.

Annie swore her heart did a backflip. "You don't know how happy it makes me to see you smile."

If it was at all possible, his smile widened. "Get used to it."

She hugged him tight, feeling his strength surge through her.

After giving Magnus a kiss, reassuring him she'd be safe in the next room, she found Amara on the living room floor with her gamma mate, Rone, their infant son, and their other two boys. Amara stood, rubbing her gut. "Ugh. I feel dizzy, but it's too soon for morning sickness."

She patted Amara's stomach. "Are you pregnant?"

"Yep." Amara elbowed her, giggling. "I swear we're rabbits, not wolves." She winked at Rone, who was pretending to drink their toddler's bottle. "I bloomed right after you left. We fucked for three days. It was a new record for me."

Heat crept into her cheeks. She'd often suspected them of being rabbit shifters, too, having lived with them for over a year and listening to them fuck almost every night. Even though she slept in the den two floors below them, her wolf-touched ears still heard the bedsprings squeaking and plenty of loud moaning late into the night. Annie suspected she and her mates would fuck as often. At least she sure hoped so.

"How is he?" Amara asked.

Annie blinked, her mind going blank.

Amara arched a brow. "My uncle?"

"He's ready for you," she answered with as much disinterest as she could manage.

Amara smiled, patting Annie's hand. "Okay."

"Amara, you don't have to do this." Though she felt bad for Roy, this was probably extremely hard for Amara after what Roy Senior had put her through.

"It's okay," Amara said. "I want to."

"You sure?"

Her smile wasn't just genuine and pure but serene, as if she'd found a way to block her ugly childhood memories. "It's not good for your soul to hold onto old grudges. Let it go, Annie. Focus on building a life with your mates. Don't let this emotional burden fester and get in the way of your relationships."

Annie was humbled by her cousin's gentle heart and ability to forgive so easily. "I'll try."

"Good." Amara pulled Annie into a warm hug. "But I can't fix broken hearts."

She wasn't aware she was crying until Amara blurred behind a curtain of tears. "Thank you." She wiped her eyes, forcing a smile.

Amara walked into the den where they were keeping Roy Senior, her second alpha Drasko following closely behind. Her cousin was amazingly humble and brave. Annie could learn a lot from her.

Amara was right. Annie had been a hypocrite to chastise Magnus for his self-pity. Her hatred for Roy Senior had fueled her own brand of self-pity. The time had come to let go of old resentments and focus on her future. When Magnus came up behind her and wrapped her in a hug, she turned into his embrace and smiled at him, knowing her future would be joyous.

AMARA SHOT DRASKO ONE more look and then expelled a shaky breath, comforted when he laid a hand on her shoulder.

"You don't have to do this," he whispered.

"I'm doing it more for me," she answered. "It will bring me closure."

"Then let's get this over with," he grumbled, following her into Roy Senior's temporary room.

Roy Junior sat beside his father's wheelchair, giving Amara a stoic nod.

The moment her uncle saw her, he started bawling. Amara had heard his health had declined, but she'd had no idea he was in such bad shape. He looked as if he'd aged significantly since she'd last seen him. He was in his mid-fifties but looked at least seventy-five. His face and neck sagged like a sock full of rocks. His legs and arms were bony, covered with paper-thin skin that appeared translucent. He looked greatly diminished in his wheelchair.

"Amara, my beautiful niece," he sniffled, a line of snot dripping from his nose. "I'm so sorry."

She sat beside him, a tear cascading down her cheek.

"Thank you for coming to see me," he continued. "You didn't have to after the way I wronged you."

"I know."

Drasko sat on a nearby stool, thumbing through the morning paper.

Her uncle's gaze flitted nervously to Drasko and then back to Amara. "If I could live my life over again, I'd have taken you from your mother and raised you as my daughter. I turned my back on you, and I'm so sorry."

"What's done is done." She absently picked at her fingernails. "No use worrying over the past."

"I guess not. Besides"—his voice dropped to a low whisper—"Karma got me for what I did to you."

"Yes," she answered tersely. Their ancient god Amarok had frightened him while he was driving home from work, causing him to flip his truck and crush his spine. Though Roy Senior had lost the use of his arms and legs, he was lucky to be alive.

"That beast who caused me to run off the road." He paused, and he looked nervously at Drasko. "He was your god."

"He is, but I didn't ask him to scare you."

He nodded, again, his gaze flitting to Drasko. "I know you didn't, and I don't blame him."

Drasko chuckled, eyeing Roy Senior over the rim of his paper before flipping to the sports section.

"Roy tells me you know all about us?" Amara stared him directly in the eye, searching for any sign of deceit. She wouldn't heal him if she couldn't trust him.

"I do."

"Thank you for agreeing to keep it a secret." She studied his facial features again and saw nothing amiss. Although if he intended on doing her people harm, Annie would've already heard his thoughts.

He drew a cross across his heart. "I'll go to my grave with it."

Amara released a pent-up breath. "What would you do if you could get up and walk out of here?"

"What would I do?" He smiled. "I would get a job and pay Roy back for my hospital bills. Pay you back for stealing your inheritance."

She inwardly flinched. That's not what she'd meant. She wasn't looking for payback. She was trying to make sure he'd live a life of gratitude. She supposed him working hard to pay them back was a sign of gratitude, though, and he appeared humbled.

She held out her hands. "May I?"

"Please." His voice cracked and he looked away, but not before she saw the naked hope in his eyes.

She placed her hands on his legs and closed her eyes, her fingertips tingling like they were being tickled by tiny butterflies as her healing magic soaked into his skin. She visualized her magic spreading from his legs to his spine and up to his neck, then down his arms and down to the tips of his toes. She had no idea how long she worked on her uncle, but by the time she felt the last of the magic drain from her fingers, she was physically and mentally exhausted. Drasko was instantly beside her, letting her lean on him for support.

She sighed as his heat warmed her. "Try to stand," she said to her uncle.

With Roy's help, he got to his feet, his eyes as wide as saucers. "Omigod, I feel my legs! I feel my legs!" Tears sprang from his eyes, and a strangled sob escaped him. "Thank you, Amara."

She tensed when she heard her youngest son crying for her.

Her uncle fell back in his chair and raised his hands, looking at them as if he was seeing them for the first time. "Amara, I meant what I said. I'm paying you back."

"Just be a decent person," she mumbled.

"Take the money, Amara," Drasko grumbled. "It was your inheritance. It rightfully belonged to you."

Roy Senior swallowed, gawping at Drasko. Her mate was intimidating, with his broad chest and long, black hair. The eyes that shifted from brown to gold were the most threatening though, and she imagined Roy Senior was on the verge of shitting his pants.

Good. He needed to be afraid, in case he ever thought about betraying the Amaroki.

"Goodbye, Uncle." She'd forgiven him, mainly for her peace of mind, but that didn't mean she wanted to spend any more time with him than she had to. Her children were her priority now.

"You're leaving?" he asked petulantly.

"I need to nurse my child." She took Drasko's hand, and they left the room. She felt as if an incredible weight had lifted from her heart. Just like Annie, she'd carried around her emotional baggage far too long, and it felt liberating to finally get rid of it.

ANNIE WASN'T FRIGHTENED when she saw tall shadows outside her window. Sliding the curtains, she opened the window. "Hello, Fathers."

Only Amarok and Fenrir were there to see her. Amarok was in protector form, an imposing black beast with glowing silver eyes. Her birth father, Fenrir, was a large black wolf with the same silver eyes.

"Will you come outside with us?" Amarok asked.

"Sure." She threw off her clothes, shifted, and jumped out the window.

We can't run the canyon with you. Amarok frowned at the crescent moon. *We can't materialize and protect you.*

I understand.

We're so happy you're safe. Fenrir nuzzled her neck, his buzzing spirit tickling her skin. *We're proud of your bravery and strength and how clever you were to catch that demon.*

Thank you, she said. How she loved affection from her fathers. *Jax told me a shadow gave him cover when he lit the barn on fire.* She gave her fathers an expectant look.

We did. A frown marred Amarok's furry brow. *We only wish we could've prevented his injuries.*

And yours, Fenrir added.

That would've been nice, but Annie wasn't bitter. She knew there was only so much they could do. *Why did you send me into the cave with the chupacabra?*

We knew he wouldn't hurt you, Amarok answered. *We wanted you to know what became of him, otherwise your mates would never have closure.*

The evil magic that Vidar and Sami used, she asked, *do you know anything about it?*

Amarok and Fenrir exchanged dark looks.

We know it is buried and best left untouched, Amarok answered in a tone so deep and forceful, she decided to drop the subject.

We've come to say goodbye, Amarok projected.

She felt a pang. *You're leaving?*

Fenrir smiled. *For now.*

We have more demons to hunt, Amarok explained. *If Balban can discover Amaroki secrets, it won't be long before more demons learn of our weakness. We must find them before they find us.*

She worried for her fathers, though she didn't voice it aloud. She had no idea what these demons were capable of.

I understand. She bowed her head, looking at them from under thick lashes. *Thank you, Fathers.*

Amarok arched a bushy brow. *For what?*

Her tail instinctively wagged, slapping Fenrir's shadow. She couldn't help it. She got so excited whenever she thought of them. *For my mates.*

Her fathers both howled, and she joined them, overcome with joy, love, and best of all, peace.

Chapter Nineteen

MOPPING SWEAT OFF HIS brow, Roy stepped out of the truck. After two days in Oregon, he had to get used to the miserable Texas heat all over again. His dad was now living with an old high school friend after his "breakthrough" surgery in Australia. Roy Senior had already lined up three job interviews and promised to pay back his family every penny he owed. Roy didn't expect it, but he secretly admitted it would be nice to afford a new truck, one with better air-conditioning.

For the past two weeks, he'd been cleaning up after the demons. First he'd helped organize the trackers. His elite team of wolves discovered several sex trafficking rings, which were subsequently raided by the feds. Then he had to fix the mess at his father's care home. Luckily Agent Johnson offered assistance. Johnson made cleaning up Amaroki messes look easy, but it wasn't.

Roy trudged up to his dad's former nursing home like he was going to his own funeral. He didn't want to face Gloria after what he'd put her through. He decided to take the side entrance, praying his gate code still worked. It did, and she was waiting for him in the courtyard, arms crossed and impatiently tapping her foot.

Shoving his hands in his pockets, he hoped the guilt he felt wasn't written all over his face. "I'm here to collect the rest of my father's things."

Her full, pretty lips scowled. "Are we going to talk about what happened to me?"

He feigned ignorance. "What about it?"

Her eyes narrowed to slits. "I was possessed, and you don't seem to be shocked."

He scratched the back of his head, wishing he could teleport elsewhere. "Huh?"

"Don't play dumb with me, Roy." She wagged a finger in his face. "What exactly do you do in the FBI?"

"I'm sorry, I can't discuss it."

She refused to back down, jabbing him harshly. "Where is the ghost or demon that possessed me? Still in your father?"

He was shocked she remembered so much. He thought she'd been knocked out. He considered lying to her, telling her she'd had a psychotic episode. That's what protocol dictated he should say, but he couldn't bring himself to hurt her. Johnson would have lied. Maybe he wasn't cut out for this job. "It's gone and won't harm anyone again."

She eyed him for a long moment before finally heaving a resigned sigh. "Is your father okay?"

Roy eagerly nodded. "He's fine. Like I said, there's this doctor in Australia—"

"Don't feed me bullshit, Roy."

"I assure you he's fine." He forced a smile, hating how much she unnerved him. "Even better than that."

"Can I talk to him?"

"No," he lied, knowing full well she wouldn't believe him. "He's in Australia."

"No, he's not."

"Gloria, listen." He released a shaky breath. This was so damn hard. "My dad is doing a million times better than he was before. That's all I can tell you. Sorry."

Her face fell and she seemed to deflate. "Then I guess I won't be seeing you around."

Did she want to see him? "I'll still be in Laredo."

"Doing what?"

"Working." A muscle twitched in his jaw. He really wasn't cut out for this line of work.

"On what?"

"Can't tell you. Classified."

She gave him the faintest of smiles. "I suppose if we met for happy hour, we'd have nothing to talk about."

A seed of hope sprouted in his chest. Was she still interested in him after all he'd put her through? "There'd be plenty we could talk about."

"I go with a few other nurses to Rosa's Cantina every Friday."

He smiled. "Good to know."

"Your dad's things are in a box behind the front desk," she said before walking away.

"Thanks. See you, Gloria." Rosa's Cantina. Men in his line of work weren't supposed to have relationships, but one drink wouldn't hurt, would it?

ANNIE SAT ON THE PORCH, sipping a lemonade with Ioana and watching the Coyotechaser children play tag. Her stomach had been buzzing with butterflies all day in anticipation of tomorrow's ceremony. It had taken two weeks to get everything for the bonding in order. She'd had to wait for Roy to straighten things out with his dad, then for Jax to finish his mission with the trackers. Even though he hadn't officially gone through basic training, Jax had been so proud to help find the sex trafficking rings. She'd worried about him the entire time, but she couldn't deny him the opportunity to fulfill his dream of being a tracker by insisting he stay for the ritual.

After the missions had been successfully carried out, the Coyotechasers abruptly stepped down as chieftains. Raine said he'd seen it coming after Cesar made a bad call regarding her rescue. Suddenly Annie's pack was in charge, which delayed their ceremony even more while she and her mates were put through a crash course on how to run a tribe.

After what felt like ages, she was finally ready to bond with her mates. Even though she was nervous as hell, tomorrow couldn't come fast enough. She set down her drink and straightened when a familiar truck came down the dirt road leading to the house. She skipped down the porch steps, as giddy as a school girl, while Magnus pulled in and parked.

Cesar Coyotechaser came outside, holding two longnecks, each with a lime wedged in the bottle and salt dusting the rims. "Evening, Magnus." He offered him a beer. "What are you doing here?"

Magnus held out a staying hand. "No, thanks. I'm here to take Annie for a drive."

She was so proud of Magnus for abstaining. He and his brothers had made a pact that they'd only drink on weekends and then only two beers each. So far they were sticking to it, as they didn't want to end up like Vidar.

"I'm not sure it's a good idea to be alone the day before the bonding," Cesar said.

Ioana grinned. "Why not?"

Ever since Tor and Van had returned to Alaska with Amara and her family, the Coyotechasers had been Annie's surrogate family, with Cesar taking Tor's place as the overprotective uncle. After tomorrow, though, she'd answer only to her mates, and they'd answer to her.

"Where are you going?" Cesar asked.

"Back to my house. I wanted to get her ideas on the furniture." Magnus gave her a surreptitious glance, then looked away, his face coloring.

He had more in mind than furniture, Annie was sure of it. Well, it was about damn time. She hadn't had any action since that one time with her mates at the pond. They hadn't returned to the waterfall since discovering those gruesome human remains. Too bad, because that place had been pretty close to paradise.

Cesar gave Magnus a long look. "How long will you be gone?"

"A few hours," Magnus answered evenly. She'd have thought him perfectly calm if not for the vein in his forehead popping out.

Cesar waved them off. "Okay."

With a squeal, Annie dragged him to the truck. She sat in the middle of the bench seat, buckling her seatbelt and snuggling up to him, relishing the feel of his big, strong body and the spicy musk smell that was all his own.

Once he pulled out on the dirt road, he looked her over with a sly smile. "Did you mean it when you said you loved me?"

She wondered what he was talking about and then recalled the night Amara had healed him. She hadn't thought much about it after that, but apparently he'd been hanging onto her words. That brought her immense satisfaction.

She playfully swatted his arm. "Of course." She smiled when his grin stretched ear to ear. "Did you really want to get my ideas about furniture?" she asked, choosing to change the subject rather than make him feel obligated to reciprocate. If he loved her, he'd tell her when he was ready.

He gave her a sly look. "You mean you haven't popped into my head to find out?"

"I'm being good." Biting her lower lip, she batted her lashes. "So, about the furniture?"

His face flushed the color of a deep Texas sunset. "Maybe just the bed."

She bit her lip, her panties filling with moisture at the thought of sharing a mattress with Magnus. "But we're not bonded yet." As much as she couldn't wait to mate with him, she wanted to save her virginity for the ceremony. Amara had told her that her virgin blood was used in the ritual.

"I won't take your virginity," he said, keeping his eyes on the road, his grip on the steering wheel so tight, his knuckles looked ready to snap. "I just want to show you how much I love you using my two hands."

She squeezed his arm, a trill racing down her spine. He loved her! "You could've shown me with one."

"And that's one reason why I love you." His grin stretched even wider. "For accepting me for who I am while pushing me to better myself."

"That sounds kind of contradictory."

Pulling onto the side of the road, he took her in his arms. "Shut up and let me love you." And then he proceeded to kiss her senseless.

AFTER PULLING OVER to kiss several more times, Annie was damned horny by the time they reached the ranch.

"Where are your brothers?" she asked when they walked inside, surprised to see how clean it was.

No cobwebs, no wall cheese. The furniture was old and ratty, but she wanted to help pick out their new stuff anyway. In the meantime the place was livable and didn't smell.

"They're out mending fences. It's just you and me."

She hauled him down the hall. "Please tell me this is the way to your bedroom."

"It is." He chuckled.

The bedroom impressed her most of all. It had a fresh coat of paint, brand new flooring, and the biggest bed she'd ever seen in her life.

"It was just delivered today," he said.

"Good." She giggled. "Let's try it out."

Swearing, she fumbled with the buttons on his shirt before finally yanking it over his head. He made quick work of her clothes and his pants before picking her up and laying her down on the bed. They kissed and kissed until her head spun with lust. He explored her breasts, pinching and squeezing her nipples into peaks. She arched into his touch with a groan, wanting more, so much more.

"Touch me down there," she pleaded, spreading her legs.

His hand moved to her mound while he kissed and sucked her breasts.

She ran her fingers through his hair, urging him to continue. He positioned himself over her, engulfing her in his warmth and tantalizing masculine scent.

She gasped when his smooth cock slid across her slick folds. She knew the game they played was risky, but at the moment she didn't care. She spread her legs wider, thrusting her hips.

"We can't," he warned, gently biting the top swell of her breast, digging his teeth in far enough to elicit a shocked cry. He kissed and licked the bite marks and then bit the underside.

"But I want it," she pleaded.

He continued to tease her outer folds, gliding across the slippery surface as more moisture spilled out of her. She tossed her head back with a groan as her pussy swelled. Every nerve ending in her body came alive as he sucked a hard nipple while rocking against her. She panted hard into his hair and then stilled when her throbbing button burst, a cascade of orgasms spilling over her. With a roar he shot his seed, coating her stomach and tits, dousing her like a firehose. He rubbed his semen into her breasts before swirling it around her labia and into her pussy. She cried out while he finger-fucked her. It only took a few strokes before she orgasmed again, her sheath pulsing around his thick finger.

She heaved a sigh of contentment while he wiped her up with a towel. They laughed, cuddled, and kissed, their hands roaming freely over each other. She admired the hard planes of his chest and abdomen while he worked her up into another orgasm. She took him in hand and kissed up and down his shaft. Soon his dick was in her mouth, spurting against the back of her throat.

They held each other until they fell asleep, and when his brothers came home and found her naked in their bed, she did for them what she'd done for

Magnus, swallowing their seed while they toyed with her clit, giving her more orgasms than she could count.

Chapter Twenty

ANNIE WAS GLAD SHE had Ioana to help her on her big day. She had only a vague idea what to expect after witnessing Dr. Lupescu's ceremony. It was *after* the ceremony she was concerned about. The part where she finally had sex with her mates. She wasn't afraid of them hurting her. She knew they'd be gentle. She wasn't even afraid of not knowing what to do after they'd marked each other. She didn't know why she was apprehensive, and then it hit her. Her fathers wouldn't be here to support her. She peered through the curtain at the starry night sky. The moon wasn't full, so they couldn't materialize.

After Ioana finished braiding her hair and helping her into a beautiful white beaded gown, she and Cesar took her to the tribal house, the barn they used for meetings, where they also conducted their rituals. She let Cesar help her out of the truck, since her dress was so tight, she could scarcely move one foot in front of the other. Her mates' truck was parked not far away, which meant they were inside waiting. The knot in her stomach swelled to the size of a grapefruit.

"You ready?" he asked, squeezing her arm.

She swallowed nervously. "Guess so."

Ioana flanked her other side. "Of course she is." She winked.

Annie didn't need to read minds to know the meaning behind that wink. Ioana had smelled mating fluids on Annie after she'd slunk into the house last night, acting like she was returning from an innocent little outing.

"It's okay," Ioana whispered in her ear. "My mates marked me before the ceremony, too. It's kind of an Amaroki tradition, even though everyone pretends otherwise."

That made her feel better. "Thanks," she whispered back, knowing full well Cesar could hear their conversation but somehow not caring.

When a shadow fell over her, blocking out the light from the lamp overhead, she turned around and saw her fathers' four smiling faces, clearly visible though they were somewhat translucent.

Cesar nearly fell over backward in surprise.

"Do you mind if we escort her?" Amarok asked, holding out his elbow to Annie. "You may still lead the ceremony."

"Of course not, Your Holy One," Cesar answered, bowing his head.

Ioana bowed, too. "It's an honor to have you here."

Annie's heart swelled with joy when Amarok and Fenrir bracketed her, and her two other fathers stood behind her.

The looks on her mates' faces as she walked through the double doors with them was priceless. After she reached her mates, her fathers backed away. Her poor brother who stood behind them looked ready to die from fright.

Magnus held out a hand. "It's an honor to meet you all."

Amarok winked at Annie. "The honor is ours to share this special night with our daughter."

Magnus beamed at Annie. "I agree. We are humbled the Ancients chose us for her mate, and we will strive each day to become the mates she deserves."

Amarok nodded with a slight grin. "That's what we wanted to hear."

Cesar took his place on the dais. "Forgive me. I'm still getting over my shock at your presence."

"Don't let us alarm you," Amarok said. "Carry on."

Magnus and Raine held her hands while Jax and Frey touched her shoulders.

"You look beautiful," Raine said softly.

"Thanks." She beamed at him and at her other mates.

"Let us begin," Cesar said, and she faced forward. "Brothers and sisters, we are gathered here today to witness the bonding between sister Annie Thunderfoot and brothers Magnus, Raine, Jax, and Frey Wolfstalker."

Cesar handed Ioana a silver goblet inscribed with images of wolves and filled with wine. Stepping off the dais, Ioana held the goblet in both hands while Cesar followed her with a long blade.

Annie was thankful Cesar wouldn't be cutting into her, like Tor had done with Dr. Lupescu. Her blood would come from her virginal barrier after the ceremony.

Cesar pricked the thumbs of her mates, then dipped their thumbs in the goblet. None of them winced.

Can't wait to take your blood, Raine projected into her head.

She blushed. She couldn't wait either.

After swirling the blood and wine together, Cesar handed the goblet to Annie. "Repeat after me," he said to her. "I, Annie, take the blood of my protectors, binding our hearts and souls as one. I vow love, honor, and loyalty to my mates, my protectors, from now until eternity."

She repeated the words and drank every last drop, surprised when her mates' thoughts popped into her head all at once. She hadn't expected the chatter to be so loud. It was nothing like her mindreading, when thoughts were almost like dreams. These thoughts were up front, and they focused on one thing—they couldn't wait to get laid. Not that she blamed them. She couldn't wait to get fucked by her four studs.

Cesar took the goblet and asked her mates to repeat after him. "I take the blood of Annie, binding our souls to hers. We vow love, honor, loyalty, and protection to our mate from now until eternity."

Their words had no meaning until they actually took her blood.

"We now leave you alone to complete the ceremony." Cesar nodded at a lumpy mattress on the floor, covered with white sheets.

She couldn't help blushing when she looked at her fathers.

"We will visit again during the next full moon," Amarok said, kissing her forehead, even though she felt nothing but a slight tingling sensation on her skin.

Each of her fathers kissed her, telling her how proud they were of her, before vanishing into the night.

Roy came up to her, rattling the keys in his pocket like he couldn't wait to get the hell out of there. "That was interesting," he said through a nervous-sounding laugh. "You look beautiful, sis."

"Thanks." She blushed.

Cesar mopped sweat off his brow. "That was entertaining."

Taking his mate's hand, Cesar left the barn, Roy following at their heels and closing the double doors behind them.

Annie looked at her mates, overcome with a sudden case of nerves. She took Magnus's outstretched hand, letting him lead her to the bed. Though it was lumpy, it was surprisingly comfortable.

"You ready?" he asked.

"Been ready for the past two weeks." She laughed.

"Good." Raine squeezed her nipple. "because you're about to get thoroughly fucked."

If ever there was a magical key to unlocking Annie's desire, those words were it. Her pussy swelled and flooded her panties.

They unzipped her dress, and she warned them to be careful with the beads. Then she helped them out of their clothes, relishing the feel of their rock-hard chests and abdomens. Frey was a little softer than his brothers, but he also had the biggest cock, which jutted at her like a torpedo. She was so enamored with it, that she bent to her knees, taking him in her mouth and smiling when he let out a groan and fell back on his elbows.

She gasped, then pressed into the thick fingers that circled her clit from behind. She had no idea who was fingering her, but she assumed it was Magnus, as he used one hand to spread her labia and the other to spear her with a thick digit. Magnus would take every opportunity to use both hands. She rocked into him while he speared her harder, faster, and slurped Frey with urgent ferocity.

Frey exploded without warning, his head swelling inside her mouth like a popped balloon. She drank his juices while smearing her saliva into his tight balls. He groaned and spurted again, his hips jerking arrhythmically while he thrust so deep inside her, she nearly choked. She pulled off his cock, batting her lashes at him.

Magnus slowed the tempo of his finger-fucking to smear her juices around her swollen folds. He trailed delicate kisses up her spine, then whispered, "Turn over."

She gladly obeyed, lying on her back and wrapping her legs around his waist. She heaved a sigh as he slowly slid into her, bursting her barrier and burying himself to the hilt.

Can you hear me? she projected.

He smiled. *Yes, my love.*

A pained expression crossed his features when he pulled out and let Raine enter her.

She dug her heels into his ass. *Deeper,* she pleaded.

He clucked his tongue and withdrew. *I'm fucking you hard and deep after we draw blood.*

Her nipples hardened when he licked them. He then grazed his teeth across them, pinching them, one at a time, between his teeth, and pulling until they gently stretched.

"Oh, Raine!" she cried. Never before had she realized that pain could feel so good.

She opened her arms to Jax when Raine moved aside. *Thank you for waiting patiently,* she said, kissing him on the nose.

You were worth the wait, he said.

After him was Frey, still as big and hard as before. *I'm impressed.* She giggled.

Baby, I can go all night.

Then Magnus returned to her, kissing her passionately and sinking deep inside her. She held him tight while he rocked into her, making tender love to her and lasting far longer than she expected. When he swelled inside her, she said his name, and a powerful orgasm gripped her hard, her pussy walls banging against his cockhead.

He cupped her face and kissed her deeply before pulling out and wiping her with a towel.

Her nipples hardened in anticipation when Raine climbed between her legs. With a predatory growl, he nipped and licked her inner thighs before biting his way up her abdomen to her breasts. He alternated between scraping her nipples with his teeth and then suckling them like a newborn babe. The combination of pleasure and pain curled her toes and made her pussy drip like a busted fire hydrant.

He was not gentle, biting and sucking until she knew he'd left bruises. Grasping his hair by the roots, she arched into him, letting him feast on her neck.

"Roll over," he growled, his deep predatory purr sending a trill down her spine.

She did as she was told, not because she was frightened, but because her hungry pussy needed to get fucked hard.

As promised, he was not gentle, and oh, how she loved it. He slammed into her with deep, fast thrusts, each perfectly timed to the wild beating of her heart. Her orgasm came too fast for her to catch her breath. She cried out, then stilled, swept under pleasure's current. He howled like a wild protector, digging his nails into her ass while pouring into her. By the time his cock finished throbbing, she was delightfully sore.

He bent over her, nibbling her ear. *You liked it rough?*

Yes, oh, yes.

Good, he growled. *Next time will be rougher.*

She shivered at the thought, and yet she couldn't wait.

Jax was surprisingly gentle and sweet, alternating between pumping into her with shallow thrusts and gently kissing each breast. She loved running her fingers across the top of his buzz cut while he slowly built her passion until she turned to putty in his arms, falling apart like an unraveling ball of yarn.

Her orgasm was sweet and pure bliss. She sang his name and then captured his mouth in a kiss when he came.

She nuzzled his nose. *Thank you, my love.*

The pleasure was all mine, my angel, he teased, tenderly stroking her breast.

Frey lasted every bit as long as his brothers, a look of pained pleasure on his face. His large, throbbing cockhead triggered another orgasm, and her fleshy sheath beat against his head with each swell.

Annie was sated and spent by the time Frey pulled out. She sank into the mattress with a tired giggle when Magnus embraced her, kissing her forehead.

She stared at the barn's crisscrossing wooden rafters with a smile. So far her first night as a mated woman was going perfectly. She could definitely get used to this.

FREY DREW A LAZY CIRCLE around Annie's nipple, enthralled at its response. Her breasts were so round and perfect, just like the globes of her ass. He could feast on her all night and never tire. But they couldn't stay in the barn all night. They had to go home eventually, where hopefully they could go another round.

Magnus nibbled on Annie's neck, growling louder each time she giggled. "Do you want to run the canyon?" he asked.

Annie sat up, her beautiful tits jiggling. "No."

"Why?"

"Sami ruined it for me. I can't get in that pool without thinking of all those skulls."

Oh, yeah. Duh. Annie had been raised with humans, so naturally she'd take it harder than they had. But the more he thought about it, the more he was repulsed by swimming in that water. How many more bones were at the bottom? For certainly Sami had lost a few along the way. Their sanctuary was literally a human graveyard. The thought both depressed and pissed him off. Tyr had warned Sami and Vidar not to experiment with dark magic. They'd almost ruined the family because of their stubbornness.

"I'm sorry, Annie," Frey said. Not only had his fathers nearly destroyed the family, Sami had never taught him how to be a good gamma. Tomorrow he was supposed to make the family breakfast, and he didn't even know how to boil an egg.

She cupped his face. "Don't be. I don't need a canyon to make me happy. I already have all I want."

You make us very happy, too. He stroked her neck, an overwhelming feeling of love making his chest swell with joy. *I love you, Annie.*

She got up on her elbows and feathered a soft kiss across his lips. *And I love you.*

Did you want to try out our new big bed again? Raine asked her, waggling his brows.

She smiled. *Most definitely.*

Epilogue

ANNIE SAT AT THE BREAKFAST table Raine had built for her per her specifications. It was a pretty white farm table with a window seat on one side and a bench on the other, plus two padded captain chairs. Annie preferred the window seat because it had lots of soft cushioning for her aching lady parts, something she especially needed after a night of delicious, hard fucking.

Her Husky Mako sat at her feet, whimpering and drooling while keeping an eye on the back door, looking as hungry as she felt.

Holding a fork in one hand and a knife in the other, she licked her lips in anticipation. Frey hadn't been the best cook when they'd first bonded but after nearly two months of reading cookbooks, watching cooking videos, and taking lessons from the Coyotechaser gamma, he was becoming a first-rate chef, quickly surpassing her skills in the kitchen, which mainly consisted of boiling macaroni and cheese.

He came in from the back porch with a smoked brisket wrapped in tinfoil, its juices dripping into the pan. "Who's hungry?"

Mako howled.

Annie banged her silverware on the table. "I want the juices!"

"Patience," he chuckled, setting the brisket on the cutting board. "We need to let it rest a few minutes."

Annie jumped up and crossed to the kitchen counter, Mako following behind her, no doubt leaving a trail of drool on the floor. "Fuck rest. It's been napping all day on that smoker. I'm hungry."

He slapped her hand away when she reached for a crunchy piece of smoked meat. She yelped when she burned her fingertips, pulling away with what she knew was an overly-dramatic pout. That seemed to do the trick, because he sliced off a seasoned corner and blew on it before popping it in her mouth. He threw Mako a big chunk of fat, but the dog didn't even savor it, swallowing it in one gulp.

She chewed slowly, savoring the delicious blend of smoke and spice. Not only was it the perfect flavor, it was the right texture, too.

"What do you think?" he asked.

She held out her hand for more. "It's every bit as good as the Coyotechasers' brisket. Maybe even better."

He beamed and sliced off another big piece. "I can't tell you how happy that makes me."

They ate an entire corner, dipping the meat in the juices until they were both full. Frey let Mako lick the cutting board and gave him several more pieces of fat.

So far, her dog had adjusted well to his new family. Though the Texas heat bothered him, he spent plenty of time outside at night, hunting small game and playing with the other ranch dogs.

Raine came in from outside, wiping sweat from his brow before grabbing the tea jug from the fridge.

"Well?" she asked, a hand on her hip. "Are you finished yet?"

Raine poured a tall glass of tea and drank it in a few long swallows. "A few minor touches are left, but I think you can see it."

"Finally!" She had no idea what this big surprise was, but they hadn't let her in the backyard for a week. Judging by all the lumber they'd brought into the yard, she suspected they'd finally rebuilt their barn full of holes that Annie had named "The Big Swiss."

Raine insisted on blindfolding her, and she played along, mainly because she was sick of being stuck in the house. The moment they stepped onto the back porch, she scented fresh water. Lots of it. Her heart hammered in anticipation. Could it be?

Raine led her down the porch steps and up another set of steps, where the scent of water was even stronger.

"Ready?" he asked.

"Hurry up!" she huffed.

She squealed with delight when he removed the blindfold, revealing an oblong above-ground pool surrounded by a stained wooden deck that offered a full-sized patio table with matching chairs and several recliners.

"Happy Birthday!" her mates sung in unison.

She threw her arms around Raine's neck, plastering his face with kisses.

"Hey!" Magnus cried. "I built that pool, too."

"We all did," Jax added.

She gave her mates big, sloppy kisses and then stripped to her underwear and jumped in. She screamed when she surfaced. The water was much colder than she'd expected, but it was so refreshing. She laughed when they jumped in and splashed her.

She swam up to Magnus, wrapping her arms around his neck. "Can we afford this?"

He pulled her to him. "Beef prices have gone up."

"Plus Father Tyr has been sending us his military pay," Jax said.

Jax had just come home for two weeks' leave after six weeks of basic training. Not wanting to be the sixth wheel, her mates' last remaining father, Tyr, refused to come home after reenlisting. He'd said he didn't know when or if he was ever coming back. Annie felt terrible for her father-in-law. She didn't know how she could go on if she ever lost her entire pack.

She swam over to Jax, giggling when he squeezed her ass and yanked her flush against the pole protruding from his swim trunks.

She traced the square line of his jaw up to the ridge of his ear. She'd missed him these past six weeks, and she'd long for him when he had to leave again next week. But she wouldn't complain. He loved his job, and it provided income and benefits for the family.

"I feel bad he's working so hard and giving us all his money," she said, running her fingers through his buzzed hair.

Jax averted his eyes. "He doesn't need it."

"How is he?"

"He's a damn good tracker," Jax said. "The Army keeps him busy. Keeps his mind occupied."

Something in his voice told her things were not okay with Tyr. She wondered if he stayed away because he'd grown tired of his sons asking him about the dark magic their other fathers had used. They didn't want to know so they could use it. They wanted to know so they could avoid it. At any rate, he must not have trusted them with the information, because he refused to tell them.

Jax had become reticent, too, pulling away whenever she tried to involve him in deep conversation.

She gave a questioning look. "And?"

He released her, ducked underwater, and swam to the other side of the pool. She hated when he shut her out. Of all her mates, he was having the hardest time accepting what his fathers had done to the family. Most days he was happy, but there were times when she saw the chasm in his soul, and she wished he'd let her shoulder some of his emotional burden. They'd only been mated two months, and he'd been gone for six weeks of that time. Maybe he'd soften to the idea after they got to know each other better.

At least Magnus had gotten better. He was no longer plagued by the nightmares of his mother's death or the fears of being an inadequate mate and chieftain. He'd taken over both roles with amazing confidence and skill. Now Annie just had to work on healing Jax's soul.

Magnus swam up behind her and gently massaged her shoulders. "He's still coping."

She didn't know if he was referring to Tyr, Jax, or both.

She buried her face against his chest and was hit by a powerful spray of water. She turned, swearing and wiping her eyes.

Raine was pointing a large water gun at her, his grin so evil, she swore she saw devil horns sticking out of his head. "Are we going to stand around and bullshit, or are we going to have fun?"

"You'll regret starting a water war with me!" Magnus boomed, shielding Annie with one hand and splashing Raine with the other.

When Frey and Jax joined in, each wielding water guns, she couldn't escape the deluge.

"Enough!" She yelled, scowling. "This is *not* my idea of fun."

"No?" Raine tossed the gun on the deck. Without warning, he dove and chased after her legs.

She tried to swim away, but he was too fast. He came up behind her and pulled her ass against his erection. "What kind of fun did you have in mind?" he asked, pinching her nipples.

She pressed into him when he slipped her panties off and pushed her toward the stairs. Hanging onto the railing, she moaned when he toyed with her pussy, then entered her with a jarring thrust. The water's friction slowed him down until her pussy's juices eased his passage. He fucked her roughly, toying with her clit. She came hard, and he fucked her through that orgasm and into another.

Each brother took turns fucking her in the pool. Afterward, spineless as a jelly fish, she floated aimlessly on a raft, sipping sweet tea and letting her mates push her around while they swam. She smiled at cloud that looked like a wolf.

"Thank you, Fathers," she whispered. "They were worth the fight."

The End.

Books by Tara West

Eternally Yours
Divine and Dateless
Damned and Desirable
Damned and Desperate
Demonic and Deserted
Dead and Delicious
Something More Series
Say When
Say Yes
Say Forever
Say Please
Say You Want Me
Say You Love Me
Say You Need Me
Dawn of the Dragon Queen Saga
Dragon Song
Dragon Storm
Whispers Series
Sophie's Secret
Don't Tell Mother
Krysta's Curse
Visions of the Witch
Sophie's Secret Crush
Witch Blood
Witch Hunt
Keepers of the Stones
Witch Flame, Prelude

Curse of the Ice Dragon, Book One
Spirit of the Sea Witch, Book Two
Scorn of the Sky Goddess, Book Three
Hungry for Her Wolves Series
Hungry for Her Wolves, Book One
Longing for Her Wolves, Book Two
Desperate for Her Wolves, Book Three
Tempted by Her Wolves, Book Four
Fighting for Her Wolves, Book Five

About Tara West

Tara West writes books about dragons, witches, and handsome heroes while eating chocolate, lots and lots of chocolate. She's willing to share her dragons, witches, and heroes. Keep your hands off her chocolate. A former high school English teacher, Tara is now a full-time writer and graphic artist. She enjoys spending time with her family, interacting with her fans, and fishing the Texas coast.
Awards include: Dragon Song, Grave Ellis 2015 Readers Choice Award, Favorite Fantasy Romance
Divine and Dateless, 2015 eFestival of Words, Best Romance
Damned and Desirable, 2014 Coffee Time Romance Book of the Year
Sophie's Secret, selected by The Duff and Paranormal V Activity movies and Wattpad recommended reading lists
Curse of the Ice Dragon, Best Action/Adventure 2013 eFestival of Words
Hang out with her on her Facebook fan page at: https://www.facebook.com/tarawestauthor
Or check out her website: www.tarawest.com
She loves to hear from her readers at: tarawestwriter@gmail.com

Made in the USA
Coppell, TX
30 January 2026

70555880R00114